T0270078

ALSO AVAILABLE FROM SQUARE ENIX BOOKS

*NieR Replicant ver.1.22474487139...
Project Gestalt Recollections—File 01*

Grimoire NieR: Revised Edition

NieR Art—Koda Kazuma Works

NieR:Automata—YoRHa Boys

NieR Replicant

ver.1.22474487139...

PROJECT GESTALT RECOLLECTIONS

FILE 02

Written by Jun Eishima

Original Story by Yoko Taro

English Adaptation by Jasmine Bernhardt and Alan Averill

SQUARE ENIX
BOOKS

NieR Replicant ver.1.22474487139...
Project Gestalt Recollections—File 02
© 2021 Jun Eishima
© 2021 SQUARE ENIX CO., LTD. All rights reserved.

First published in Japan as *NieR Replicant ver.1.22474487139...Gestalt Keikaku Kaisouroku* in 2021 by SQUARE ENIX CO., LTD.
English translation rights arranged with SQUARE ENIX CO., LTD. and SQUARE ENIX, INC.
English translation © 2024 by SQUARE ENIX CO., LTD.

Based on the video game NieR Replicant ver.1.22474487139...
© 2010, 2021 SQUARE ENIX CO., LTD. All rights reserved.

Library of Congress Cataloging-in-Publication Data

Names: Eishima, Jun, 1964- author. | Yokoo, Tarō, 1970- author. | Bernhardt, Jasmine, translator. | Averill, Alan, translator.
Title: NieR Replicant ver.1.22474487139...: project gestalt recollections / written by Jun Eishima; original story by Yoko Taro ; English adaptation by Jasmine Bernhardt and Alan Averill.
Other titles: NieR Replicant ver.1.22474487139. English | NieR (Video game)
Description: First edition. | El Segundo, CA : Square Enix Books, 2023- | "First published in Japan as NieR Replicant ver.1.22474487139...Gestalt Keikaku Kaisouroku"
Identifiers: LCCN 2023009048 (print) | LCCN 2023009049 (ebook) | ISBN 9781646091836 (file 01 ; hardcover) | ISBN 9781646096619 (file 01 ; ebook)
Subjects: LCGFT: Dystopian fiction. | Novels.
Classification: LCC PL869.5.I7 N6613 2023 (print) | LCC PL869.5.I7 (ebook) | DDC 895.63/6--dc23/eng/20230412
LC record available at https://lccn.loc.gov/2023009048
LC ebook record available at https://lccn.loc.gov/2023009049

ISBN (hardcover): 978-1-64609-184-3
ISBN (ebook): 978-1-64609-662-6

Manufactured in the United States of America
First Edition: March 2024
1st Printing

Published by Square Enix Manga & Books, a division of SQUARE ENIX, INC.
999 N. Pacific Coast Highway, 3rd Floor
El Segundo, CA 90245, USA

BOOKS

square-enix-books.com

CONTENTS

A NOTE ABOUT THE CONTENTS

This book is an updated and expanded edition of *NieR RepliCant Recollection: Gestalt Keikaku Kaisouroku* (NieR RepliCant Recollection: Gestalt Project Retrospective), originally published in Japan in 2017.

REPORT 09

It's been one unexpected situation after another lately, and we've got our hands full dealing with everything. However, the biggest headache is the little tiff we had with Nier regarding what to do with Number 7 and the Shade-possessed woman.

As protectors of this village, we need to nip conflict in the bud right away. People always direct fear toward the different and unknown, and fear has a way of morphing into violence and savagery—which is why we decided not to allow Number 7 or the possessed woman into the village. We made this decision with the best of intentions, and Popola and I continue to stand by it.

But we had no idea Nier would be *this* furious with us. Honestly, I don't even understand what caused him to react like he did. We've been on good terms with him for so long, and he's never expressed anything but support for our methods. I figured this decision would be much the same, but hoo boy, was I ever wrong.

Luckily, Number 7 and the Shade woman seemed to understand; they both agreed to stay out of the village, which settled the matter. Nier was still angry, but since they were all right with it, he couldn't push it. He's clearly not over it, though, because his face was still clouded and angry when he stormed out of here.

It was awful timing too. Just before this whole thing blew up, I'd finally pinned down the Shadowlord's location. Turns out he's been a stone's throw away this entire time (or "right under our noses," as the old saying goes). I wanted to tell Nier immediately, but the fight sort of threw a wrench into that plan.

Anyway, I'll keep an eye on him for the next few days and try talking to him again. Even if he's still angry, I bet he'll listen if we mention the Shadowlord's whereabouts. He'd do anything to get Yonah back after all.

This update wasn't quite as long as anticipated. End report.

Record written by Devola

ADDENDUM: Turns out Nier approached *us* the other day to make amends, at which point Popola told him about the Shadowlord's castle. However, he still seems to hold some distrust toward us, and I don't think that will go away for a while. It's all making me a bit uneasy— we've never seen him act like this before.

NieR Replicant
ver.1.22474487139...

The Man 2

1.

EVEN WHEN POPOLA told Nier she'd learned the whereabouts of the Shadowlord, he found it hard to believe. Part of him even thought she'd made some kind of mistake. After all, it had been five long years of panic and anger, years where each thread of hope ended with him empty-handed once more. But the next thing she said was even more unexpected: The Shadowlord could be found at the Lost Shrine.

"The temple where I was first discovered!" exclaimed Grimoire Weiss when Popola delivered the information. "It was right under our pages the whole time!"

"Yes." Popola nodded. "It seems the Shadowlord's lair is connected to it somehow."

Hearing the location, Nier finally started to feel it could be true. While he'd spent all this time searching far and wide for his foe, he never considered searching so close to the village. The image of the Shadowlord flying off into the sky was burned into Nier's retinas; he'd simply assumed the villain had gone somewhere far, far away and had thus never considered venturing into the vicinity of the Lost Shrine.

"Still, the bridge leading to it is unusable," he pointed out after a moment. This was another reason he hadn't bothered to search the Lost Shrine: The road was cut off. Thankfully, Popola already had a plan in place.

"So take a boat," she said.

"A boat?"

"Yes. It took longer than we wanted, but the canal has been repaired."

Popola's words brought a memory back to Nier of how the village had been planning to repair the canal five years earlier. It seemed the work was finally complete.

"I also asked them to provide a boat at the path to the Lost Shrine's back entrance," she continued. "The ferryman will let you use it free of charge, which should make it easier for you to move from town to town."

The canal project's progress hadn't come up since Nier first heard of it five years prior. Perhaps Popola had kept quiet about it so as not to get him excited at the prospect before it was even close to done.

"Thanks, Popola," he said. "I feel like you've done so much for me."

At the end of the day, he would have been helpless if not for Devola and Popola constantly pitching in. Well, perhaps not *entirely* helpless, but there was no doubt his trials and tribulations would have been much more difficult to overcome. That point could not be argued.

Their conversation concluded, Nier headed straight for the village docks and found someone unexpected waiting for him.

"Hey, look who it is!" cried the man. "Remember me?"

Truth be told, Nier had forgotten his face, but the red bag slung around the man's body made it clear who it was.

"You're from Seafront, right?"

"You *do* remember me!"

Nier nodded, deciding not to mention the man's arguments with his wife. Grimoire Weiss, however, clearly didn't feel such consideration was warranted.

"It's one half of the quarrelsome couple!" he barked. "Whatever could you be doing here?"

"I've been sailing the waterways since you found me. They said I did really good work, so they hired me on as the ferryman."

"Oh yeah, huh? Congrats!" said Nier.

"Thanks! Still, it's not all puppies and unicorns—the ol' ball-and-chain is always harping on me now about how much I work."

Thinking back on it, Nier hadn't seen the man with the red bag in Seafront during the past five years; it made sense that he'd been away from the city working the waterways. Still, he should have expected the couple's arguments to remain a staple of their relationship.

"Anyway, never mind that," continued the ferryman. "If you got a place to be, just let me know and I'll take you there."

"We need to get to the Lost Shrine," replied Nier. "I heard we can get there by boat."

"You sure can! There's a dock in back of the place."

Nier felt a slight sense of unease as he placed one foot inside the boat. For as long as he could remember, the adults in his life had warned him about falling into water. And while he'd grown used to the boats that glided over the sand in Facade, boarding one that sat on liquid felt entirely different.

Once he finally settled into the boat, they pushed off. The ferryman handled the oars with a practiced hand—no surprise considering the people of Seafront were so at home on the water.

"Would you mind stopping when we get out of the village?" Nier asked.

"Why? Forget something?"

"Just meeting up with some people. Is that okay?"

"You got it."

Once he brought it up, Nier recalled the back-and-forth that had taken place with Devola and Popola the night before. He'd been *so* furious when they asked him to keep Kainé and Emil out of the village; without Kainé's sacrifice five years prior, there wouldn't even be a village to keep her out of, nor a single resident left to complain. Kainé and Emil had saved every villager—including Devola, Popola, and Nier himself—and Nier found it selfish beyond belief that they might ask the very people who'd saved their lives to stay away.

"Please try to understand," Popola had said when she explained the situation. "People are tired and scared, and . . . I'm sorry. I'm sorry you have to bear the brunt of that."

The handful of villagers who were afraid of Kainé and Emil felt fear for a simple reason: One wasn't human, and the other was host to something that wasn't human. Regardless, it still struck Nier as a selfish line of reasoning.

Strangely enough, it was Emil who showed understanding and managed to bring Nier down from his fury.

"People are afraid of us," he'd said. "And really, I understand. I mean, look at me. It's okay. We can sleep outside."

"I'm used to sleeping outside" was Kainé's only thought on the matter. When she said that, Nier couldn't help but remember something she once said to him: *I like being alone.* He'd never seen her attempt to enter any village or city they visited and eventually came to understand that she preferred being alone to dealing with people who loathed her for being possessed by a Shade.

Would the ferryman come to fear and hate the pair as well? If so, it would be the end of their boat rides and force them to find another way to access the Lost Shrine.

Nier braced himself, but the ferryman showed no signs of fear or panic. He merely widened his eyes slightly at the sight of Emil.

By the time Nier introduced them as friends, the ferryman had already returned to his regular countenance.

"Thank you for letting us use your vessel," Emil said with a bowed head as he stepped on board.

"Glad to be of service!" replied the ferryman as he extended a hand to help Emil into the boat. This caused the boy to hesitate for a moment, but he ultimately reached out to grasp the proffered hand.

As Nier suspected, the idea his friends' presences alone would cause unrest was wrong. Not everyone who saw someone strange and different immediately began hating them. They might be surprised or bewildered at first, but they would quickly settle into a state where they tried to accept the other person. Sadly, those accepting sorts were few and far between in his village.

The boat glided over the water. The air was still, and the sun shone brightly overhead, so their journey went smoothly. No Shades assaulted them, and wild animals kept a respectful distance.

Finally, the ferryman moored the boat at a small dock just outside a cave. Once Nier stepped onto solid ground, he felt a sense of familiarity. Glancing around, he realized from the shape of the mountains that they were on the outskirts of the northern plains. While he'd come to this river countless times to fish, there was no bridge, so he'd never considered crossing to the opposite bank.

"The Lost Shrine's up ahead, just past this cave," the ferryman said.

"As well as the Shadowlord's castle," added Nier.

The area was so peaceful, Nier had to express that thought out loud in order to make it feel real. He recalled that, though Shades appeared frequently on the opposite shore, so long as one rooted those out, that was it—there were no sheep or goats to worry about. Fishing here had been a good way to relax.

"Take care," the ferryman said as he watched them venture into the cave.

The cave was short, and the companions soon found the Lost Shrine looming before them. There was a moat surrounding the building that could only be crossed by a long wooden bridge that was falling apart. Clearly no one had used the path in a very long time.

The shrine's outer wall stood tall on the other side of the bridge. Once there, they found a long ladder as old as the bridge itself leading up. Nier felt tired just looking at the ladder but swallowed his dismay and climbed until he reached an ancient outside passageway. Nier began carefully making his way across the shaky boards, but Kainé simply strode briskly ahead.

"Kainé, wait!" Emil called. "Don't run off by yourself! . . . Aaand she's gone."

Patience was not one of Kainé's strong suits; she often ran ahead or otherwise separated herself from the others. Nier sometimes wondered if she'd been doing less of that since Emil joined the party but figured he was probably imagining it.

"There she is!" cried Emil suddenly. "Kainé!"

No. He wasn't imagining it. Kainé wasn't just standing on the path ahead—she was actually *waiting* for them.

As Nier continued on, Emil and Grimoire Weiss floated through the air toward her. Though the boy had legs, he remained airborne instead of using them. In fact, Nier hadn't seen Emil attempt to walk since the moment he took on his new form. Nier once asked if using magic to float all the time ever made him tired—a complaint voiced on occasion by Grimoire Weiss—and Emil responded that walking took much more effort. He then went on to explain that having a higher vantage point gave him a better view of his surroundings, which let him home in on danger more quickly. This fact apparently gave him peace of mind.

I want to do everything I can to keep everyone safe, he'd said to Nier. This was likely the real reason for his floating: He didn't care how tired it made him so long as he was able to keep his friends safe.

Kainé was stopping to wait for them, and Emil was watching over them from on high. Nier thought once again about how kind his friends were, and when he finally reached them, it was with a new determination in his heart.

"Kainé? Emil?" he said. "Look, from now on, I'm going to sleep outside with you."

"Why?" Emil asked.

"I can't accept that you aren't allowed in the village. It's stupid."

That feeling only grew stronger when he saw how normally the ferryman treated his friends. Of course, he was a man from Seafront, which meant he was used to interacting with the new and unusual. But just because someone lacked experience with a thing didn't make it right for them to hate it.

"So you're staging a protest?" asked Emil. "Fun!"

"Don't waste your time," Kainé interjected.

"But it just feels wrong," Nier explained.

"Well, that's really nice of you, but you still don't have to stay out here with us."

Nier felt a bit of relief when Emil said that and wondered if perhaps his sudden new desire to stay with his friends was actually a selfish one. After all, Nier was the only one of them who seemed to have any trouble with the arrangement.

"You can't sleep out in the rain," continued Emil. "What if you catch a cold? Besides, you've got a super-important mission."

Emil knew that Nier had been searching frantically for the Shadowlord for half a decade now, and Emil wanted to emphasize how close they suddenly were to that goal. He'd been there when Yonah was kidnapped, after all, and he knew full well how formidable the Shadowlord and Grimoire Noir were as enemies. These were not foes one could march up to and subdue before dinner. Nier and his companions might have to attempt it once, twice, or more before finding success. They might even need to go to the trouble of improving their weapons and buying new equipment. In his own way, Emil was gently reminding Nier that even a case of the sniffles might be enough distraction to cost him his life.

When Emil noticed Nier had fallen silent, he continued with a light, cheerful tone. "Besides, I like camping with Kainé! Sometimes we sit around the fire and tell stories or roast—"

"Emil, that's enough!" Kainé interrupted. "I got a fucking image to maintain."

The conversation was enough to reassure Nier that his friends would be all right. He'd brought up the topic in an attempt to be kind, but they ended up showing consideration for *him* instead. At least he was mature enough to realize it.

2.

"SO DO YOU actually have an idea where the entrance to this Shadowlord's castle is?"

Kainé brought this up because both Nier and Weiss seemed to be moving with conviction. The layout inside the Lost Shrine was complicated, with crumbled walls and stairs leaving it in a haphazard state. At some point in their wanderings, she realized she had no idea where they were going. But since Nier had been to the place before, she figured his confident steps meant he at least had some idea of what he was doing.

"It's where I first found Weiss," he replied. "That's the only place I can think of that fits the bill."

He went on to tell her about a room on the roof that contained an altar of some significance, as well as two large Shades who had been standing guard over the book.

"I have a feeling they were protecting more than just Weiss," he continued. "But since I was there to take Yonah home, I didn't spend a lot of time looking around the altar."

"I can think of nothing that has equal or greater value than myself, save the entrance to the Shadowlord's lair," huffed Weiss. The book's opinion aside, there had to be *something* more to that altar—especially since it had a barrier that prevented anyone from accessing it.

"There are way more little Shades here than there were five

years ago," Nier muttered as he entered yet another room packed with tiny Shades and began mowing them down.

"Ain't ya excited, Sunshine? We finally get to bathe in blood!"

An uncomfortable chill ran through Kaine's left side as Tyrann began to ramble; he was likely desperate to let loose after being petrified for so long.

Don't talk to me, Kaine thought to her other self as she kicked away a horde of little Shades. But no matter how many she sent flying, they just got up and shambled back toward her. She could hear them screaming at her to "turn back," but there wasn't any force behind it. They were weak, helpless creatures who could barely walk properly, much less mount any kind of proper attack. It was almost as though they were only approaching the group in order to die. The fact they had the intelligence to tell the group to turn back meant they understood the concept of danger, yet they kept walking toward their own demise all the same.

"These are certainly not your garden-variety Shades," Grimoire Weiss remarked, sounding as though he had the same thoughts as Kaine. A moment later, Tyrann suddenly piped up with what seemed to be an answer to Kaine's question—although she doubted he would ever actually be that helpful.

"Say, I've heard of this! A cursed area where incomplete Shades gather!"

Incomplete? You mean their bodies weren't fully functional? Why would they need a place like this?

"The hell do you care, Sunshine? All that matters is that you can mow 'em down and drink their blood! Kya ha ha!"

She should have known asking him would be a wasted effort; what kind of answer could she ever expect from a creature that thought only of malice and death?

"Turn back!" screamed the little Shades. *"Turn back!"*

Even without the shrieking, the dark masses jostling together in such a tiny space was enough to irritate Kainé to no end. Add their voices on top of that, and it was more than she could stand.

"That's why you gotta kill 'em all and get some peace and quiet, eh, Sunshine?"

Tyrann was right, but there was no way in hell she'd let him know it. Instead, she ignored him and continued swinging her sword.

The higher into the Shrine they went, the louder the Shades became. As they spoke, Kainé realized she understood how the weak could resist in their own desperate way.

"Don't go . . . We protect . . . It's precious . . ."

Fragments of their voices came to her, but she kept telling herself it was all just sound and noise without any significance.

They needed to get to the roof as soon as possible; Shades couldn't appear in places that were exposed to the sun. That was Kainé's only thought as she clambered up ladders and rushed up various outer passageways. But when she finally reached the roof, she was dismayed to find hordes of Shades there as well. They were lurking in the shadows, hiding between the gaps in the rubble where the light couldn't reach. Some even carried ragged little umbrellas.

"Just kick 'em aside!" snarled Nier. Kainé followed his lead and continued cutting them down. Even if Nier couldn't hear it, Kainé knew the Shades were trying to protect something behind the door. Whatever it was, that was their destination.

Once Nier cleared the roof, he pushed open the doors. This was Kainé's first visit to this place, and the room was much longer than she'd expected. She was also surprised at how she had to crane her neck to take in the vaulted ceiling.

"Something's heeere!" cried Tyrann. She could almost hear him licking his lips. Of course, he had neither a tongue nor lips, but her imagination wouldn't let the image go.

A moment later, Kainé began to sense an extremely powerful Shade that stood out from the noise of all the little ones. She tensed, searching for the source of the feeling. The moment she realized it was above them, a terrible rumble rattled in her ears and shook her bones. A few paces ahead, Nier came to a stop and snapped his gaze upward. The ceiling immediately crumbled. For a moment, Kainé thought a boulder had come crashing through.

"This thing's still alive?!" cried Nier.

He was facing one of the two Shades he and Weiss claimed to have defeated five years earlier. Though it looked like a stone statue at a glance, it was a full-fledged Shade. It also lacked an arm, which aligned with at least part of Nier's story. And though Nier had no idea, Kainé knew it was called Gretel because the little Shades kept babbling the name.

"I'll get you this time!" cried Nier. He unsheathed his blade, causing the little Shades to mob around him.

"*Don't you touch them!*" cried Gretel. But Nier couldn't understand its words—all he heard were a series of eerie groans. With nothing to stop him, he brandished his greatsword and prepared to strike. The horde of little Shades cried out as they swarmed him, but he rendered them to dust in an instant. Regardless, each time he cut one down, two more appeared in its place.

"*Stop, little ones!*" cried Gretel. "*They're too strong for you!*"

The Shades pressed forward, paying no mind to Gretel's warning. Either they weren't intelligent enough to understand the situation or they wanted to protect Gretel regardless of the cost.

As Nier marched forward, cutting down enemies, Grimoire Weiss brought him to a halt. "These creatures cannot abide the sun! Lure them to the light!"

Kainé glanced up and realized the hole Gretel had made in the ceiling was allowing a shaft of sunlight to illuminate the middle of the room.

"*Stand down!*" called Gretel, who clearly saw what Weiss and Nier were attempting to do. "*Don't follow them!*" But the little ones paid it no mind. Their tiny forms rushed straight into the sunlight before melting away. Unlike Gretel, who wore stone armor, the little Shades had no way of protecting themselves.

"*Stop! Please!*"

Gretel howled. Gretel raged. But it did nothing to stop the Shades' death march.

"Aim for that statue!" Nier called. "It's the leader!"

A leader of Shades. That's all it was in Nier's eyes—and Weiss's and Emil's as well.

"*I am not their leader! It is I who rely on them! It is they who saved me!*"

Kainé's eyes went wide. Gretel understood Weiss and Nier, which meant Shades could understand human speech even though humans couldn't understand them. Thinking about it, she realized the Shade that killed her grandmother had enjoyed the conversation between itself and Kainé. At the time, she thought it was because it liked to see human faces twisted in agony and hear human voices colored by pain, but now she realized it understood every word the entire time. In fact, it was *because* it understood human speech that it was able to cast a spell and speak to Kainé as if it were her grandmother. That thing had been perfectly aware of the entire situation and *still* chose to mutilate her only family while toying with her feelings.

Her gut lurched at the thought. That *thing* and this Gretel were both Shades, and she hated that fact.

"*Grimoire Weiss was taken away,*" Gretel cried out to the little Shades. "*And when Hansel died, I thought there was no reason for me to exist anymore. But because I had all of you—because you listened to me—you saved me! I thought we'd be able to spend the rest of our lives together!*"

Gretel appeared ready to say more, but Tyrann's mad cackling drowned out the words.

"Kya ha ha ha! Oh, you're funny! I'm gonna start cryin' here!"

Kainé felt herself beset by dueling urges—one to scold Tyrann into silence and one to thank him for preventing her from hearing the rest of Gretel's speech. But she didn't want her possessor to notice how she felt, so she pushed both thoughts down and leaned into the weight of her blades.

"These little bastards just keep coming!" she yelled. Her voice was as loud as she could make it—a desperate attempt to drown out the others around her. But Gretel only yelled back even louder:

"Stop hurting my friends!"

Gretel raised its weapon, a cross between an axe and a spear, but Nier's magic hand suddenly came crashing down. Gretel used its weapon to deflect the hand, but the bigger the weapon, the bigger the swing—and the bigger the opening. Kainé slipped under the blade as Gretel defended, closing the distance between her and it in an instant before raising her swords as one.

The power of her blades—and her inhuman Shade strength—sent Gretel flying. Its massive armor-clad frame soared into the air. Immediately, Nier brought his greatsword down, slamming Gretel into the ground. The Shade now lay motionless, the impact of its own weight against the hard floor having apparently taken a toll.

"Have you felled the beast?" cried Grimoire Weiss. Gretel roared out a moment later, as though answering his question.

"Stop! Those are my . . . my friends!" Gretel writhed against the floor for a moment before using its weapon as a support to bring itself to its feet. It then launched into a fearsome, violent rampage that was more flailing randomly than it was a counterattack. Covered in wounds, the creature no longer knew where any of its foes were, nor where it was going.

"This is one stubborn son of a bitch!" Tyrann cackled.

"Dammit!" replied Kainé. She fired a bolt of magic at Gretel, who was now moving too quickly for swords to work. "Dammit, dammit, dammit!"

They needed to subdue this thing *now*. She wouldn't let it speak any more than it already had—she couldn't take it.

"Hey there, Sunshine! You ain't feeling bad for this freak, are ya?"

Shut up, Tyrann! What do you care?!

Kainé continued to blast the Shade with spell after spell, emptying her mind so she didn't have to think, and Tyrann would have nothing to question.

"Ain't no turnin' back now," said Tyrann, his voice suddenly quiet. *"Gotta lust for blood. Embrace the slaughter."*

I know.

"All we know is the thrill of battle. Ain't that right?"

My hands exist to kill Shades. That's it. Now that my grandmother is avenged, I kill Shades for Nier. I made up my mind. I . . .

She heard the sound of metal clashing with metal, followed by someone calling her name. When she snapped back to reality, she saw something flying right at her.

"Kainé!"

A powerful force slammed into her.

"Oh, you're kiddin' *me!"* cried Tyrann. It was clear from his tone that she hadn't evaded the attack, and a quick examination revealed that Gretel's weapon was now embedded deep within her chest.

The world spun.

Her body collided with the floor.

Then came pain.

She couldn't breathe. She couldn't move. She couldn't even lift a single finger. While the battle wasn't over, her panicked urge to get up and keep fighting was quickly withering away.

"Move . . . Move!"

For a moment, Kainé thought she was hearing her own voice. But when she saw Gretel out of the corner of her hazy vision, she realized the Shade was talking.

"Come on, you stupid arm, move!"

Gretel continued to scream from its position on the floor. It still seemed willing to fight, despite how heavily injured it was. But in that case, what was Kainé doing?

"We are incomplete. But our friends make us whole!"

What was the Shade talking about?

"We are mocked, abused, and hated. But our friends keep us strong! That is what keeps us going!"

Kainé understood the individual words, but the way they fit together made no sense.

"Do not stand in the way of our lives!"

She could hear Emil scream for someone to strike it down, then felt a thud as the creature fell to earth again. Clearly it had righted itself at some point, but Kainé wasn't sure, because none of her senses were working properly.

"Kainé, are you all right? Kainé!"

Nier's voice grew distant as Kainé's vision went dark. All she could hear was Tyrann laughing. This was bad. Soon—very soon—her body would be overrun by the Shade that was blood-thirst incarnate.

Get . . . back . . . was what she wanted to say, but she could scarcely speak.

"It's all over for you, Sunshine!"

With Tyrann's triumphant screech came darkness.

3.

"WHAT IS THIS?!"

Grimoire Weiss was the first to speak, or perhaps it's fairer to say he was the first to remember *how*. The sight before the party was so unbelievable that Nier and Emil had forgotten speech was even possible.

Black letters floated across Kainé's body, reminiscent of the symbols that appeared on Yonah's limbs when her Black Scrawl was flaring. However, Yonah's symptoms were a result of illness and lacked the aura of a Shade.

The symbols on Kainé's body writhed, exuding a thick Shade aura, covering her entire body. Eventually the symbols lost their shapes and morphed into dark mist that grew thicker by the moment, staining her skin black.

Nier could feel incredible power wafting from her. The weapon that had pierced her chest melted like hard candy over a fire. He only had time to think two words—*Oh no*—before he felt his body lift into the air. A moment later, an impact on his back and head confirmed he had been flying.

He struggled to get up. His world spun. He tried and failed to focus his eyes on something—anything—but the entire process was taking far too long. Finally, out of the corner of his hazy vision, he spotted Kainé—or at least the thing that *should* have been Kainé. But instead, it was a Shade with her silhouette, and the growling voice of a strange animal. Her limbs were twisted in unnatural directions, and her eyes glinted red like a monster in the dark.

"It's Kainé's Shade . . ." Emil began before trailing off. He couldn't find a way to say the words they were all thinking: The Shade that possessed her had finally assumed total control.

Kainé had long worn provocative clothing despite the gawking stares and unnecessary comments it produced. But there was a reason for this: to keep Tyrann's encroachment in check. Both regular Shades in the field and those that possessed humans were weak against the light of the sun, and neither could exist in flesh that was constantly exposed to it.

Yet Kainé had kept the left half of her body bandaged, blocking the sunlight. She wanted to keep the Shade in check, yes— but she *also* wanted to use its power. She needed it alive inside her in order to maintain her superhuman physical prowess. It was a dangerous dance, but she'd managed to find a way to coexist with it for some time. However, the balance had tipped too far in the opposite direction.

Now entirely a Shade, Kainé leaped in the air and began scuttling across the wall like a lizard. The wound in her chest was gone. Nier had heard from Kainé about the Shade's physical and regenerative abilities, but seeing it for himself was astonishing.

"What should we do, Weiss?" he asked as Kainé began peppering them with an outpouring of magic. Not the magic she normally used but *Shade* magic.

"We'll make no progress in this state!" cried the book. "Strike her down!"

Nier fired off a magical spear but found it hard to aim while constantly dodging Kainé's attacks.

"I'll handle this!" called Emil as he floated through the air and approached her. "Kainé! Come back!"

The moment Kainé's attention turned to Emil, Nier fired another spear, causing her to howl as she fell from the wall.

"Now!" Grimoire Weiss exclaimed. "Pin her down with magic! Do not use your blade!"

It was the same method they used when Emil had been almost overtaken by Number 6. Nier slowly approached Kainé, firing magical bullets as he did, but it wasn't enough to keep the Shade in place. As he watched, the writhing black mist that was her body suddenly rose and leaped back onto the wall in one smooth motion.

"Emil, get back!" Nier yelled as he protected Emil from the spell Kainé cast as she leaped.

But Emil would have none of it. "No! Let me handle this! I'll be fine—my sister's power will *make* it fine!"

Emil flew straight toward Kainé and her endless barrage of magic. She was clearly injured—her leaps were not as frequent as they had been earlier—and she was within range of Nier's magical hand. Even if it didn't hit her, it might at least draw her attention away from Emil, so Nier unleashed the spell and sent it straight at her.

"It's do or die time!" yelled Emil. He raised his staff, closing the distance between himself and Kainé. A moment later, their magic clashed in a ferocious display that proved just how powerful the two of them actually were.

"Provide support!" called Grimoire Weiss, who didn't have to tell Nier twice. He knew his attacks would land if he used them now, so he sent out a magic spear, hoping to be of at least a *little* use to Emil.

The attack struck home, piercing right through Kainé. A moment later, Emil's magic finally overcame that of Kainé's, sending her crashing back to the ground.

"Kainé, please! Come back to us!" Emil called.

Nier fired all the magical bullets he could in an attempt to keep Kainé down. Emil raised his staff, firing magic that clashed with Kainé's once more. This created a flash of light that burned Nier's eyes, followed by a deep rumbling that deafened him. After that, there was a long, long silence—one finally broken by the voice of Grimoire Weiss.

"Oh, dear."

The Shade coloring vanished from Kainé's body. The black mist returned to its place beneath her bandages. Yet her eyes remained closed and seemed content to stay that way.

Emil began calling her name, doing so with the same distress he'd felt in the library when she was freed from her petrification. There was no way a voice so pure and honest could fail to reach her, and after a long moment, her eyes slowly peeled open, blinking in the light.

"Kainé!" Emil cried.

Kainé's expression was clouded. "I . . . I couldn't hold it back . . ."

Had she been conscious while the Shade took control? If so, it must have been a terrible thing to experience. But in the end, it didn't matter if she realized what was happening or not; a Shade made her attack her friends, and there was no one to blame for it but herself.

"I can't be with—"

You anymore was what she was going to say, but Emil cut her off.

"We're always going to be together, Kainé." Though her eyes were cast downward, he took her hand in his own. "If you transform again, we'll just stop it again. As many times as it takes. I don't care how tough it is, we're gonna get you back!

"I like sleeping outside because I'm with you, Kainé!" he

continued in a tone that would brook no argument. "I'm able to ignore my appearance and keep going because of you! I'm weak, and I'm sad, and I'm lonely, but you make me strong! You're my friend and I need you, so don't you dare leave me!"

Tears began to stream down Emil's face. Everything he said came out of him in a single breath, and he was incapable of doing anything more than sit there and sob.

As Kainé watched Emil, a gentle hue colored her eyes.

"All right," she said, running a hand over Emil's head. "All right. Stop crying."

As she sat up, an inquisitive hum came from Grimoire Weiss.

"What is it, Weiss?" asked Nier—but the tome ignored the question and instead made his way to the altar. At some point, a door had appeared behind it. It hadn't been there when they first entered the room, and Nier didn't recall it being there five years ago. Perhaps some sort of seal had loosened when they felled the stone Shade.

"This might lead to the Shadowlord's castle," said an excited Nier.

"But it seems it will not let us simply waltz inside," replied Weiss. "Something else has appeared along with the door."

"Is that a barrier?"

Whatever it was, it was clearly meant to prevent people from getting in through the door. Indeed, a similar barrier had been in a similar spot five years ago. That one had vanished when Nier killed the one-horned statue, but now the other statue was dead and this barrier remained. What could they kill, then, to remove this one?

"This must be of some significance," murmured Grimoire Weiss.

Nier walked over to where his companion was concentrating

and saw he was correct: A pentagonal drawing with a stone fragment inside sat before the barrier. The stone hadn't merely fallen into that location; the lines of the drawing clearly matched the shape of the stone, indicating it belonged there.

"What's this?" asked Nier. He picked the fragment up and saw it was carved with strange patterns. They were similar shapes that appeared with regular frequency, meaning it had to be some kind of writing, though it wasn't a system he was familiar with.

"It's got some kind of writing on it, but I dunno what it says. You have any idea, Weiss?"

"How remarkably useless of you," responded the tome. "Let us go ask Popola."

His prim tone helpfully glossed over the fact he was also unable to read the text.

4.

WHEN POPOLA LAID eyes on the fragment, her brow furrowed lightly.

"It's a cipher of some kind."

"I thought so," Grimoire Weiss murmured. The reason he'd been unable to understand the writing was because it was written in code. "Can you determine its meaning?"

Popola, who was sitting with fingers pressed to her temple, suddenly looked up. "You said there was a pentagonal outline, yes?"

She reached into her shelf of old books. She repaired those that were worse for wear in her free time, but her office was still filled with worn and tattered tomes.

"Here, look at this."

The book was ancient enough that the binding looked ready to crumble at any moment. With great care, she opened to a certain point, causing Nier's mouth to fly open. The design on the page was the same as the pentagon carved on the altar.

"But how?!" he exclaimed.

"I thought this might have been the thing you saw," said Popola. "That should mean that what's written on that fragment is an encoded version of . . ."

"The language in that book?"

"Yes. The fragment you have is called 'The Stone Guardian,' and I think the lines inside the pentagon signify the shapes of stone fragments. That means there are four others—like this one, for example."

"The Law of Robotics," Grimoire Weiss said as Popola pointed to a bit of writing.

"You can read that, Weiss?" asked an increasingly shocked Nier.

"I am the great tome of knowledge, Grimoire Weiss! Every written script in every book is known to me. Also, that one there reads 'Sacrifice,' does it not?"

As Popola nodded, he continued. "The others say 'The Memory Tree' and 'Loyal Cerberus.' Given that you found 'The Stone Guardian' in the Lost Shrine, the others must signify other locations."

"I get that we'll make the pentagon shape if we put all five fragments together," Nier began. "But is there any *actual* significance to that?"

Indeed, if names like "The Law of Robotics" and "The Memory Tree" were pointing to the locations of the other fragments, why were they kept separate? Why weren't all five of them waiting on the altar?

"I think this is the key to unlocking the Shadowlord's castle," Popola began.

"And what makes you say that?" Grimoire Weiss cut in sharply. "What could you possibly see in these shapes and fragments that allows you to say so with such conviction?"

He sounded more accusatory than doubtful, as if he were questioning not the explanation but rather Popola herself.

"Weiss," Nier spoke up. "You can't just doubt Popola like—"

"It's fine," Popola interrupted, seemingly unbothered. "I should have said that first. The information is in this book—it claims the entrance to the Shadowlord's castle is located in the Lost Shrine."

When Popola first told them about the Lost Shrine, Nier wondered how she came about the information. But Popola knew a lot of things—and a lot of people. No matter how far Nier traveled or how remote the village, there were always one or two folks who asked after her. At the time, he'd figured one of her many acquaintances had given her the information.

But it turned out the answer was in the library the whole time. That made sense because the only thing Popola had more of than acquaintances was books.

"I guess it figures we'd learn this information in a library, right, Weiss?"

Nier turned to his friend for confirmation but received none. Instead, the book doubled down on his grilling of Popola.

"How did you know the answers to the Shadowlord's castle would be in that book, mmm? You have a near-infinite number of texts in this building—what ever made you decide to look at *that* particular one?"

"It wasn't me," replied Popola. "It was Devola. She found this years and years ago. Apparently it was all a big coincidence—she was just puttering around and happened to pick up a book that had the Song of the Ancients in it."

"That's the one she's always singing, right?" asked Nier.

Popola nodded and began reciting the lyrics: "From distance eternal come black wings o'er the land. Feathers fall, bringing ruin. Only white wings may silence its echoes of arrival."

There's a terrible black book that shows up and starts spreading disease all over the place, but then a white book appears and saves the world is what Devola told them it meant five years prior. Those lyrics were what sent Nier and Weiss out in search of the Sealed Verses in the first place. Nier believed with all his heart that collecting them and defeating Grimoire Noir would cure Yonah of the Black Scrawl. But in the end, they hadn't been able to bring

Grimoire Noir down, and Yonah had been stolen away by the Shadowlord.

"It's an old song, and I didn't think it meant much," Popola explained. "But it turned out that Grimoire Weiss *did* exist, as did the Sealed Verses and Grimoire Noir. I figured if that was true, it might also contain information on the Shadowlord, so I decided to read it cover to cover."

"You read *that* thing cover to cover?" marveled Nier. It was as thick as three or four of Yonah's favorite picture books stacked together, with pages crammed full of tiny writing. He couldn't begin to imagine how long such a task would have taken.

"Yes, although it was more difficult than I imagined and took a great deal of time. I was hoping to find what I needed and tell you earlier, but I did my best with what I had to work with. I'm truly sorry."

"You don't have to apologize, Popola," said Nier. From the corner, Grimoire Weiss cleared his throat awkwardly. If there had been any doubts remaining in his pages, her explanation seemed to have cleared them away.

"So about these four fragments," said Popola, resuming the conversation as though nothing had happened. She grabbed a pen and paper and quickly wrote down five phrases: *Sacrifice. The Law of Robotics. The Memory Tree. Loyal Cerberus. The Stone Guardian.*

"'The Law of Robotics' probably refers to the Junk Heap," she said as she finished. Though it had been left abandoned to rust, the Junk Heap had once served as a large military facility. Nier had no idea what its original use was, but the name "Junk Heap" certainly fit what it had become.

"Also, I think The Memory Tree might be the Forest of Myth," continued Popola.

"Right," said Nier. "That makes sense." A strange disease

where people were pulled into others' dreams had broken out in the Forest of Myth. After going there, Nier and Weiss discovered a Sealed Verse in a great tree at the forest's center; it only made sense that would be The Memory Tree.

"As for the other two, I don't have a clue," Popola finished.

"'Sacrifice' and 'Loyal Cerberus,' mmm?" Grimoire Weiss mused.

"Cerberus is likely talking about a dog, but I'm not aware of any particularly unusual dogs."

Popola and Grimoire Weiss fell silent, as though admitting defeat in the face of the final two clues. In Nier's eyes, however, the entire affair was absurdly simple. They knew a gigantic Shade had been guarding the altar at the Lost Shrine. That altar was the entrance to the Shadowlord's castle, *and* the thing that housed The Stone Guardian. And since they'd needed to kill the Shade to secure the fragment, the only logical conclusion was . . .

"So we just have to kill the big Shades guarding these fragments to claim them, right? That's easy. It'll be like when we collected the Sealed Verses." While the only specific place names they had were the Junk Heap and Forest of Myth, the Shades they'd be looking for weren't your run-of-the-mill types. Nier figured it would be a simple thing to find them.

Grimoire Weiss snorted. "Oh, splendid. By all means, let us undertake a murderous rampage."

"This will be a dangerous task," Popola reminded him.

Why is she telling me this now? Nier wondered. He'd taken jobs killing Shades to raise money for Yonah's medicine, and he felled a number of enormous ones to collect the Sealed Verses. He killed and killed and killed to look for clues on the Shadowlord's whereabouts; what she considered "dangerous" was merely something he'd been doing for a long time now. And besides . . .

"Yeah, well, Yonah's in even more danger," he finished aloud.

"But how can you even be sure that she's—"

"Because she is! All right?"

Popola's gaze dropped to the floor as she fell silent. Even the normally loquacious Grimoire Weiss had nothing to add.

"The Junk Heap and the Forest of Myth, yeah?" Nier continued. "I'm on my way."

"Please," Popola said in response, her voice barely a whisper. "Be careful."

It was something she always said to him, yet for some reason, her eyes remained downcast this time.

REPORT 10

At long last, we've discovered the Shadow-lord's location. We wanted to square this away ourselves as soon as possible, but Gretel was guarding the entrance to his castle, and that Shade was beyond our capabilities. Thus, we told Nier that the Lost Shrine connected to the Shadowlord's lair.

Surprisingly, however, the Shadowlord has sealed off the entrance. I surmise it was Grimoire Noir's idea to lock the door and not simply leave a Shade to guard the entrance—he likely anticipated our approaching the Shadow-lord in order to prevent the failure of Project Gestalt.

The fact Nier brought useful information back was a stroke of good luck, but unfortunately, the key to the Shadowlord's castle has been turned into a cipher. Still, considering how the Shadowlord's subordinates need to share this information among themselves, I imagine it will be relatively easy to solve.

My plan was to send Nier out to collect the pieces while I begin work on that aspect, but I did not anticipate Grimoire Weiss having doubts about the scheme. He was eventually calmed with proper reasoning, but we could have been in real trouble had that gone a different way.

We'll have to be very careful around him in

the future. I assumed his amnesia would render him mostly harmless, but in fact, it may instead be causing him to engage in unexpected behavior. At present, I feel Grimoire Weiss is our single largest cause for concern.

End report.

Record written by Popola

The Man 3

1.

HOW MANY YEARS had it been since Nier last visited the Junk Heap? When he heard the answer, he was shocked. *Five?* He'd dropped by to have one of his weapons reinforced right after Yonah was kidnapped, but apparently that was the last time.

"This place hasn't changed."

The metal bridge. The ladders. The fence at the entrance. The mesh door to the shop. It was all the same. Emil was the only one who seemed even remotely curious about the place; he flew up to crooked scaffolding and chased mice that scuttled at his feet. For her part, Kainé was wholly uninterested, preferring to lean against the fence and close her eyes. As the two of them settled into their respective positions, Nier and Weiss ventured into the shop.

"Oh, hey there," said a voice. "It's been a while."

It was the elder of the two brothers greeting them, and like the location, he also hadn't changed. Except . . . No, wait. It wasn't the *elder* brother at all.

"You're the little one, aren't you?" said Nier. "You've grown up."

Despite how strikingly similar the face was to the older brother, Jakob, it was the younger brother, Gideon, who stood before them. Nier figured the elder must be in the Heap scavenging for material, and Grimoire Weiss clearly had the same thought.

"How fares your brother?" he asked. His tone was that of an old man speaking to a child, likely because Gideon had been so small when they first met. But when the brother answered, his words could not have been more unexpected.

"My brother died in an accident four years ago."

"Oh, I see," said Weiss solemnly. "Please forgive the question."

With the boy's mother dying five years prior and Jakob's more recent passing, that left Gideon all alone in the world.

"It's all right," he reassured them. "So how can I help you today? Do you need your weapons improved? Or something else, perhaps?"

Gideon had probably spent the last four years coming to grips with what happened, so Nier did his best to stay calm and not make things gloomier than they were.

"I need to ask you something," he said.

"What is it?"

"Have you heard any rumors about Shades around here? Not the little ones—I'm looking for one that's unusually big and powerful."

"No, I haven't heard about anything like that. But I haven't really been listening."

Something suddenly felt off. The boy's tone had turned bright—strangely so.

"All I want to do is destroy robots," he continued. "Just rip 'em up."

Despite a chuckle at the end, there was a faint chill to his expression, and Nier began to wonder if perhaps he'd spent the last four years drifting away from sanity instead of toward it.

"Uh . . ." Nier hesitated, unsure of what to say. "Okay? Never mind then. See you later."

"Wait!"

"Yes?"

"I recently got my hands on a weapon. A very powerful weapon. I thought you might get some use out of it."

Gideon pointed to a weapon resting against the wall. It was a greatsword, one that looked particularly heavy at a glance but also oddly short.

"Hmm," remarked Weiss. "This sword has seen better days."

As Nier examined the weapon, he realized the short length was because the tip of the blade had been broken off. "Can you repair it?" he asked.

"I can repair anything with the proper materials," Gideon replied.

"Well, if you'll fix it, I'll get the parts."

"Eee hee! I'm so glad I decided not to throw it out!"

With that, Gideon took out a small piece of paper and began to write. He looked shockingly similar to his brother when he did so—both in the way his shoulders were drawn up and how his hand clenched the pen. Nier almost thought he could hear Jakob saying, *Here's the passcode!*

But Gideon spoke faster than his brother and also didn't attempt to make eye contact. Now that Nier was having a conversation with him, the differences between the two stuck out more.

"Here's everything I need to repair it," Gideon said after a moment. "Only the real big enemies on the second basement level have them, so watch yourself. Oh, and here's the passcode to get down there. Use it on the elevator."

After thanking the boy, Nier pushed open the door, passed through the outside area, and ventured into the Junk Heap just as he had five years prior. The robots waiting for them at the entrance and the pungent smell of oil were exactly the same; it brought up memories of the past, causing Grimoire Weiss to speak in an unusually grave tone.

"It's a shame about the older lad. He was but a child."

"Gideon said it was an accident," Nier added. The death had

probably been sudden. More likely than not, Jakob had no idea when he woke that morning that the day would be his last.

"The elder brother postponed his joy for the sake of his sibling. Do you think he was ever truly happy?" Grimoire Weiss mused.

Nier nodded. "Just making his little brother happy would have been enough. That's what being an older brother is like."

His only regret would have been leaving Gideon alone in the world to fend for himself. But if Jakob's death had been sudden, he wouldn't have had time to think about such things. So of course he was happy to help his little brother. He had to be.

"Maybe we should start coming back a little more often for upgrades," Nier mumbled.

"Are you trying to make up for five years' worth of lost custom?"

"No! It's just that we'll be fighting the Shades guarding these fragments, right? Quality weapons will be important."

"Mm-hmm."

The excuse was clearly forced, and Weiss saw right through it. But perhaps there hadn't been any need for excuses; Weiss had also seen how the little brother cried for his mother and no doubt thought about coming to check on him from time to time as well.

When the group reached the second basement level, they found foes who were powerful but manageable, and Nier soon had the memory alloy he needed. He was better with a sword now and had both Kainé and Emil by his side; he even had the time and energy to grab some other useful materials while they were there. It was all a result of the hard work he'd put in over the past five years. He couldn't help but think about how that was such a long time—for both him and Gideon.

Upon their second visit to the store, however, he realized time had not been as kind to the young boy as he'd assumed.

"I need to ask you a favor," said Gideon. He looked at Nier with sharp eyes, the repaired weapon lying on the counter before him. It was a familiar look—Kainé had worn the same one while facing off against the Shade that killed her grandmother.

"I want you to avenge my brother."

He *was* the same as Kainé. "Avenge" was something one said about someone or something that had killed another, which meant the boy's brother hadn't died in an accident at all. Time had likely come to a halt for Gideon the moment his brother was killed, just as it did for all those whose families had been needlessly taken from them.

"That is a rather ponderous favor," Grimoire Weiss remarked.

The boy aggressively shook his head. "It's my mission! It's the whole reason I've been creating these weapons for the past four years. I don't care about money! I only care about making a weapon strong enough to kill those bastards!"

"Which bastards?" Nier asked.

"The ones in the mountain. That little Shade and his robot!"

"There's a Shade in there?"

In that moment, Nier realized his own sense of time had come to a halt the moment Yonah was stolen away. He and the boy in front of him were exactly the same in that respect.

"You've got to avenge my brother!" Gideon pleaded. "Kill him! Kill that damn robot! Rip 'em up!"

"Oh, we're gonna kill it," said Nier as he reached for the greatsword with its dully gleaming blade.

2.

KAINÉ SUDDENLY UNDERSTOOD what it was like to be a cat whose fur was standing on end. Her instincts were pounding with an unpleasantness that made her feel sick. She'd been hoping to avoid having to do any of this a second time, and yet here they were, the merry-go-round spinning all over again.

"Revenge, huh?" she said to herself. The moment she heard the kid's desperate plea from behind the mesh door, she was annoyed. The last thing she wanted to do was go into the Junk Heap again, but she knew there was no way Nier would tell the kid no.

Still, she understood—perhaps too well—which was why she fell into step behind Nier without a word. As they crammed into the small elevator, she clicked her tongue at the floors that slid past and wrinkled her nose at the metallic, oily odor.

When it came to the actual combat, things were surprisingly simple. When robots came pouring into open spaces, she kept her distance and took them down with magic. When she encountered them in close quarters or her field of view was obstructed, she ran up, struck their weak point, and leaped away again. It was a trick she'd learned from Nier, and a very effective one.

She'd had no idea a robot was about to self-destruct the first time one shut down in front of her, and she paid for the mistake by being sent flying across the room. If not for Tyrann's restorative abilities, it likely would have been the last mistake she ever made. Kainé had begun to doubt her ability to control her power back at the Lost Shrine, but she was now painfully aware she couldn't do without it in the thick of a heated battle.

"I've never heard of a Shade living with a machine," Emil said with wonder as they moved through the Junk Heap. "What's that about?"

"Don't know, don't care," Nier spat. "All that matters is that we kill them both."

"Right," added Kainé. Nier hadn't been looking for agreement, but she answered anyway. His bold words were just what she needed to hear right now, so she decided to try her hand at it as well.

Still, a Shade and a robot were both enemies, which meant they'd launch an attack the moment the group encountered them. For Kainé's part, she felt it would be easier to kill the robot since they didn't talk. Even the Shades that only strung together meaningless, nonsensical sequences of words would have been all right. But more than that? Actual speech? She wasn't sure she could handle it.

"How'd it go again, Sunshine? 'Don't hurt my friends'?"

Kainé scowled when Tyrann spoke. He had *such* a talent for saying the exact right thing to make her feel completely despondent.

"So you did *sympathize with that big ol' thing? Aww, I feel the tears coming—and* the laughs! Kyaaaa ha ha ha!*"*

Arguing would only make Tyrann happier, so she kept her mouth shut. But she still couldn't help thinking about it. Why were some Shades so intelligent? Why did they mourn the deaths of their companions? Their only function was to attack people, which meant their mental capabilities should be beneath that of worms.

Then again, was that *really* the case? Tyrann was crafty, cruel, and clearly very intelligent, and he was a Shade. The prospect that some of the creatures might have one of those traits shouldn't come as a surprise.

"*Hey, now!*" cackled Tyrann. "*Cruel? You're cruel—even if you're right! So what are you gonna do if this Shade talks, huh? What if it's intelligent but also nice and polite? What if you get an earful of a sob story? Then what, sister?*"

Instead of telling him to shut up, Kainé leaped, letting gravity drag her down as she plunged her blades into a robot near a large wooden crate. She withdrew her swords, then thrust again, throwing all of her momentum into the action. Over and over. Again and again.

Suddenly, sparks flew and there was a horrible noise. Panicked, she leaped away, the blast of air from the explosion knocking her onto her ass, causing her to bark with laughter.

Not exactly graceful there, huh?

"Kainé!" Emil cried.

"You okay?!" Nier called.

They started to approach her, but she held up a hand to stop them and picked herself up.

"Yeah. I'm fine."

She plucked a few shards of metal out of her arm. Blood poured out momentarily, but skin soon scabbed over the wound as the pain receded. Even if she was wounded—even if she bled—Kainé always returned to normal. This was the power of a Shade—and it meant she wasn't human.

She told herself that even if their next foe was an intelligent Shade, she would still kill it. Even if it was kind and considerate, it was still a Shade. Not a person. *All that matters is that we kill them both* was what Nier had said, and Kainé knew he was right.

As they went deeper, they realized the map Gideon gave them was technically correct but missing a few key elements. When they reached the second basement level, for example, they were forced to ride a small trolley through a swarm of flying robots. After that, they had to climb a long spiral ramp and ride an elevator up again. Now they found themselves standing before a massive pit.

"It seems we have found the entrance to our robot friend's hideout," Weiss said. His tone betrayed how fed up he was with the whole exercise. A hole without a ladder could hardly be called a passageway.

"Right," said Nier. "Let's head down."

"Are you mad?!" Grimoire Weiss replied in utter shock. "We've no idea what lies below!"

It was a fair point: Weiss and Emil could both float, and Kainé had the boon of a Shade. A fall from a great height would be no real bother for them, but for Nier, it could easily prove fatal.

"Beats going the long way around," said Nier. "Come on."

The rest of the party stared at one another, unsure what to do or say considering the one person in danger didn't seem to care.

"Okay, wait here," said Emil finally. "I'll see what's down there."

"Oh, screw this," said Kainé as she leaped into the hole without waiting for a reply. She knew Emil would be in danger if the hole was filled with robots or Shades or any other kind of evil fiend. And besides, he'd take forever to gently float down, while she could rocket straight to the bottom like a stone.

As she expected, it took less than a second. Just as she started hearing wind howling past her ears, a heavy shock traveled from the soles of her feet and through her legs. That was a good sign; it meant the drop wasn't long enough to splatter any normal person who decided to try it.

Kainé scanned the area, ready to confirm the absence of

enemies and give the signal, when Nier suddenly landed next to her. She glared at him—what the hell was the point in her jumping down first if he was just going to do it anyway?

A moment later, however, she was glad he had. When she looked away from him, she saw the robot. There wouldn't have even been time to check for enemies or send any kind of signal. The map might not have been user-friendly, but it did get the facts right.

"There it is!" cried Nier.

As he readied himself, Grimoire Weiss floated over to his side and said, "Good lord, it's enormous!" It was a fair comment, considering the machine was far larger than any of the robots they'd seen so far.

Suddenly, a voice rang out with the words "Intruder detected." It wasn't the voice of a Shade, nor was it human. Kainé's eyes immediately began looking around to find the source.

"Get 'em!"

Now *that* was a Shade. Reflexively, Kainé called out to the others and pointed. Resting atop the massive robot was a little Shade, one that seemed to be lounging about rather than concerning itself with any particular purpose.

When Kainé heard there was a Shade working with a murderous robot, she'd pictured an enormous, ferocious sort of creature—Gretel from the Lost Shrine or the thing with the giant head that attacked Nier's village. But the one atop the robot seemed more like the inconsequential, incomplete Shades that had inhabited the Lost Shrine.

The robot's eyes suddenly lit up, as though signaling the start of the battle. "Intruder detected" came the voice again, at which point Kainé realized it had been the source of the strange words she heard moments ago.

"Intruder detected. Scanning. Scanning. Exterminating."

As the robot stomped the ground, the Shade atop it threw up both arms.

"Do it, Beepy! Beat 'em good!"

Kainé couldn't believe her ears. That didn't sound like something a Shade would say—it was more like a phrase you'd hear from a human toddler. A childlike Shade? A talking robot? She'd figured their foe was going to cause her at least a little heartburn, but this was something else entirely.

The robot stomped the ground again, causing the floor to shudder and bring Kainé to her knees.

"That thing is commanding the robot somehow!" Grimoire Weiss cried.

Wrong, book. Those aren't commands.

"Aim for the legs!" yelled Emil. "Knock it down!"

It didn't seem Emil could hear it either. In fact, none of Kainé's companions had any idea what the Shade and robot were talking about.

"C'mon, Sunshine! Rip 'em to shreds! I thought you were gonna kill every Shade you could find, so LET'S GET TO KILLING ALREADY!"

Tyrann was jabbing right where it hurt, but he was right. She was going to kill every Shade—she *had* to.

"Take out the Shade!" Kainé yelled as a way to encourage herself. Her voice was louder than normal; without that effort, she wasn't sure she'd be able to keep a handle on her swords. As she yelled, Nier plunged his blade into the joint of the robot's leg, and Emil fired his magic. When Kainé followed suit a moment later, the robot's voice began to stutter.

"Exterminating . . . ing . . . ing . . . ing . . . ing . . ."

A dull sensation ran up her arms as she swung her blades, almost like she was cutting into stone. The horrid sound of metal on metal reached her ears. She slashed again and this time felt something pop loose. She'd harbored doubts as to whether swords would work on a robot so thoroughly covered in metal plating, but the joints were weaker than she had expected. Once the outer plates were dealt with, the insides were surprisingly fragile.

"*Beepy, stop!*" the little Shade cried out. "*That's enough! You're gonna be destroyed if you keep fighting!*"

Cried out? No. That wasn't right. That was a different voice. It had to be. Shades couldn't cry out in distress.

"Dammit, that's a Shade," growled Kainé. "It's a Shade!"

When the robot raised its foot, Nier rolled out of the way, taking the opportunity to send forth a volley of magic. Kainé heard something break, and a moment later saw a crack appear on the robot's leg.

"Must defend . . . my mission . . ." sputtered the robot.

"*No!*" yelled the little Shade. "*I can't live without you! I don't wanna be alone again!*"

"It is . . . my job . . . to protect . . ."

The static in the robot's voice made it sound like it was running out of breath. But the machine's strained gasps meant nothing to Nier, Emil, and Weiss, who continued to mercilessly assault its metallic frame with magic and steel. Every time an attack connected, there came a loud creaking noise, almost as if the robot was groaning in pain.

"*Kill 'em!*" cackled Tyrann. "*Kill 'em real good!*"

"Dammit!" screamed Kainé. She swung her swords again, keeping her eyes averted. She thought she'd miss, but her blade slotted right into the crack on its leg, bringing the massive automaton crashing to the floor.

"Attack now!" ordered Weiss. As Nier plunged his sword into the robot's back, Emil melted its metal with his magic.

"*Beepy!*" the Shade screamed again.

"Military Defense Robot P-33 will protect Kalil."

Now Kainé understood: The robot was called P-33, while the Shade's name was Kalil. As that thought crossed her mind, the discarded pieces of metal littering the arena began to shudder. Banging and clanging, they swirled toward P-33; all their hard work to chip its armor away was being undone in an instant.

"P-33 will defend Kalil," proclaimed the robot. As it spoke, the discarded metal bits began forming a pair of enormous wings.

"This thing can transform?!" Nier exclaimed.

P-33 stretched out its awkward-looking wings and stood. It then began to flap the newfound appendages, creating a massive gale with each up-and-down motion.

"Get into cover!" Grimoire Weiss shouted.

"Beepy! What are you doing?"

"Escape. Escape. Escape. Escape."

It seemed impossible for such a large metal being to fly, and had you asked Kainé before this moment, she would have expressed doubt it would even be able to get off the ground. And yet there it was, bobbing in midair amid dire gusts of wind.

"Go . . . see the world-ld-ld-ld-ld," stuttered P-33 as it lifted higher and higher into the air with Kalil in its arms.

"Where do you think you're going?!" Nier shouted as he and Emil let fly a volley of magic. But their attempts to shoot the robot only caused scraps of metal to rain down everywhere.

"Look out!" cried Weiss. "Get out of the way!"

Kainé craned her neck as she dodged debris and saw P-33 ram straight into the ceiling. It was impossible to tell if the rubbish falling all around them was robot parts, ceiling parts, or both.

"You taught me much . . . Kalil," said the robot in a halting voice. "You have helped to expand . . . my vocabulary. You . . . have instructed me . . . in the ways of the outside world."

P-33 rammed against the ceiling again. Black smoke poured from its torso, but it showed no signs of stopping. Words Kainé wished she could block out pelted her along with scraps of metal.

"We . . . explore the world . . . together. We . . ."

But that was all. P-33 slowly began coming back to the ground, unable to keep its altitude. Even from this distance, Kainé could see sparks bursting from its body.

"Aim for the wings!" instructed Weiss, an order with which Nier and Emil were more than happy to comply. P-33's body began to tip in midair as their magic struck home, a wing peeling from its back. The remaining one continued to flap violently, but it wasn't enough to keep the robot airborne.

The sound of cascading metal caused the entire room to shudder as P-33 fell forward and at last remained still. Kalil, however, was still moving. It rolled away from the body of the robot, a small, faint thing that resembled the incomplete Shades from the Lost Shrine.

"*Stop!*" it cried, throwing its arms wide. "*Beepy's my best friend in the whole world! Stop hurting him!*"

The way it was trying to protect someone besides itself was the same as those incomplete Shades. And just like them, it was too weak to do so, fated only to disappear into mist. As it approached them, arms raised, Nier's sword flashed, tearing the Shade neatly in two and causing it to start melting.

"*I'm sorry, Beepy,*" Kalil whimpered as it collapsed to the floor. "*I'm not strong enough . . . I wanted . . . to be with you . . . forever . . .*"

As the lines of Kalil's silhouette began to fade, it crawled toward P-33. This was different from the other incomplete Shades—how it so desperately wanted to be with its friend to the very end.

"Kalil . . . Together . . ."

P-33's arms shuddered. Even though it was so horribly injured that it could barely function, the robot continued to reach out for its companion. But Kalil was already gone, its darkened form turned to mist.

"Beepy alone . . . Beepy . . . cry?"

The light vanished from P-33's eyes. The whirring of machinery fell silent. All Kainé could hear was Nier's breathing. Both robot and Shade were no more. But in the silence that followed, she heard another noise: the soft clatter of something falling from P-33's motionless body.

"Nier, look!" Emil cried. "It's a fragment! It's part of the key to the Shadowlord's castle!"

The party hadn't come to the Junk Heap to take out a random robot; they came because of the phrase "The Law of Robotics." The fact the robot contained what they needed only meant it was doomed to die in the first place. Knowing its death had a purpose made Kainé feel slightly better about the entire affair—and yet she hated that she needed to be reassured at all.

"It appears we've found what we came for."

As Grimoire Weiss peered at the fragment, a sudden noise ripped through the silence: the sound of hard soles on ground. The group turned to see Gideon, who had apparently been following them the entire time. With the party having taken out the dangerous robots, it had been a simple matter for the young boy to move through the Heap.

"You stupid machine! You killed my family! You took everything from me!"

Gideon grabbed a nearby pipe and brought it down on the wrecked remains of the robot. The sound of the impact rattled the acrid air in the chamber in a most uncomfortable way. "Why did you have to be here?! Why you?! *Why?!*"

Kainé knew Gideon's mother had been killed by a machine; Weiss once mentioned her being shot by some kind of defense robot. Still, she found it unlikely P-33 had anything to do with it.

"You took everything from me!" Gideon howled as he pounded the robot. "You killed my brother! You killed my mother! If it weren't for you, they'd still be *alive!*"

Wait—P-33 killed his brother? The robot who called the Shade Kalil and who was called Beepy in turn? The one who vowed to protect and stay with his little Shade friend and wanted to see the outside world with him? The one who reached for him as he died? *That* robot?

"Hey, come on. That's enough," Nier said gently.

"I did it!" Gideon shrieked. "Can you believe it?! I did it! I DID IT!"

In truth, it was Kainé, Nier, Emil, and Weiss who took down P-33. But Gideon was too far gone to worry about such minor details.

"Now that this goddamn thing is dead, I can forage wherever I want! Just wait, you goddamn freak! Now I can make all *kinds* of powerful weapons! I'm gonna make a fine weapon! Gonna rip those machines apart! *Every single one of them!* Aaah ha ha! So many weapons! I'll rip 'em up!"

The laughter pouring from Gideon's throat caused Kainé to shiver.

"Just leave it to me! I'll rip every robot to shreds!"

"Look, we get it, okay?" Nier placed a calming hand on the boy's shoulder, but he kept laughing.

"Yesss. Goooood!"

Kainé had been waiting for Tyrann to chime in. This kind of dark emotional outpouring was right up his alley.

"*People always pretend like they did nothing wrong. They always find a way to blame something else. And I freakin' LOVE IT!*"

Something else? That meant Tyrann, too, thought it wasn't P-33 who killed Gideon's brother.

"*Don't you get it, Sunshine? Kid pinned the blame on the robot so he had an excuse to kill it. Remember how he said Big Bro died in an accident? Well, I'm betting this psycho caused the accident HIMSELF! Kyaaa ha ha ha!"*

Though Kainé hated the idea, she knew Tyrann—the supreme connoisseur of the ugliest and most horrible parts of the human mind—knew all there was to know about such emotions. So perhaps it wasn't an idea at all but a fact.

"Beautiful. What a perfect example of humanity!"

This? Humanity? Some kid smashing a pipe against a corpse while he howls in anger and madness is *humanity*?

Kainé remembered the way P-33 said the word *alone* in his last moments. She remembered how Kalil begged them to stop hurting him. So which of these things was the true example of humanity?

Kainé had no answer.

REPORT 11

Popola warned me earlier that my reports are unnecessarily long. I do tend to write down every little detail, so please bear with me.

As one might expect from her warning me about such things, my sister works quite quickly. And the same can be said for Nier. When we told him "The Law of Robotics" was a reference to the Junk Heap, he went there that day, just like he did when we told him about the Lost Shrine.

At first, he was told there'd been no word of a big Shade out at the Heap, so he came back disappointed. (We were honestly shocked by that as well but glad to learn it was false. Details to follow.)

Thing is, Popola doesn't make mistakes in her work, and the fragment was indeed waiting in the Junk Heap. Several days later, Nier returned with The Law of Robotics prize, which means the mistake came from the person who told him there was no giant Shade in the place. (That would be the weapon-shop kid who only thinks about robots, by the way. I guess people only pay attention to what they want to see.)

Despite a job well done, Nier seemed down when he came back. Sure, he was energetic as ever, but it was like a shadow had been cast over him. Maybe I should have chalked it up to my imagination, but since we argued not long ago, I put out feelers to Grimoire Weiss just in case. That book is always by Nier's side, so we exchanged a few words while the kid was talking to another villager. Long story short, it didn't help. All Grimoire Weiss said was "Hatred and madness will never heal a wounded heart." *No* idea what that means, but it sounds like things weren't all hunky-dory out in the Junk Heap.

Anyway, now that I know Grimoire Weiss won't be any help, I've decided to collect information another way. The next time a traveling merchant comes to town, I'll come up with a job to send them to the Junk Heap. I know one particular merchant with wit and tact who'd be perfect for such a task. Plus, she's used to strolling through dangerous places without breaking a sweat.

Only problem is, I never know when she'll show up. Really, I'd like to learn as much as I can before Nier gets back from the Forest of Myth, but . . .

Well, anyway, that's the state of things. I'll stop here before Popola gripes at me again. End report!

Record written by Devola

The Man 4

1.

"THE WIFE AND I had another fight."

The ferryman with the red bag gave a heavy sigh as his boat leaned precariously to one side. He said the same thing every time Nier and his friends hopped onboard, so it was rather obvious they fought even on days the group *wasn't* taking the boat. Clearly their reputation as a quarrelling couple was warranted.

"Turns out that when she asks me to do something," he continued, "what she actually means is *do it NOW*. Last night I tried to put a chore off until later, and boy howdy, that did *not* end well . . ."

"My sister used to tell me I had to do things right when I was asked!" chimed in Emil. "She said I always forget otherwise."

"I mean, sure, I get that. But I'm a busy man, you know?"

"Oh, I *completely* understand."

Nier hadn't expected Emil and the ferryman to hit it off on that particular topic, but their heated conversation was so delightful that he decided to stay silent and listen.

"Anyway, I asked the postman to pick up these collectible stamps from different regions for me during his run."

"Stamp collecting? That sounds fun! I like the ones with flowers on them. They're pretty."

"Right? I'm right, right? But whenever I ask the wife, she tells me I'm, quote, 'wasting our money,' unquote."

"What?! No, you're not!"

"Exactly!" replied the gleeful boatman. "I'm *absolutely* not!"

Kainé, oblivious to it all, snored softly. *We're at peace*, Nier thought. *For now, at least.*

"You seem down, lad," noted Grimoire Weiss.

It was a keen observation, though a sensible one; the group was presently on its way to the Forest of Myth in search of the stone fragment called "The Memory Tree."

"Though I cannot blame you," Weiss muttered as a follow-up. "I myself am less than enthusiastic about those people."

The residents of the Forest of Myth loved to chat. They had been a taciturn bunch while under the influence of the Deathdream, but the second they awoke, they blathered on and on about nothing in excruciating detail. Sadly, such conversations rarely led to any kind of salient point.

"But we still have to talk to them if we want any clues," said Nier.

"Then let us hope our business finishes quickly."

"Yeah, it'd be nice . . ."

Talking to them was not a task either Nier or Weiss looked forward to, seeing as the forest residents seemed locked in a competition to string together as many words as humanly possible.

"Still, I'll take conversation over getting dragged into another scripted dream."

"That's how we'll have to look at it," Grimoire Weiss said wearily as the boat came to a stop along the shore. The dock on the northern plains wasn't all that far from the village.

"Take care out there!" called the ferryman. In response, Emil waved enthusiastically to his new best friend.

2.

THOUGH NIER AND Weiss hadn't visited the Forest of Myth since dispelling the Deathdream five years prior, the mayor still remembered them.

"We are truly indebted to you," he said as they approached. "In fact, your being here reminds me of a funny story—"

"We actually have a question for you," Nier said, hurriedly cutting the mayor off. He couldn't worry about being rude or hurting feelings right now—there were bigger fish to fry.

"Has there been anything unusual happening here? Any big Shades around? Or it doesn't even have to be a Shade—it could be a big and dangerous *anything.*" Nier knew he might miss out on meaningful information if he concentrated solely on Shades—that was a lesson learned in the Junk Heap.

"Unusual things, eh? Hmm . . ."

The mayor folded his arms and fell into thought, seemingly unconcerned about Nier's interruption. "Well, I *have* been feeling a strange presence lately whenever I visit the Divine Tree."

"The Divine Tree?"

When the mayor named it as the tree in the heart of their village, Nier remembered it was said to hold a Sealed Verse. And while he'd received a Sealed Verse from it, that had been in the midst of the Deathdream, so he didn't remember many of the details.

"Did you investigate the cause of this presence?" asked Weiss.

"No." The mayor answered without a moment's hesitation, as if any other answer was inconceivable.

"And why not?"

"Well, we're not really supposed to go near the tree."

"And why is *that*?" continued Weiss, each of his questions more irritated than the last.

The mayor shrugged. "I don't know. It's just how things have always been."

"Odd," Grimoire Weiss muttered, but Nier knew that was the only answer they'd get. Well, they'd come here to investigate any strange goings-on, so might as well get to it.

"Understood," said Nier to the mayor. "Thank you."

"Just don't go near the tree, okay? Please."

"We won't."

Of course, Nier had no intention of respecting the mayor's wish. Grimoire Weiss knew this and silently followed behind his companion as he walked away. Though the mayor watched them anxiously, the forest was a dark place, and the sky overhead was overcast. A few paces later, the pair had disappeared from his sight.

When Nier first looked at the tree in the center of town, he was struck mostly by its size. But now that he knew it was called the Divine Tree, his impression had changed: There *was* something different about it.

It wasn't because it was the largest tree he'd ever seen or that the branches were twisted in any particular way. It was more the peculiar aura that surrounded it. Perhaps that presence was why the villagers kept their distance.

Nier took a step toward it, then another. By looks alone, it was nothing more than a large plant. Its bark was a dull brown, its leaves dark green. He stepped over the twisting roots at his feet and approached.

"We are the grass . . . We are the trees . . . We are the woods . . ."

He and Grimoire Weiss exchanged a glance at the voice. "Why do we seem to encounter nothing but odd people lately?" muttered the tome—an amusing observation, considering how grandiose his own statements tended to be.

"You should talk, Weiss," needled Nier.

"Pah! As if Grimoire Weiss is capable of spouting such—"

"Hang on."

Nier cut Grimoire Weiss off. The strange words were continuing, and he didn't want to miss a single one.

"The dark form that governs all memories. May the words form themselves to your liking."

He wondered if that meant the tree would tell them what they wanted to know. That would be nice, but should they be taking the statement at face value? This was the village that succumbed to the Deathdream after all. But the moment memories of that scripted world came back to him, it was already too late.

```
Black. Pure darkness. Painted over
everything.
```

                    NIER
```
This again?
```

              GRIMOIRE WEISS
```
I believe this is a touch different than our
last predicament.
```

                    NIER
```
You think?
```

              GRIMOIRE WEISS
```
True, we are following a script as we did
last time, but this place is in a most
haphazard state.
```

Words. Scattered here and there across the blackness. Kind words. Difficult words. Amorous words. All sparkling in the dark like jewels.

NIER

Yeah, I'm not following.

The words are few now, and time is short. The TREE grabs the words in desperation and turns to the sky.

TREE

This is wrong. This is not how it was supposed to be.

The TREE's voice is the wind through the leaves. Once, long ago, the TREE remembered everything about the world. This was its task. Its function. Its purpose. It shivered with something approaching joy as it collected the memories of mankind. This was no accident; emotions were as much a part of the tree as root and bark. Memories collected like dew on the thick green leaves of the tree.

NIER

Is that . . . a plant?

The memories once formed a web that spanned the entire world. Words collapsed into sunlight before passing through leaves and into the pool of memory. From

the pool, the words joined together
to form colonies, the colonies united
into whirlpools of light, and the light
coalesced into stars.

GRIMOIRE WEISS

I would be hard-pressed to call that a
plant, lad. See how it expands like a mesh?
I believe I've seen this somewhere before.
Where was it? Was it from long ago? I
cannot recall . . .

TREE

Look at my memory.

There is a BOY here, brought low by
disease. His only friend is a healthy
GIRL. Despite their closeness, they
do not speak. Eventually, the GIRL
disappears. The BOY dies alone.

Etched upon the memory is a single word: envy.

TREE

Look at my memory.

A battle rages against a BEAST with red
eyes. Fighting it are a FEMALE WARRIOR
and her FELLOWS. Her foe is so large that
it blots out the sky. The WARRIOR laughs
and laughs as the town that contains her
DAUGHTER collapses into a pile of dust.
She laughs until her final moment. This
memory has been stored for a very long
time with a single word: loss.

TREE

Look at my memory.

A red dragon falls from the heavens.

TREE

Ah, that memory has been lost. A shame.
It was a favorite of mine.

After many centuries of existence, the
TREE sees that its carefully labeled
memories are beginning to dwindle. The
TREE does not feel sadness at this; grief
is an emotion beyond its comprehension.
It does, however, have the distinct
feeling that something is missing.

TREE

My careful collection of memories is
disappearing.

The TREE stretches its branches as far
as it can, but new memories refuse to
flow. The pool of memories is a black,
empty pit; a hollow place where life once
flourished.

TREE

I have lost my purpose. There is nothing
left.

This is why the TREE is pleased when the
young man and his companion enter the
room. Someone other than itself exists.
Someone other than itself speaks. There

are no words to describe its happiness at this discovery.

NIER

The hell is this place?

GRIMOIRE WEISS

A gloomy spot if I've ever seen one.

NIER

There's something on the ground.

There are crystals haphazardly scattered across the ground. NIER picks one up and peers at the scene inside it.

NIER

Hey, I remember this.

The crystal shows the Forest of Myth, its villagers prisoner to the Deathdream. NIER is shocked to see himself and GRIMOIRE WEISS in the scene. The TREE had seen everything.

TREE

I apologize. That is all that remains.

NIER

Who was that?

I must tell them, *thought the TREE.* For a voice had sounded from within the depths of its body. I must ask this of those before me, *thought the TREE.* For that order was absolute.

GRIMOIRE WEISS

Look there!

NIER

It's a Shade!

A small, shadowy presence appears from beneath the floor. It appears to be a SHADE. NIER and GRIMOIRE WEISS are shocked. The SHADE grasps several jewels in its hand. More tumble out of its mouth like shards. Some are labeled. Some are not. Some are crystalline. Some are not. Various scenes appear and disappear inside the jewels.

GRIMOIRE WEISS

This Shade appears to be consuming the memories.

NIER

Those are memories?

GRIMOIRE WEISS

(Exasperated)

Were you not paying attention to the stage direction?

A scene from five years ago is reflected in one of them.

The TREE disregards their remarks and extends a branch toward NIER. NIER brings his sword down on the SHADE, tearing its stomach wide. Jewels burst out and scatter across the floor.

TREE

Ah. There's my Conviction memory.

I must tell them, *thought the TREE. For that order was absolute. The TREE opens its mouth but finds no voice.*

A millennium of silence and solitude has caused the TREE to forget certain things. Focusing all its power on the riddle of speech, the TREE forms makeshift vocal cords and tries again.

TREE

Ahem. I . . . I implore . . . (cough)

A jewel is ejected from its mouth. It must try again. One more time.

TREE

I implore you. What was the color of the lost envy?

Its speech is perfect, but the TREE does not know what to do next. After a thousand years of solitude, the TREE finds itself lost.

GRIMOIRE WEISS

It spoke! This Shade has intelligence! And emotion!

NIER

Who cares?

NIER's sword slices through the SHADE's right arm. With its remaining arm, it

*reaches out to NIER. It must touch him.
It must make contact.*

*The moment its fingers brush against NIER,
the TREE feels a warm sensation begin to
burn. Something hot courses through its
fingers, up its arm, and out to its entire
body. It is emotion. Feeling. Passion.
The TREE cries out, its vocal cords
completely still.*

*One thousand years alone. One thousand
years in quiet contemplation. The TREE
had felt as if it was going to break
apart. New, powerful sensations began to
take hold. They are more than the simple
emotions it had been designed to feel:
They are the beginnings of a soul.*

The TREE has more questions.

TREE
*I implore you: How many were lost by the
warrior who—*

NIER
Okay, riddle time is over.

*I'm gonna kill this stupid Shade once and
for all!*

*The wound on its stomach burns. Something
spills from inside.*

NIER
What's that?!

GRIMOIRE WEISS

A key to the Shadowlord's castle! Secure it, quickly!

TREE

Ah, that's right. I remember now. That's the key.

(pause)

No, the man is the key to freeing trapped souls.

I must hurry. I must find my next words.

GRIMOIRE WEISS

This world is falling apart!

NIER

How can a script fall apart?!

The pool of memories begins to crack. The walls erode aw ay. But t he TREE m us t conti nue wit h it s questi on.

TREE

I implore . . . most important thing wo rld

NIER whirls around. His mouth forms words. Why does he feel the need to answer? He does not know, but the TREE is thankful for his whims.

Light fills the area. All memories vanish. The TREE loses sight of the boundary lines. The end of the script looms. The time for NIER and GRIMOIRE WEISS to return to regular prose is nigh.

And the TREE is satisfied.

Vision suddenly returned. Small, glowing bugs danced through a dim blanket of mist. Nier saw bark of dull brown. Leaves of deep green. He and Grimoire Weiss stood before the Divine Tree, finally free of the scripted world.

Nier unfurled his fist to find The Memory Tree. They had obtained it just as they had done with the Sealed Verse, though the details of how that had been accomplished were just as vague as last time. In that moment, Nier decided he didn't care for the scripted world; everything was at the whim of someone else, and he found it exhausting.

Still, this made for three fragments. All that was left now was to track down "Sacrifice" and "Loyal Cerberus."

"I never realized Shades were capable of rational thought," Grimoire Weiss mused.

"I don't care if they can tap dance and play the fiddle," replied a grumpy Nier.

"The script was not as coherent as it was five years prior, perhaps because the Shade had been weakened. Or mayhap because it was not using the villagers' dreams as a medium?"

As a piece of literature himself, Grimoire Weiss regarded the script with interest, despite abhorring the experience of being in it. Nier, however, didn't care what might have been different from their last visit. His surprise was finding a Shade in the tree, one that had been responsible for both the unusual presence and the Deathdream. Clearly, it was the reason the residents of the village revered the tree as divine.

But the fact a Shade hid within the tree did not erase the truth of the villagers' worshipful reverence, and Nier felt a responsibility to explain the situation. He slowly approached the mayor, fully prepared to receive stinging criticism, but the man's response was something else entirely.

"The Divine Tree . . . ? Oh, you mean that big ol' tree?"

Nier was blindsided. The mayor was now speaking of the tree the way he might any old shrub that sprouted up in the woods.

"Uh, you called it the Divine Tree, remember? You've always worshiped it? I wanted to talk to you about it because . . . Look, this isn't an easy subject to bring up."

As Nier fumbled for the right words, the mayor saved him. "Oh, you're going to tell me about that strange presence, right? Well, I don't feel it anymore."

"You don't?"

"Nope. It's gone. Poof! Like whatever was possessing the tree just up and disappeared."

That was most certainly because they had killed the Shade. Now perhaps the mayor and other villagers could approach the tree without any qualms.

"Still, I wonder why we revered that tree so much, you know?"

The mayor cocked his head in a puzzled fashion; the expression on his face made it seem like he'd just awoken from a dream.

"I don't want to go through that ever again," sighed Nier as he glanced back over his shoulder at the Forest of Myth. The forest was as quiet as always; all he could hear were bugs murmuring and birds singing. It was hard to believe they had been fighting a Shade there earlier.

"With the tree defeated, we no longer have to worry about being trapped in its scripted world," said Grimoire Weiss.

That was exactly what Nier was hoping for, considering his mind was still incredibly frazzled. But just as he was wondering if it was possible to feel more out of sorts than he did right now, Grimoire Weiss spoke up.

"Unless, of course, time itself begins to rewind."

Weiss spoke in a dramatic tone, as if expressing an ominous portent. Nier could only laugh. Of all the things to say.

"Over here!" came Emil's voice. Nier looked up to see him waving, while Kainé leaned against a tree with folded arms. It was like they hadn't even moved.

"Did you find the fragment?!" cried Emil.

Nier gave an enthusiastic nod as he waved back.

REPORT 12

This report details our circumstances regarding our efforts to collect the key to the Shadowlord's castle and solve its cipher.

The cipher has proven more difficult to solve than anticipated. Though Nier has brought back The Law of Robotics and The Memory Tree, I am still unable to decipher them. I will have to think of a better approach, and quickly.

Meanwhile, the areas of Shade activity have been expanding at a frightening rate. Shades are now found in the northern plains regardless of weather, and strange activity has been reported in and around the desert. The most serious case, however, is thought to be in The Aerie, where behavior that may threaten the project has been observed in a portion of the residents.

As such, I decided to use the village as a kind of observational test case. Its residents provide the perfect sample size, and since their lack of contact with other districts will give us untainted data, it fits perfectly with the rest of our plans.

As I was considering this, however, a letter arrived from The Aerie's village chief stating he is willing to share information on Sacrifice. That said, there is no proof the fragment is even *in* The Aerie, and I feel there is a very high possibility this is nothing more than an attempt to lure Nier into a trap.

On the other hand, our best option to ascertain the veracity of this claim is to send Nier, which is why I showed him the letter. Grimoire Weiss agreed it's likely a trap, but Nier insisted on going anyway. It would be nice if he found the fragment there, but even if he didn't, I don't expect him to run into anything he can't handle. Either way, we don't stand to lose anything.

We must use every method in our arsenal to stop the Shadowlord's rampage.

End report.

Record written by Popola

NieR Replicant
ver.1.22474487139...

The Man 5

1.

HEARING THE HINGES creak, Emil rushed toward the village's northern gates, where it sounded as if someone had put all their weight into throwing them wide. The village guards, terrified of Shades, would never open the gates with such force. There was only one person with both the strength to push them open like that and the courage to face the Shades.

"Welcome back!" called Emil as he caught a glimpse of silver in the gate's opening. Yet as it widened, he was surprised to find not Nier, but . . .

"Weiss?"

"What is the matter, lad?" asked Grimoire Weiss. "Have you taken ill?"

Though the book was showing appropriate concern, Emil didn't have the heart to ruin that kindness by admitting he'd been hoping to see Nier first.

"Er, it's nothing," said Emil, gathering himself. "So where are we going next? Did you find any clues? Popola must have told you something, right? What did Popola tell y—"

"Choose one question and stick with it, boy! Even one of my greatness would be hard-pressed to respond to so many queries at once!"

"Sorr—"

"We're heading for The Aerie."

As Emil was struggling to apologize, Nier called out their next destination, shutting the gate behind him as he did so. Considering he was leaving the village through the gates, it was clear they wouldn't be taking the ferry to their destination. Anytime that happened, Nier would tell him and Kainé where to meet up, then return to the village. And of course, when they knew where to go ahead of time, everyone would just reconvene at the spot directly.

Guess I'm not seeing the ferryman today, Emil thought. That was disappointing, but he was also excited to be heading somewhere new.

"The mayor sent Popola a letter," Nier explained. "Apparently there's a villager who knows something about the Sacrifice fragment."

Emil was touched. Though Grimoire Weiss scolded him for asking too many questions, Nier took the time to answer all of them. Weiss was kind in his own way, but Nier was much kinder.

"The Aerie, huh?"

Emil had heard that name somewhere before. Since it seemed they would be getting there on land via the northern gates, that meant it had to be in the area of the northern plains.

"What a soul-crushing place," sighed Grimoire Weiss.

"Why?"

"It's filled with a sorry, gloomy people, all of them unsociable and clannish."

Grimoire Weiss sighed again, this time with such force that Emil thought some of his pages might fly free of their bindings.

"But wait!" Emil piped up in cheerful protest. "They told us about one of the fragments, right? So even if most of them are a bunch of grumpy geese, at least there's *one* who isn't!"

Nier and Grimoire Weiss exchanged a glance. Just as Emil thought there had to be a meaning behind the gesture, the tome spoke up.

"Strange things are afoot in that village, mark my words.

When Popola sent letters to all the village leaders she could think of, a missive came back from The Aerie *instantly* stating they had information on the Sacrifice fragment. Does that not strike you as unusual?"

"Maybe it's a coincidence! Although it *would* be weird if the mayor told her before she'd even sent the letter . . ."

"That is not all," continued Weiss. "The letter stated that the villagers have decided to set up a mercantile. For *shopping*! Wholly unbelievable, if you ask me! Not a single resident of that village deserves to run a shop—unless they have truly opened their minds, which I very much doubt!"

This screed caused Emil to wonder if the description of The Aerie as *unsociable* and *clannish* was, in fact, no exaggeration.

"Yeah, I got my doubts," Kainé interjected in a low voice. "Unless something else changed, I don't believe a word of it."

The way she spoke made Emil think she knew the people of The Aerie.

"You've been to The Aerie before, Kainé?" he asked. But his friend stayed silent, forcing Nier to answer in her stead.

"She used to live there."

"Really?!"

That must have been where he'd heard the name before! People always bring up places they've lived at least once—and though Emil didn't recall discussing the matter at length, the name likely came up in relation to another topic.

"Aren't you glad to be going back home, Kainé?" he asked in his ever-chipper way.

Her eyes narrowed—a sign she was unhappy. "That place is a shithole."

Emil didn't understand what that meant, exactly, but he was acutely aware of how upset she was. Perhaps she'd had some bad experiences in her old hometown.

No. This wasn't a "perhaps" situation—she *did* have bad experiences. Emil knew full well the cruelty people who believed they were "normal" could show toward those they deemed otherwise.

This thought led him to recall what happened after he took on his current form and he and Nier set out to undo Kainé's petrification. While Emil had been to the village library to check on Kainé before, that trip was different. People stared. They looked away. Some even made a display of scowling at him or whispered among themselves. Far from finding a friendly face, Emil encountered only hate and disdain. He was certain he would have faced even worse treatment—perhaps even had a stone or two tossed his way—had Nier not been with him.

So when Popola asked Emil to stay out of the village, he understood. Even walking the short distance between the eastern gate and the library showed him all he needed to know. And when Popola explained that he and Kainé were actually the ones at risk, Emil agreed at once, but he wasn't very happy about it.

When Kainé said she was used to sleeping outside, Emil took that to mean she'd been subject to discrimination and shunning in the places she'd lived before. He knew now that had been her situation in The Aerie, and he felt ashamed he'd called it her home.

As she began to walk away with the rest of the group, Emil whispered a silent apology in his heart.

2.

"ARE THOSE HOUSES?! Wow, that's so cool! How'd they get 'em up so high? I sure hope they don't fall!"

Emil emitted a nonstop stream of wonder when he saw the tanks plastered to the cliffside in The Aerie. He'd listened with great interest when the others told him the village houses were different, and he was thrilled when Nier offered to bring him along. Since the residents never ventured outside, Emil wouldn't be subjected to strange looks or harsh words. Sure, they might peek through cracks in the shutters and whisper awful things, but he would never hear it.

However, Emil was less interested in the tanks than the village's rooster weather vanes and suspension bridges. He entertained himself by floating up to the vanes and poking their tails, then drifting beneath the bridges to see what he could find.

I'm glad we brought him thought Nier as he watched his friend explore. He only wished Kainé would have agreed to join as well, but she stubbornly chose to remain outside.

They crossed a bridge, went up and down ladders, then crossed another, encountering not a single villager all the while. No doubt they were cooped up inside their tanks as always. But when Nier casually glanced to the side while crossing yet another bridge, he was shocked.

"There are *people* over there!" he said.

Indeed, there were people in the plaza built over one of the trestles—and not just one or two, but an entire crowd. He could see items lined up and available for purchase in a number of open-air stalls.

"That must be the market," he continued. "I almost can't believe it."

"To think the letter was correct," Grimoire Weiss mused.

"You think that means the Sacrifice information is too?"

"We will have to confer with the village chief in that regard."

Nier nodded and began climbing a ladder to the chief's house. He felt his mood rising in spite of himself. If the villagers now felt open enough to start a market, perhaps that meant the chief had turned a friendlier page. But the moment he knocked on the tank, the response dashed his hopes.

"It's all over . . ." said a mournful voice from behind the door.

"Uh, hello?" replied Nier as he collected himself. "We're here from Popola's village."

"I'm scared . . . Terrified . . ."

"We're here to ask about the letter you sent?"

"Our days are numbered . . . Our village is doomed . . ."

"As cheerful as ever, it seems," Grimoire Weiss remarked dryly. But Nier wasn't about to give up.

"You're the one who wrote the letter, right?!"

"I don't know about any letter."

"But you told her there was a villager who could tell us something about Sacrifice!"

"No . . . I don't know . . . Leave this place . . . I know nothing . . ."

That meant there was no way to know if the rest of the information was accurate or not. Nier looked around, at a loss for what to do next.

"Perhaps we should ask the villagers themselves," Grimoire Weiss suggested.

"Yeah," agreed Nier. "If the chief didn't send it, someone else must have."

According to Popola, the postman delivered the letter from The Aerie, which meant someone must have left it in the mailbox. Though Grimoire Weiss regarded this tale with doubt, she insisted the letter was genuine, even if she couldn't speak to the veracity of its contents.

But if the chief didn't write the letter, who did? The group decided to visit the tank nearest to the chief's to ask and were promptly met with a cynical reply from behind the door:

"I don't believe anyone anymore!"

No matter how hard they knocked or how loudly they called out, the voice did not speak again. With no other choice, they moved on to the next tank.

"Leave! We're not coming outside!"

"You don't have to," replied Nier. "I just want to talk."

"Go away!"

"Someone sent a letter to—"

"Go!"

Nothing had changed over the past five years; Nier couldn't even hold a proper conversation. He continued knocking on the doors of every tank between the chief's abode and the plaza, but the results were very much the same.

"It's over for us . . . And for you . . ."

"The Shades attacked again last night . . ."

"My wife's been acting weird . . ."

"I'm scared . . . Make it stop . . ."

"If you're not a Shade, then prove it . . ."

"What will become of our village . . . ?"

Every word was filled with suspicion and anxiety. Just listening to their voices brought Nier's mood low.

Thankfully, the gathering of people in the plaza seemed to

promise a bit of relief. People had ventured outside on a sunny day to chat with neighbors and do a little shopping. Such a thing likely felt commonplace in other villages and towns, but for The Aerie, it was a rare thing indeed.

"Wow, there's so much stuff on sale," said Emil. "Plus, everyone looks like they're having fun!"

There was a hint of jealousy in the boy's voice at these words, and it suddenly occurred to Nier that Emil had never been shopping before. He'd scarcely left his manor once his petrification powers took hold, and while his new form now permitted greater freedom, he never tried to enter other settlements. The fact Devola and Popola forbade him from entering their village had clearly left a mark.

"I think we have time to nose around if you want," said Nier.

"REALLY?!" cried Emil.

"Sure. Just don't leave my side, okay?"

"Okay!"

Emil gave a delighted nod that reminded Nier of Yonah's excitement when he invited her on shopping trips. It was a memory that came to him out of the blue, and one that caused panic over her current situation to rise just as fast. A moment later, he calmed himself. Panic would only lead to him missing clues and making poor decisions. Taking a deep breath, he stepped into the plaza and its rows of stalls.

"Got some new items in stock today" came a cordial woman's voice. She sat behind baskets overflowing with fruits and vegetables. The look on her face was so bright, Nier almost couldn't believe she was a resident of The Aerie.

Behind him, he heard villagers saying things such as "I'd almost forgotten what the breeze felt like" and "I could feel myself cramping from staying inside all the time." It was hard to imagine such cheerful voices being lumped in with those they heard from the tanks.

"Would you like a flower?" asked a smiling florist. But as she grinned at him, Nier felt something was off. Markets were a common sight in any town or city, yet this one seemed . . . *wrong*. Was this because he was so firm in his preconception that the people of The Aerie were gloomy and closed off?

. . . No. This didn't matter. Right now it was more important that they look into who sent the letter. He placed the strange sensation to the side and called out to a passing villager.

"Excuse me. We're from Popola's village, and we're looking for the person who sent this letter."

"A letter?" said the villager.

"We thought the chief sent it, but he apparently didn't."

"Hmm. Sorry. Can't help you."

"Okay."

"Good luck though!"

"Thanks."

This exchange was typical of the ones that followed. Even though he hadn't gotten any tangible leads, the fact Nier could hold an actual conversation with someone felt like a win—even if setting the bar so low painted The Aerie in a rather unpleasant light.

"I'll try asking someone else," said Nier. But though he asked every villager who passed by, the responses were the same. The people were pleasant enough—if a bit mundane—but no one had any useful information.

"To think not a single one of them knows of the letter," muttered Weiss.

"Yeah," agreed Nier. "I was hoping we might find at least one."

Nier scanned his surroundings again. He was starting to wonder about the odd sensation he felt earlier. What had that been about anyway? Where had it come from? And why was he still worried about it?

As his thoughts whirled, Grimoire Weiss floated over and said, "Why not ask that guard over there? I think you've yet to pick his brain on the matter."

Nier looked up to see that a guard had stationed himself in the corner of the plaza. "Yeah, you're right. Good idea."

This was the first time Nier had seen a guard in The Aerie—although it was also the first time he'd seen any people at all. As he wondered if perhaps that was the source of his unease, he approached the guard and began questioning him.

"A letter, huh?" the guard replied absently. His nonchalance caused Nier to wonder anew if this was all just a big waste of time, but then the man added something else:

"Yeah, I think I heard about that."

"So you know about the letter?" replied a very relieved Nier.

What confidence the guard had quickly drained away. "Hmm. Maybe I don't? I mean, I'm not sure . . ."

"Bah! Which is it, man?!" barked an irritated Grimoire Weiss. But the guard's unfocused eyes remained trained in Nier's direction.

"If I may ask, are you friends of Kainé?"

"You could say that," Nier replied.

He was a bit blindsided by the sudden change in topic, and even more bewildered that said topic was Kainé. Still, she *did* used to live here, so perhaps it wasn't all that unusual for her name to come up. And yet he couldn't shake the feeling that all of this was just so damn *odd*.

"Ah, I've heard the rumors," continued the guard. "Here to hunt Shades, are you?"

Nier remained silent, forcing Grimoire Weiss to answer in his stead. "Indeed. Our aim is to defeat every last one."

The guard's voice abruptly changed. "Every . . . last one? Every one? Every one, every one, everyoneeveryoneeveryoneeveryone . . ."

"Weiss!" cried Nier as a black mist suddenly came over the guard's body.

Emil, who had been floating beside Nier, whirled around to protect his friend's back as the outline of the guard's body blurred into a fog.

"Beware!" Grimoire Weiss shouted. "This man is a Shade!"

3.

THE HUT WHERE Kainé used to live had scarcely changed over the past five years. She sat down on crates she once used as a bed and felt their familiar shape beneath her.

"It's still a crappy little shack, and it's gonna be one forever!"

"Cram it, Tyrann."

Even though Kainé told him to be quiet, she doubted he would take her up on the suggestion. The villagers never came out here, and with Nier, Weiss, and Emil having gone to town, there was no one else to talk to.

"You sure you don't wanna join 'em? It's not like you to abandon your wittle fwiends! Kyaaa ha ha ha!"

I'm not abandoning them, she replied in her head. She'd just determined it was best not to join them in town. They didn't need to get hassled by villagers for hanging around with the weird Shade woman—and since they were just going to the chief's house, she doubted they were in any real danger.

"You sure about that, Sunshine? You really *sure?"*

The insinuating tone in Tyrann's voice was because he sensed Shades in the village as clearly as Kainé did. But Shades being in The Aerie wasn't exactly news, and she didn't detect any abnormally large ones lurking around. Her three companions could handle the small fries on their own, just as they'd handled the incessant waves of Shades in the northern plains on their way to The Aerie.

"Small fries, eh? Yeah, I guess they are pretty small. Sure are a lot of 'em though!"

The only thing bothering Kainé was the fact the Shades' presence was growing thicker by the minute. She'd thought about catching some shut-eye while waiting for Nier, but sleep wouldn't come. There was a heightened buzz in her mind, most likely owing to the Shades.

"You suuure you wanna go into the village?" cackled Tyrann as she took blades in hand and stood. *"It's full of sooo many tewwible wittle memowies, remember?"*

Who gives a crap?

Kainé didn't care a lick for the people who threw rocks, mud, and awful words at her. All they were capable of was bullying the weak—their skinny little legs would tremble if they saw her now. But they weren't what was on her mind at the moment.

"Shades, eh? Yeah, there's a lot of 'em. Hell, this village is chockfull of the things! I can't wait!"

Kainé dashed off, the sensation of Shades growing thicker with each step. There was nothing whatsoever normal about this, and she found herself deeply regretting not tagging along when she had the chance.

When Kainé reached the bridge leading to the village, she was shocked. Uncountable numbers of Shades were blocking the way, and the pathways and bridges crisscrossing the area were packed with even more.

"Well, shit," she observed.

Kainé let fly a volley of magic as she charged the bridge. It buckled and swayed beneath her, making it impossible to wield her swords with any kind of precision. But she didn't have to kill them—she just needed to knock them off the bridge.

She frightened the one at the front of the bridge with her magic, plunged a blade into it, then swept it off its feet with a kick. The Shade staggered, then fell. Kainé instantly lowered herself into a crouch and held the position. When the bridge swung, she thrust her blade forward, causing another Shade to fall. She sent creature after creature plummeting to their deaths on her journey across the chasm until she finally found herself safely on the other side.

"Hey, didja hear that? Didja HEAR that, Sunshine? It's your wittle fwiends!"

Rather than answering, Kainé kicked the face of a heavily armored Shade standing before her, then sent it stumbling backward with a swift slice. Though they didn't sway like the bridge, the platform passages were narrow and difficult to navigate. Unable to support its own weight, the armored Shade fell, spouting curses at Kainé all the way down.

She'd heard Shades whispering the moment she entered the village. They apparently knew all about her and were saying she was cursed—a monster.

"Pretty rich comin' from them, eh? I mean, hell, they're the real *Shades, am I right?!"*

You can say that again.

The first Shade she'd knocked into the abyss had been screaming at her to leave the village. It was something she'd already heard a nauseating number of times in her life.

"One-trick ponies, the lot of 'em! But when did these ponies get here?"

Who knows? Kainé replied, mowing down a Shade that was about to shoot her with magic. As it fell to the depths of the ravine, she heard it screaming another thing she'd grown weary of: *"If only you never existed."*

She continued down the passageway and toward the plaza, where she saw the rest of her party. Thankfully, they were all still in one piece.

"You guys sure are taking your goddamn time!" she yelled.

"A thousand apologies!" Grimoire Weiss replied in a tone that was anything but apologetic. "We were distracted by the local welcoming party!"

Tyrann abruptly cackled like that was the most delightful thing he'd ever heard.

"*I think he means the local* murdering *party!*" he screamed in her mind. His sick play-by-play made Kainé glad once again that she was the only one who had to deal with him.

"Kainé, the villagers are possessed!" Emil cried in a voice thick with tears.

"But not all of 'em!" Nier added. "Some are still human, so be careful!"

Now Kainé *really* regretted not coming along at her first chance. The plaza was chaos, containing a mixture of Shades, humans, and Shades that *looked* like humans. Since Nier and the others couldn't tell human from Shade, they weren't going to be able to handle the situation with any kind of precision.

"Follow me!" yelled Kainé. As she cut down a Shade that had taken the form of a person, a human kicked it away to clear a path. She spotted a few people she recognized in the melee, but many were strangers. People who once bullied her as a child and people she'd never seen before had both been turned into Shades, and she killed both kinds without mercy.

"*We just wanted to live our lives in peace!*" sobbed one.

"*We do not desire conflict!*" pleaded another.

"*MURDERERS!*" screamed a third.

"*That one there hit the nail on the head! Murderers, the lot of you! Humans can't ever see what's on the inside!*"

But Kainé still had to kill them; if she didn't, they would do the same to her and her friends. There was no other choice when it came to Shades.

Finally, the party escaped the plaza and ran across a nearby bridge. All they had to do was make their way through a narrow passageway, cross another bridge, and run like hell for the exit. As Kainé calculated their route in her head, a young woman suddenly appeared in her path. She held a sword in one hand, trying desperately to guard a boy behind her.

Kainé saw steel flash in the light. She managed to block the attack, but it was a close thing. Had her reactions been a second slower, she would have been dead.

"Kainé!" Nier shouted. "What's going on?!"

"Don't be fooled by this lady!" replied Kainé. "She's a Shade!"

It took all of Kainé's strength to say that; the lady was going to break her guard if she hesitated for even a moment. The power of her foe wasn't normal, and Kainé soon found herself being pushed toward the exposed edge of the passageway.

But then something unbelievable happened: The woman turned to the boy behind her and yelled, "Get out of here!"

"No way!" he cried back. "I'm not going to abandon my own sister!"

Kainé couldn't believe her ears. The thought a Shade would protect a human was unbelievable enough, but a human calling a Shade "sister" was *unthinkable.*

"D'aw, wouldja look at that! They're pretending to be family!"

The Shades Kainé had thrown from various bridges and platforms had screamed curses at her just as the villagers used to. They did so because they knew her well—and Kainé finally understood why.

"You monster! You possessed monster! Why have you done this?! We just wanted to live our lives in peace!"

The woman's voice was thick with tears, the force of her blade unrelenting.

"Aww, she's protecting her pwecious wittle brother! It's so beauti-ful, I'm gonna laugh!"

Shut up, shut up, shut uuuuup!

Kainé pushed back with everything she had. Her anger at Tyrann and her irritation at the Shade standing before her gave her a new, beastly strength. The force pressing against her blade suddenly slackened, and a moment later the woman fell to the floor.

"No!" screamed the boy as he rushed to her side. The woman lay still where she fell, as though in death. But she had yet to turn to the traditional black mist of a deceased Shade, which meant she was still alive.

Kainé approached, swords still at the ready. She needed to end this Shade; that was the only option.

"Stay back, you possessed monster!" cried the boy. Now it was *his* turn to block Kainé's path. As his eyes flashed, Kainé found herself momentarily stunned by the power of his hate.

"Stay back, kid," Nier said quietly. "Your sister is one of them now."

"I don't care what she is! She's my sister, and I love her!"

None of them had a ready reply. What could they say to a boy who knew his sister was a Shade yet chose to steadfastly love her anyway?

"You people are the monsters here!"

The boy's words dug thorns into Kainé's heart as the previous words of other Shades echoed in her mind.

"We just wanted to live our lives in peace!"

"We do not desire conflict."

So who is really seeking battle here? she thought. *Who's the one blazing a trail of destruction and slaughter?*

Me. It's me.

"Kainé!"

Kainé snapped back to reality when Emil called her name, but it was too late. The thing that had once been the boy's sister had risen up in full Shade form behind him and was launching a massive arm directly at her.

"KAINÉ!"

There was an impact. A breath. Pain. And then Kainé knew no more.

4.

"EMIL, WATCH KAINÉ!" ordered Nier.

After hearing a small voice of assent behind him, Nier turned his full attention to the Shades. They were an endless wave of enemies, and he cut down every one without mercy. While some of their number might have been true humans, he lacked the leeway to worry about that; a moment's hesitation now would come at the cost of his life.

"Murderer!" came a yell as something flew toward him. He raised his arm out of instinct, but the projectile landed harmlessly in front of him. It was a ceramic vase. As that strange fact registered, a cup, a spoon, and an egg quickly joined the pile at his feet.

None of these things were enough to kill him even if they did manage to land, yet Nier had never felt more hurt in his life. A small part of him started to hope they'd give up on the kitchen supplies and just start throwing rocks instead.

"We're trying to save you from the Shades!" cried Emil. "Please, you have to stop!" But though there were tears in his voice, the villagers did not listen. He had both hands extended, protecting Kainé.

Why had everything come to this? The party had gone to The Aerie in search of information on the stone fragment. They happened upon a Shade, so they killed it. That was all. Yet everyone here seemed to think *they* were the villains.

"Kainé, wake up! We need to get outta here!"

Nier called out to Kainé as he continued cutting down everyone in his path. That was the only way they'd ever escape the village now.

"Kainé, you gotta get up!"

How many had he killed so far? He dodged and weaved, swinging his sword for what seemed an age, until the passageway finally fell silent. The time had come for them to flee this place, so Nier hoisted the unconscious Kainé over his shoulders and began making his way down the path.

"Look at that!" Emil cried.

Nier followed the pointing hand, and his jaw dropped in shock when he saw a black swirling mist in the center of the ravine.

"What in heaven's name . . . ?" wondered Grimoire Weiss.

To Nier, it looked like what happened to Shades when they died, only if the black dust they usually dissolved into stuck around instead of scattering to the winds. But the sheer amount of dust in the vortex was as far from normal as one could imagine: the swirling mass was so large, it had already consumed the entire market plaza.

The vortex whirled faster and faster. As writhing Shades around it were sucked inside, a solid outline began to form around the amorphous mist.

"Are they combining?" asked Nier. He remembered Kainé saying once that Shades could occasionally merge together—and that the more there were, the more powerful the resulting creature became. But the black mist was now doing more than just absorbing Shades: It was also sucking up the villagers. Those who had waited too long to flee the plaza were the first to go, followed by any who sought safety inside their homes, along with their houses.

As the black vortex grew more and more ominous, it began to take on the form of a massive sphere. Its spinning grew irregular as the black mist surrounding it dissipated.

"By my pages," groaned Weiss. "Is this beast a Shade as well?"

And indeed, the surface of the sphere *did* look like the skin of a Shade.

"But all the villagers are inside that thing!" shouted Emil.

Had the villagers been swallowed up and killed, the group's next logical step would have proven easier on their consciences. In that case, they needed only to kill the Shade the same way they had countless of its kind before. But this time, the villagers were *still there*. The group could hear human voices coming from within the black sphere, mixed in with the chittering noises of Shades.

"I can't trust anyone . . . I can't trust anyone . . . !"

"My wife's been acting kind of strange . . . My wife's been acting kind of strange . . ."

"Hee hee! Oh, that child's just fine. That child's just fine!"

"Oh god, help us! Help us, please! We aren't Shades!"

"I can't tell who's human anymore . . . I can't tell who's human anymore!!"

"Ow! It hurts, Mom! It hurts!"

"I can't take this anymore . . . What's happening to us?!"

"Our village . . . Our world . . . Where am I? Who am I?"

As words poured out of the sphere, Nier had to fight the urge to cover his ears. Not that it would have helped; the villagers' utterances of resentment and madness were so loud, they caused the entire ravine to shudder as they echoed endlessly between the stone cliffs.

"I feel something from within the creature," Grimoire Weiss murmured.

"Like what?" asked Nier.

"Behold!"

Nier looked again, expecting to see the same amorphous, curse-spewing sphere he'd seen a moment ago. Instead, he noticed something beginning to twitch in the center of the sphere. After a moment, it turned into a reddish circle that formed itself into a massive bloodshot eye. As the red orb glowered at the party, its gaze suddenly became corporeal.

"Look out!" Nier shouted. He leaped to the side while Emil and Weiss took to the sky. All that was left on the empty bridge and passageway were a set of blackened scorches; the enormous eyeball's gaze had unleashed a searing beam of light.

"We would have been toast if that thing hit us!" said Emil as he floated down and stared at the burn marks left in its wake.

"We can't just leave this thing here," replied Nier. All he'd been thinking about was getting the injured Kainé out of the village, but that plan had fallen to the wayside in the face of the enormous Shade before them. Its destructive power was simply too dangerous to ignore.

Nier fired a magic spear at the creature's new eye. As the spear flew through the air, the sphere appeared to blink. A strange mass—perhaps fins or tentacles—spread out from the sides of the sphere, covering the front. This made it look as if an eyelid with luscious lashes had closed tight.

"Those horrid tentacles appear to deflect magic," Grimoire Weiss stated. Indeed, the moment the spear made contact with the tentacles, it vanished harmlessly.

"Then we just need to dodge its attacks and fire back!" snapped Nier. As long as the tentacles were in place, the eyeball couldn't use its beam. The eye needed to be open for them to fall under its gaze, which gave them an opening to strike. Realizing this, Nier paused, waiting for an attack and readying himself to let fly with a volley of magic.

He did not have to wait long.

"Now!" Grimoire Weiss commanded. "Focus your magic on the beast's center!"

Nier's magic spear flew out and pierced the red eye. The eyeball shuddered, its tentacles writhing in pain. "Did we get it?" he asked.

The answer came in the form of a powerful arcane blast. While Nier's attack hadn't been entirely ineffective, it clearly wasn't fatal. The eyeball sent out waves of magical bullets as though irritated; Nier cut them down with his blade as he dodged to the side, but there was no way he could keep up such a defense for long.

"It will take more than a barrage of magic to stop us!" Grimoire Weiss shouted.

Nier had no intention of halting his attack, nor would he let a few successful blows from the creature slow his own. As magical bullets slammed into his side, he let out his own barrage in return. When the tentacles again fell into place and dispelled the attack, Weiss suddenly cried out with an idea.

"Go to the back! The beast is weak at its back!"

While the eyeball was tough, it seemed to lack something in the smarts department—it only strengthened its defenses on the side where it was being attacked.

"I'll keep it busy!" Emil yelled as he flew toward the creature. He let fly a barrage of magic as he dodged bullets to either side of him. "You should be able to attack from behind!"

Nier nodded and dashed off. He thought he could reach the thing's back from the bridge near the village entrance, so he ran for it with everything he had.

"Hurry!" Grimoire Weiss urged. "Emil is about to falter!"

"I know!"

Nier clambered up a ladder, then continued running. He

crossed a bridge, trying to ignore the way it swayed beneath him, until he found himself facing the creature's rear side.

"Strike it with care!" cautioned Weiss.

Nier mustered all the magic he had and fired. The backside of the sphere had no tentacles to protect it, and when his multitude of spears connected, the eyeball shuddered with more force than before. A moment later, its defensive wall came crashing down.

This is our chance, Nier thought, but the eyeball still refused to give in.

"It's still going?!" cried an incredulous Nier.

"Yes, but its defenses have fallen," replied Weiss. "All that is left is the beast itself!"

They were so close. A few more attacks, and it would all be over.

Nier looked up to see Emil swooping down on the beast. "Help me take it out," he cried from midair. "Now's our chance!"

"On it!"

Until that moment, Emil and Nier had been splitting their efforts between the front and back of the beast, but now its protective coverings were gone. If the power of the ultimate weapon and Grimoire Weiss combined on a single spot, they could deal damage beyond anything previously possible.

When Emil began to cast his spell, the area around him started glowing a brilliant white. As he thrust his staff into the air, Nier let fly a volley of magic. The power of the ultimate weapon and Grimoire Weiss came together, creating a massive magical force that pierced straight through the creature's eye. But Emil did not relent, and when the eye shuddered in defiance, he overwhelmed it with his own brilliant white light.

"We did it!" exclaimed Nier.

A deluge of blood sprayed from the eyeball as its movements

stilled. The Shade had been almost unbelievably powerful, but they had managed to subdue it.

"Emil?"

There was no response. Even though the enemy was still, Emil was raising his staff once more.

"Emil? Emil, wait!"

The air around Emil began to glow anew. Instead of calming after the end of the fight, the white light around him was growing more powerful and more blinding. A moment later, the boy threw his arms wide.

"*Emil!*" cried a despondent Nier.

"He's gone!" replied Weiss. "His instincts have taken hold! The ultimate weapon is being deployed!"

Weiss's words were drowned out by Emil's screams. Heat rolled off the light in waves. Nier rushed to Kainé, who was still out cold, and began dragging her to the village entrance as the suspension bridge creaked ominously beneath them.

Emil's magic continued to spiral out of control. The air shuddered. Light swelled. Tanks began to fall off the sides of cliffs as the passageways around them crumbled. The moment Nier brought Kainé's body to the other side of the bridge, the swollen light burst forth, swallowing the canyon whole.

All that remained was a brilliant blue sky.

Emil sat on the ground, sobbing. Occasionally an apology would slip through his teeth, only to be replaced by more wailing. Unsure what to say, Nier simply sat beside him in silence. Kainé, who had awakened in the meantime, remained quiet as well.

"I killed . . . innocent people . . ." sobbed Emil.

The white light had been so powerful, Nier could still see flashes of it when he blinked. When his vision had finally returned after the explosion, he was shocked to see . . . nothing.

The enormous eyeball? The bridges? The passageways? The tanks? The rooster weather vanes? All of it had been obliterated by the arcane light, swallowed up and dispelled from the world. Even the walls and depths of the ravine had been carved into new shapes, completely altering the geography of the land. When Nier tried to imagine how Emil must feel, his heart ached to the point of bursting.

"It's okay," he said softly. "You don't have to cry anymore."

"But I killed them all . . ."

Emil shuddered as he sobbed. Nier reached out and gently ran a hand over his head, but it did nothing to calm the tears.

"Yeah," he said finally. "And you saved us."

Emil looked up at last, confused.

"If it wasn't for you, we'd all be dead," continued Nier. He didn't think his words would be enough to soothe Emil's conscience—it had been too cruel an act for so kind a person— but he still wanted to try. Even mentioning how most of The Aerie villagers had been absorbed by the vortex before he went out of control would likely do little to assuage Emil's guilt. Yet Nier still had to try *something*.

"We owe you," he said.

"But I . . ."

"It's all right."

Nier placed his hand on Emil's shoulder before standing up. The deep gouges in the ravine were blanketed by a white mist. As he looked across it, he was greeted by reshaped mountainsides and a callously blue sky. It reminded him how great the destruction had been—and also how great the sacrifice.

"Don't look back."

He said this as much to himself as he did to his companions. They could not let this stop them. Considering the weight of what had been lost so far, they *had* to keep going.

He opened his clenched fist and held it out to Emil, showing him the meager compensation for all that had been broken and lost.

"That's . . ." began Emil before swallowing his words. In Nier's palm was the Sacrifice fragment—the entire reason they had come to The Aerie to begin with.

REPORT 13

The Aerie has been destroyed. While Nier successfully brought the Sacrifice fragment back, he seemed to be hiding something, so we decided to investigate and analyze the situation personally. (Naturally, we chose a time of day when folks were asleep and wouldn't see us—we're always careful.)

To our surprise, The Aerie had been erased from existence. In fact, it looked like something had scooped out the ravine entirely. After observing traces of powerful magic in the area, we believe this was Number 7's doing.

The villagers must have known Popola was searching for information on Sacrifice and sent her the letter in the chief's name. The purpose of this was to lure Nier to the village and kill him; since the villagers were living alongside Shades, he posed a threat. Sadly, the plan backfired rather spectacularly.

Popola and I knew a small portion—hell, a *large* portion—of the villagers had been exhibiting problematic behavior, and we'd been wracking our brains for a way to deal with it. We'd considered treating the village as a test case and attempting to peaceably resolve the situation, but now that we see what's happened, I think that might have proved too difficult. There are too many problems in the coexistence of Shades and humans, and it would have been a major challenge for us. So, it seems we have no choice but to proceed with the project.

As such, we need to stop the Shadowlord's rampage as soon as possible. While we can't pin the blame for all the recent abnormalities on him, he's certainly at the root of most of them. At the very least, the sheer increase in Shades and Black Scrawl cases reflects the deterioration of his mental and emotional stability.

I know it's been one bad piece of news after the other, but there *is* a little light at the end of this particular tunnel: We only have the Loyal Cerberus fragment left to find. After that, we just have to wait for Popola to solve the cipher.

We've also prepared a trump card that we're hoping can stop the Shadowlord in his tracks. We thought we could use Nier to control the Shadowlord at first, but his combat prowess has grown beyond our initial estimations, so controlling *him* might not even be possible anymore. In fact, we're a little worried his increased power might instead bring about the worst-case scenario.

However, the trump card is something we can control—and as a bonus, it's flexible. We believe it will prove effective in stopping the Shadowlord. We'll keep it up our sleeve for now and let Nier collect the remaining fragment.

I know this ended up on the long side [AGAIN!], but I had lots to write about. At least I didn't go off on any tangents this time, right? Anyway, please forgive me. End report.

Report written by Devola

NieR Replicant
ver.1.22474487139...

The Man 6

1.

IT HAD BEEN a long time since Nier walked across the southern plains.

All their trips to Seafront had been by boat of late. And unlike the plains, which were home to medium-size, armor-clad Shades, the waterways were peaceful as could be. Traveling on the ferry was safe, fast, and allowed them to bring as much cargo as they liked. There was no reason to ever travel by another method. However . . .

"The Shades keep getting stronger," Nier mused. It was true: Even with the reliable support of Kainé's twin blades and Emil's magic, it still took considerable time to eliminate them.

"It seems the vile creatures are learning," Grimoire Weiss agreed.

"Yeah, and everyone is going to be in trouble if the ferry doesn't start running again."

Popola had informed Nier that the ferryman with the red bag hadn't come to work for a few days—which explained why he'd not been seen on the village docks of late. This exchange took place at the same time Nier was thinking of taking Emil to Seafront via the ferry. The boy had been feeling low since the incident in The Aerie, and Nier thought a boat trip might be just the thing to cheer him up. So when Popola asked Nier to go to Seafront and check on the ferryman, Nier agreed at once. While it was partially for Emil's sake, he also knew how much his village had come to rely on the ferry. If food stopped being shipped in from Seafront, the situation would grow dire almost immediately.

That day, Nier met up with Kainé and Emil outside the southern gate, and the trio headed for Seafront. He thought the three of them would cut through the southern plains in no time, but they ended up taking much longer than he'd imagined.

"The ferryman must be sick," Emil said as they walked. "I should go check on him."

"We don't know that," Nier responded. "Let's just have me and Weiss look into it first."

"But—"

"You should go say hi to Sebastian, Emil. I know you haven't seen him in a while. Maybe take Kainé with you."

Going on foot through the southern plains took them by the manor where Emil used to live. The moment Nier took the job in Seafront, he decided to send Emil off to see his old butler, hoping that might do a better job of cheering him than the absent ferryman.

Nier said goodbye to Emil and Kainé at the bottom of the hill that led to the manor, then continued on with Grimoire Weiss.

"This all feels very familiar," he mused. Five years ago, Popola had asked them to check on the man who was supposed to repair the waterways because he stopped showing up for work, and now they were taking on the very same mission.

"Pah!" Grimoire Weiss barked. "I'm sure that couple is merely having another one of their inane spats."

The tome took the words right out of Nier's mind. The reason the ferryman stopped coming to work five years ago was because his wife had left home. Nier recalled the sight of the man sitting despondently in front of his house.

"His wife probably ran away again," said Nier.

"I would not put it past her. Regardless, we must take care not to get too deep into their petty quarrels."

Once again, Weiss had stolen a thought from Nier's mind.

Nier and Weiss turned out to be slightly off the mark. When they approached the couple's home, they didn't find the husband sitting outside, but the wife.

"Oh god, it's over," she moaned. "My life is over!"

"Ah, another bout of déjà vu," Grimoire Weiss muttered.

"What's wrong?" asked Nier.

"Hey, I remember you," said the woman as her eyes darted between Nier and Weiss.

"Seeing as we've come all this way, I suppose we had best ask: What is the matter?" Grimoire Weiss said, sighing.

"I had a fight with my husband and he ran away from home."

"A reversal of roles, is it? Mmm, yes. You may color me utterly flabbergasted."

"But it's all that idiot's fault! I was saving up a bunch of apples, and he went and ate *all* of them!"

One thing the couple had in common was that they both *really* liked red things. They always wore the matching red bags they bought for their anniversary, and apparently they ate red apples nearly every day.

"I get how you feel, but they were just apples."

The woman's brows shot up unnaturally fast; Nier had clearly crossed a line.

"Just apples? *Just* apples?!" Despite how listlessly she'd been sitting earlier, she suddenly leaped to her feet. "Listen to me. He ate ten of them. *Ten!* He ate ten of my apples all by himself!"

"That's . . . actually sort of impressive."

"It is not! It's *awful*!"

Nier felt like everything he said was coming out wrong, so he decided then and there to reply as little as possible.

"Uh, yes, ma'am."

"Under the circumstances, can you blame me for what I said to him? Anyone would have done the same!"

"Of course, ma'am."

"Look, I admit I may have lost my temper a little. But I can't believe he just up and left! He's been gone for a week now, and it's . . ."

The woman suddenly choked up. As her raised brows knitted together, tears began to stream down her cheeks.

"All right, all right," Nier said in a voice weary with surrender. "We'll help you find him."

"Really?" The woman's tears came to a sudden halt, replaced by a brilliant smile. "Oh, thank you so much!"

Both of them are sure . . . interesting people, thought Nier. *In many senses of the word.*

Though Nier had been planning to follow Weiss's advice and not get wrapped up in the couple's marital affairs, his plan had fallen apart. He couldn't escape their problems five years prior, and he apparently didn't stand a chance of doing so now.

After agreeing to help, Nier and Weiss headed for the tavern just as they had five years before. It was the perfect spot to ask around; it was always busy, and the people gathered there were always ready to talk. Luckily, the pair's trip across the southern plains had taken up so much time that it was now evening, the time of day when the tavern was busiest.

As Nier entered with a meek greeting, he spotted a familiar face. It was a woman he'd gotten a clue from five years ago, and he was hopeful she might be able to help again.

"I'm looking for the man with the red bag," he began. "You know, the one who runs the ferry? Have you seen him around?"

"Reeeally? Is that couple fighting *again*? Or maybe he just ran away!"

"His wife said he took off and hasn't been seen since. I take it this isn't a surprise?"

"Hardly! Their arguments are legendary—we're actually considering selling tickets as a tourist attraction."

Last time, the two had simply been known about town for arguing. It seemed they'd upgraded to "legendary" status during the past five years.

"Oh, I remember now!" continued the woman. "I think he's from that town with the library, right?"

She clearly meant Nier's village; it was the only one that contained a library.

"So yeah, maybe he went back home. Remember last time the wife ran away and caused a huge commotion, and it just turned out she went back home? It's probably the same thing."

Her voice filled with confidence, she reached for her glass and threw back the rest of its contents. "Oh, and I think his brother is a guard out there or something."

"Is he?" replied Nier. "Thanks for the tip. I'll go back and ask right away."

"Right away? C'mon, you're pretty handsome. Stay here and I'll buy you a drink."

Despite the force with which she tugged on his arm, Nier managed to beat a hurried escape.

2.

NIER AND WEISS stayed the night in Seafront, then they left early the next morning to meet Kainé and Emil in the southern plains.

"Whoa, the ferryman's from your village?!" Emil exclaimed. "I had no idea!"

"Me neither. Thought I knew everyone's face, but I guess there are some people I never met."

As they chatted, they mowed down more Shades. Kill, rest, walk, kill; it was rinse and repeat all the way back to the village. But no matter how many Shades they killed, more appeared to take their place, to the point where Nier found himself irritated. Where were they all coming from anyway?

The group was exhausted when they returned to the village, but there was no time to catch their breath until they tracked down the missing ferryman. Two guards stood at each of the gates of the village, so they decided to ask the pair at the southern ones first.

"Oh, hey," a guard greeted them. "What's up?"

"You know the ferryman who carries a red bag?" Nier asked.

"Yeah, he's my little brother," the guard replied.

Bull's-eye on the first shot.

"Have you any idea where he may have absconded to?" Grimoire Weiss asked.

"Not a clue. I haven't seen him in a while."

"Well, that's unfortunate," Nier muttered.

As he thought about it, he realized Popola wouldn't have asked him to check on the ferryman if he'd been in the village recently. Devola was constantly hanging around the tavern; she would have known the moment he set one foot in town.

"Oh, but the last time I *did* see him, he said something about using his ferry to deliver letters," continued the guard. "Maybe you should try talking to someone at the post office."

"I guess we could ask the postman over in Seafront," Nier offered aloud.

"Just once, I would enjoy receiving a quest that can be solved in the general vicinity of the asker," sighed Weiss. His tone suggested he was fed up with the whole affair, and Nier thought he was right to feel that way. Passing through the southern plains meant they'd spent a majority of the day fighting Shades, which was tiring work now that they'd gotten used to traveling by boat.

"So you looking for my brother or something?"

"Yeah. Popola said he hasn't shown up to work in a few days," replied Nier, who wisely decided not to mention the whole "fighting with his wife" part.

"I see. Well, if you happen to run into him, you mind telling him to stop home and see his family every now and again?"

The work of a ferryman was busy, and it was unlikely the boatman had time to step away from the docks whenever he found himself back in the village. Still, that was a sad burden to bear for his family, who would have wanted him to drop by and say hello while he was in the area.

"I'll tell him," Nier replied as he took his leave.

"Well?" asked Emil. "Did you find him?"

"No. He hasn't been back, apparently."

"Oh."

"If I'd known that, I would have just had you stay at the manor."

"Huh?"

"We're headed back to Seafront. We got word the postman might know something."

Nier had assumed they'd find the ferryman at the village, which was why he'd picked Emil and Kainé up at the manor. If the man had indeed been in the village, it would have meant they'd return to boat travel and wouldn't be crossing the southern plains again. If he'd known he'd be heading back to Seafront by land, he could have waited until that point to get his friends. Emil, however, furiously shook his head, as though Nier had given a most outrageous suggestion.

"No! It's too dangerous for you and Weiss to make a round trip through the plains alone!"

"I guess killing Shades *does* take a lot longer without you two around," admitted Nier.

"I thought so!" said Emil as he pulled himself straighter with a huff of pride.

"Look what trouble we're going through for the sake of one man," Grimoire Weiss muttered.

"Sometimes it's nice to go out of your way to help people," replied Nier. Their recent fragment-collecting meant constant battles with Shades far larger and more dangerous than those of the southern plains. Compared to that, Nier wasn't about to argue with a mundane job like finding a missing ferryman.

"I certainly hope this is no calm before the storm," Grimoire Weiss said in his most pessimistic tone.

This time, Emil and Kainé accompanied Nier and Weiss to the outskirts of Seafront. That way, they'd be ready to either take the boat once they found the ferryman or head out immediately if the search led them to a different city—although the idea of further travel was a possibility Nier didn't want to consider.

Leaving their friends to ready their camp for the night, Nier and Weiss made for the post office. Along the way, they stumbled across the woman with the red bag.

"Hey!" she cried. "It's you! Did you find my husband?!"

"Uh, no. Not yet." The honesty of this answer caused the woman's expression to fall, so Nier hastened to add a follow-up. "Uh, but the postman might know something, so I'm thinking we'll figure out where he went soon."

The woman's crestfallen expression immediately brightened. "You *will*?!"

"Er, I think so? Maybe? We might."

Though Nier made a couple attempts to hedge his answer, she had stopped listening.

"Oh, I'm gonna give him an earful the next time I see him!"

"About what?"

"About leaving me alone! Oooh, I am gonna give him nine kinds of hell when he gets back!"

"I cannot imagine why he hasn't returned yet," Grimoire Weiss muttered.

You can say that again, Nier quietly agreed.

When Nier and Weiss finally reached the post office, the postman was nowhere to be found. Instead, an annoyed local fisherman stood behind the counter.

"Uh, where's the postman?" asked Nier.

"Beats me," growled the fisherman. "I just swung by to pick up a letter and wound up running the damn place. You here for a package or something?"

"No. There's this couple who's always fighting, and the husband took off, so I'm trying to track him down."

"Oh sure, I know them," said the fisherman, driving home once more how the couple had become infamous throughout Seafront.

"So do you have any idea where he is?"

"Sorry, pal. You're asking the wrong guy."

"That's all right. Thanks."

"I suppose we have no choice but to wait for the postman to return," Grimoire Weiss muttered.

As he said that, the fisherman spoke up again. "Still, that's pretty weird; my buddy's daughter took off too. Maybe running away is the cool thing to do now."

"I find it exceedingly unlikely this pair of runaways is mere coincidence," Grimoire Weiss mused. "Especially considering it happened within the same time frame."

"Any idea where she might've went?" asked Nier.

"That *is* the question, isn't it?" said the fisherman, nodding. "She's just a kid—hard to think she got anywhere else to be. Unless . . ."

"Did you think of something?"

"This is a wild guess, but there was a shipwreck that drifted into the inlet the other day. All the kids have been talking about it. How could they not? Damn thing was huge."

"And you think she went to check it out?"

"We've been telling the kids to stay away from it, but you know how the little devils are. Tell 'em no, and they just wanna do a thing all the more."

An image immediately popped into Nier's mind of a child getting stuck in a shipwreck and calling for help and the ferry-man rushing in to save her. Nier thanked the fisherman, left the post office, and made for the western inlet with all speed.

3.

". . . BUT I CAN still pour you some, if you like! We could also start making food, even though it's a bit early."

Kainé could hear Emil talking to her as they sat by the fire, but his words went in one ear and out the other. Finally, he looked over with a puzzled expression.

"Kainé?"

"Hmm? Oh. Thinking. Sorry."

"That's okay! I'll make some tea anyway!"

Seemingly unbothered by her lack of attention, he began boiling a pot of water over the fire. As he did, Kainé's left side bubbled and Tyrann sprang to life.

"*You feelin' that, Sunshine?*" he asked in a voice filled with strong implication.

Yeah, she replied. In truth, she'd picked up on the scent way before they even came to Seafront.

"*There's some reeeally weird magic goin' on here.*"

Weird was indeed the word. Kainé had never felt anything like it, and at first she thought her imagination was playing tricks or there was something odd about the weather. But while the winds were indeed ominous, the closer they came to town, the stronger the feeling got. Once she and Emil started setting up camp, she was certain there was more to it than wind or whims.

A Shade, maybe? But for a Shade, it was so . . .

"This ain't like you, Sunshine. I'm startin' to think your two legs work faster than your two brain cells!"

Though she knew Tyrann was mocking her, there was a truth to his words. No matter how long she thought about the problem, a solution remained out of reach. It was strange enough that she was just going to have to go see it for herself.

"You okay, Kainé?" asked Emil. "Is something bothering you?"

She was about to say no but stopped. "I'm sensing something like a Shade inside the city."

"A Shade *in* the town? That's not good."

"Yeah, I don't know if I'd call it a Shade, exactly."

"But it's still dangerous, right? Is that why you're worried?"

When Kainé didn't respond, Emil doubled down. "Then let's go!"

"It's in town though. We should wait until everyone's aslee—"

"No! We have to go now! The others are still in there!"

He was right—it would be bad to wait. Even though Shades were more spry during the day now, their natural period of activity was still at night. They were likely to be more docile during the day, even if only by a little.

"It's okay," continued Emil. "The ferryman lives here, so it *can't* be full of bad people!"

"Fair enough. Let's move."

After putting out the campfire, Kainé followed Emil into town. The moment they stepped through the gate, she stopped caring about the townsfolk completely. The presence was so bizarre and eldritch, she didn't have the brainpower to worry about anything else.

"It's this way," she said after a moment. All her instincts were screaming at her to stay away from that direction, which meant it was where they'd find the mystery presence.

"This magic's baaad news, Sunshine!"

Shut up. You're distracting me.

They left the main street and passed through a narrow road that led to a grotto. Whatever Kainé was feeling, it lay farther inside.

"Hey! You listenin' to me?"

A noise suddenly rang out from the direction of the presence. It went high, then low, then began oscillating back and forth between the two extremes, causing the air to shudder.

What the hell? Is this supposed to be sound?

If so, Kainé doubted a regular human would be able to hear it. As that thought swirled in her mind, she suddenly heard her name.

"Kainé! Emil!"

She looked up and saw Nier rushing toward them. He'd mentioned going to see a postman before going into town. Maybe this was where the post office was.

"What's going on?" he asked breathlessly. "I haven't seen you two come into Seafront in . . . Well, ever, I guess."

"Sorry for the surprise," Emil apologized. "Kainé said she sensed something strange in the area."

"Strange how? Like a Shade?"

"Maybe," Kainé responded. "Not sure. There's some kind of . . . sound or something coming from up ahead."

"There's an inlet up ahead," Nier informed her. Kainé didn't know much about the layout of Seafront, so the fact there was even an inlet at all was news to her.

"Yeah, okay," she said. "Then that's where the . . . Shade or whatever it is will be."

Shade didn't exactly feel like the right word, yet Kainé also felt certain that it *was*. Whatever the case, it was a creature more powerful and unusual than any Shade she'd encountered before.

"What an incredibly specific piece of information the hussy

has graced us with," quipped Weiss. Kainé had a vague inkling her companion was trying to rile her up, but it didn't register. She only realized what was happening when Emil began to scold the book.

"What's going on, Kainé?" asked a worried Nier. Under normal circumstances, she would have had a retort at the ready regarding Grimoire Weiss's state as a book, but she'd remained silent.

". . . Nothing," she said finally. "Let's get moving."

She marched ahead. Though her instincts were sounding alarm bells and her legs threatened to freeze in place, she forced herself to move anyway.

Whatever's going on, this is some bad *shit right here. I don't want to go forward. In fact, I just want to go home.*

"*You and me both, Sunshine. I wanna go home and lock all the doors and windows. 'Cause this thing? Woof.*"

Tyrann felt somehow calmer today, his usual glee absent. The reason was clear enough—the Shade inside her loved violence and slaughter if he was the party responsible. It wasn't nearly so enjoyable when he was the one at risk of being murdered.

"Wow! Look at how big this boat is!" Emil exclaimed as they exited the grotto. An enormous wooden ship lay stranded on the beach, practically closing off the inlet. It was in a terrible state: Its masts were snapped, and the hull was dingy with dirt. Clearly the thing had been adrift for a very long time before finally running aground.

"*It's in there.*"

The bizarre presence was emanating from inside the ship, and it caused the left half of Kainé's body to shudder.

"*It's resonating,*" Tyrann murmured.

The Shade part of her body was reacting independently of Tyrann's will. Nothing like this had *ever* happened before, and it could only mean she was facing something bigger and more powerful than anything she'd come across before.

"We're gonna need to figure out some way to get inside that thing," Nier mused aloud.

"This ship is in a state of wanton decay," replied Weiss. "Surely we can find a hole or some such if we put our minds to it."

Keen on going inside, Nier and Weiss began eagerly roaming the perimeter of the ship.

"The entrance is probably near the bottom," said Nier. "I mean, kids got in after all."

"*Kids?*" asked an incredulous Kainé.

"Yeah. Some kids from town have gone missing over the past few days."

Nier gave Kainé the quick rundown of what he'd learned. A fisherman at the post office mentioned a girl going missing, while several elderly people chatting on the street told him about two absent boys.

"Everyone thinks they went to play in the ship and couldn't find a way out," Nier concluded.

"Right," Kainé replied. It took all of her energy and concentration to say that one word. Whatever was wafting out of that ship was making her sick.

"Hey, look!" Nier shouted as he rounded the stern of the ship. Waiting there was a hole big enough for a person to climb through. The inside, however, had been covered by wooden planks, which was why he'd missed it the first time around. It didn't help that the craft was in such a state of disrepair.

"The planks aren't even nailed in place," he said. "We can probably get in if we move 'em out of the way."

Nier deftly moved the boards to one side and stepped through, followed closely by Weiss. All Kainé could do now was prepare for the worst, so she swallowed briefly and forced herself to move toward the hole.

"Oh baby, that is one hell of a smell. We got somethin' real nasty nearby, Sunshine."

Tyrann was right—the odor was beyond foul. Strangely, only she and Tyrann seemed to notice it. All Nier said was that the place smelled vaguely of fish.

Suddenly, Kainé took an inadvertent step back, causing a horrible creaking sound to echo from under her feet.

"Do not thrash about and bring this ship's timbers down around us, hussy," Grimoire Weiss scolded.

". . . Whatever."

It took great effort for her to squeeze out a reply. She didn't want to open her mouth anymore. She didn't want to breathe a single molecule of the ship's air.

"You've picked up on it, haven't ya? You of all people gotta know what this smell means."

Kainé didn't want to think about what the odor meant. Because—

"You sure you're all right, Kainé?" Nier asked, interrupting her thoughts.

"Yeah, you really shouldn't push yourself," Emil chimed in.

Despite both friends voicing their concern, all Kainé could do was stay quiet and try to breathe.

"Hey, I've got an idea!" Emil piped up. "How about you and me search the outside and get some fresh air in the process?"

". . . Sure. Let's do that."

Though she managed to keep a straight face, Kainé was at her limit. When she stumbled onto the beach outside the boat, she gasped for air, breathing in huge lungfuls. As her frigid cheeks and fingers finally began to warm again, Kainé thought she had never been so thankful to encounter the blazing sun and ocean breeze.

4.

ONCE KAINÉ AND Emil left the ship, Nier decided to walk around the inside.

"It's dark," he noted. Though faint rays of light squeezed through gaps in the planks, it wasn't nearly bright enough to help in his search.

"Look there—on the floor," stated the sharp-eyed Weiss. "I believe we have found ourselves a lantern!"

Nier reached down and picked it up, pleased to discover it was still filled with oil.

"Nice."

"There is no guarantee any outside light will reach every inner room. Let us spark it while we can yet see."

Grimoire Weiss was right. They'd only taken a few steps before they found themselves out of the sun's reach. Without a light source, they'd have to stop the search and pull back, and they might even find themselves hopelessly lost.

The floor was littered with empty bottles, splintered crates, and metallic fragments weathered beyond use. Nier lowered himself to keep steady and aimed the lantern to the floor to make sure he didn't stumble, which was why he only saw the shadow of a moving figure from the corner of his eye.

"What was that?!" he cried.

"I saw it as well," said Weiss.

"It looked like a girl."

The figure was small, and Nier thought he saw long hair flutter behind it.

"This may be one of the missing children. We should retrieve her with all haste."

"She went in there, right?" said Nier, aiming the lantern's light at an open door. It showed crates, barrels, and empty bottles—all things they'd seen plenty of thus far.

"No one's here," said Nier. He stepped inside and lit the corners around the barrels and crates, but there was no girl to be found.

"Weird. Maybe we saw a ghost."

"Still your tongue, fool!" barked Grimoire Weiss. "I'd sooner assume the waif vanished herself behind a secret passage."

Wow, Weiss really hates talking about ghosts, Nier thought, remembering the first time they'd explored Emil's manor.

"Actually, wait," he said suddenly. "This isn't a secret passageway, but there *is* a door. I didn't see it at first because there's no handle."

"And Grimoire Weiss is right once again! The lass surely ventured—"

"Nope. No one's there."

Nier pushed the door open and held up his lantern but found nothing. He could hear Grimoire Weiss gasp in fright.

"Oh, but there's another door," said Nier. "Looks like we can keep going. C'mon."

As he was about to take a step forward, he noticed something round at his feet.

"Huh? It's an apple. It's a bit bruised, but it's not super old or anything." The moment he said this, he remembered the red-bag woman's words about her husband eating her apples.

"Oh dear," said Weiss. "Perhaps that fruit-loving ferryman absconded to this ship to wait out the storm after yet another spirited debate with his wife. Goodness, what a troublesome couple."

There was also the possibility the ferryman couldn't leave the runaway girl alone and was trying to convince her to come home. Regardless, it wasn't as though either one had found their way in and gotten stuck. The shadowy figure in the hall didn't seem to be injured either. If she managed to walk this far, she could easily walk out again.

"Let's keep moving," said Nier.

As they proceeded farther in, they came across a staircase leading up. Lighting it revealed only a dark, impenetrable abyss—but as Nier held the lantern high, there came the sound of a heavy object colliding with something else.

"Wh-what was that sound just now?" cried Weiss.

"It came from upstairs. You think it's the girl?"

The stairs were in poor shape, and Nier worried any extra weight might cause them to come crashing down. With the utmost care, he placed his feet on one plank, then another. Each step brought a series of horrible creaking sounds. He doubted even the lightest child could use them in silence but decided not to point that out. He wasn't here to scare Grimoire Weiss after all. But after taking the time to walk up the steps, Nier quickly saw what caused the noise.

"This barrel's been knocked over," he said. He held up the lantern, which showed flour scattered across the floor.

"Surely it was the girl who toppled this. Ah, but wait! Cast your eyes to the floor, lad."

There were white footprints on the floor under Grimoire Weiss. The flour must have stuck to her feet, because the prints continued down the hall.

"I expect we will find our way to the child should we follow these tracks," Grimoire Weiss remarked.

She'd left behind not only footprints but handprints on the walls as well, most likely because she had fallen over when she ran into the barrel. However, the prints came to an abrupt halt at the door at the end of the hallway, which they found to be locked.

"Weird. She came through here, so why is it locked?"

"Are you suggesting it was a ghost? Preposterous! She . . . she simply locked the door behind her! Yes, that must be it."

"I never said it was a ghost, Weiss. Now, look around. There has to be a copy of the key somewhere."

The room next to the mystery door wasn't locked, and the interior was in the same messy state as the lower part of the ship. Chairs lay on their sides, pitchers and buckets were scattered about, and books and ledgers cluttered a writing desk by the wall.

"This seems to be this ship's logbook," Grimoire Weiss remarked. He left Nier's side to float to it, likely an indication he was eager to read the contents. Seeing this, Nier helpfully flipped open the book and held up the lantern.

"Records of the routes it traveled, the weather it encountered, and the places it made port—all in a painstaking level of detail. I would expect no less for a vessel of this size."

Nier flipped through the pages in line with Grimoire Weiss's reading speed until he revealed a blank page. They had come to the end of the log.

"And the records suddenly cease," muttered Weiss ominously.

"Doesn't that just mean they finished their trip?" Nier asked.

"The end of a seafaring voyage would include records of their final docking at port. This log, however, ends with the vessel still well at sea."

What had happened here? Had the pair simply found themselves amid a disaster that left the victims no time to keep records, or . . . ?

"What about this ledger?" Nier said, pointing to another book. "It's crammed full of writing and numbers."

"Let me see. It's a record of cargo. Perhaps an account book? Hmm . . . Oh dear."

As Grimoire Weiss scanned the ledger, he fell silent. After a brief pause, he made a disgusted sound. "By my pages, this ship was used by slavers! How simply atrocious."

"You're telling me they sold *people*?"

"And made out quite handsomely from the transactions, it would seem."

"How could they do something like that?"

"I do not know, nor do I care to ponder it. Let it suffice to say there are monsters who trade coin for misery in all corners of this accursed world."

Grimoire Weiss separated himself from the writing desk. He was right: There was no point in analyzing ship logbooks and ledgers any more than they already had, even if they could spare the time to do so. But just as Nier was about to place the ledger back on the desk, he spotted a ring of neglected keys nearby.

"Weiss! I found keys!"

The whole reason they'd come into the room in the first place was to search for a key that fit the door at the end of the hall. Nier prayed the one they needed might be on the ring as they hurried back to the passageway.

Luckily, it was. As the door swung open, they were met with the familiar sight of dusty white prints. Suddenly, they heard a sound from the far end of the room.

"Do you hear that?" asked Nier.

"What could it be? Is someone singing?"

It sounded both like an ambient noise and a voice. If it *was* a voice, however, it didn't seem to be speaking. Nier followed the sound and ventured deeper into the room. As he got closer, he could tell it was indeed a voice and not a noise. The pitch went up and down, which led him to believe it was a song—albeit one terribly out of tune.

Though the white prints had vanished, the singing continued. Nier scanned the room and finally found the source: a metallic pipe bolted to the wall.

"Is this the girl's voice?" he asked. As his hand came to rest on the pipe, the noise stopped.

"Huh. I wonder what that was all about. You think that girl was singing?"

"This is a voice pipe," Grimoire Weiss explained. "It is a contraption by which one's voice can travel to a faraway location."

"Which means the girl is in whatever room it connects to."

"Hold a moment. I spy a chart of the ship's layout on the wall. This room must have belonged to the one responsible for minding ship-wide communications."

Grimoire Weiss floated toward the chart and examined it. "Ah, I see. This pipe connects to a cabin in the ship's stern."

"Got it. Onward and, uh, inward, I guess."

They returned to the hallway and kept going. The layout of the ship was complicated, and it was hard to remember where things were. Belatedly, Nier realized they should have torn the chart off the wall and brought it with them.

Eventually, a toppled barrel blocked their path. As Nier tried to scoot past, something slid out.

"Is that a notebook? Why is it in a barrel?"

He flipped it open and found what appeared to be a diary filled with pages of dates and notes.

●● / ●●

A monster appeared after the storm. Thing ate my crewmates right in front of me.

●● / ●●
I can hear the captain screaming.

●● / ●●
Crunching. Then silence.

●● / ●●
Went to the hold to get water, but our goods were destroyed. Came back fast as I was able.

●● / ●●
The door was broken, so I hid in a barrel.

●● / ●●
I hear screams from the rooms above me.

●● / ●●
I hear screams from the room next to me.

●● / ●●
Hungry.

●● / ●●
Hungry.

●● / ●●
So hungry.

●● / ●●
I don't hear the crew anymore.

●● / ●●
I hear the monster. It's close now.

The writing grew messy partway through the record, presumably because that was when the author was inside the barrel. The last few pages contained only the word *help* scrawled over and over in an increasingly unsteady hand.

"Do you think this actually happened?" Nier wondered aloud.

"I cannot say," Weiss replied curtly.

All the rooms they'd seen so far had been littered with debris, and the corridor they stood in now was in an equally messy state. At first, Nier thought it might be the result of a storm at sea, but now he wondered if the mess was something left in the wake of the "monster."

"Hey," he said, looking down. "Another apple."

"Just how many apples *does* that quibbling husband keep on his person while he's out and about?"

Considering he'd put away ten apples in one sitting, Nier thought he might have crammed his bag full of the things— but finding them scattered about the ship haphazardly gave him pause. If the man loved apples so much, why didn't he come back for them?

As this thought rolled in his mind, Nier flung open the door and was hit by a stench so powerful, he nearly dropped his lantern.

"The hell is this *smell*?" he gagged. It was strong enough to make him take a step backward and a scent wholly unfamiliar to him. Was this what rotting fish smelled like? The creatures were so valuable in his village that they never got to the rotting stage, so he had no way to know if that was the case or not.

"Perhaps it is wafting from further inside," suggested Weiss.

"That's where we'll find the pipe, right?"

Nier wanted to turn back, but he felt he had to bring the girl home now. After solidifying his will, he took a step forward. The floor gave a terrible groan under the weight, but by the time he realized his mistake, it was too late.

"AAAAAAH!"

He tumbled through the air before landing with a dreadful *crack* and *crunch* that caused him to yelp in pain.

"Speak to me, lad! Are you hurt?!"

Nier heard Weiss's voice but was unable to locate the source in the midst of the utter darkness in which he found himself.

"Been better, but I'll live."

"I suspect we may have fallen into the ship's hold."

"It smells *terrible* down here."

Nier sat, trying to locate up from down, and thrust his hands out to grope around.

"Yeowch! That's hot!"

Well, that was one problem solved: He'd found the lantern by placing his hand directly on the wick.

"Weiss, I found the lantern!" he cried happily.

"Might I suggest you cease the celebratory fanfare and light the blasted thing? I can hardly tell if my eyes are open or closed."

"Okay, okay."

Nier figured he'd end up stepping on a rotting fish if he didn't do as Weiss said, and that was a fate he desperately wanted to avoid. But once the device flickered to life, he realized old fish were the least of his concerns.

"Oh dear," whispered Weiss.

The lantern's light revealed a human corpse.

"It's the ferryman," murmured Nier.

But his was not the only corpse at the bottom of the ship. There was also the girl and two boys the adults suspected of running away, plus a number of adults. All the bodies were in terrible shape: The children were missing their lower halves, while the adults were only torsos. As for the ferryman, his stomach had been ripped open, scattering its contents across the floorboards.

"This can't be real," someone said—Nier only realized moments later that the voice belonged to him. "This can't be real.

This can't be real. This shouldn't have happened. This can't be real. It can't be. *IT CAN'T!*"

"Enough, lad. Avert your eyes." Grimoire Weiss's voice snapped him out of his mania. "Now pull yourself together; the culprit who murdered these poor folk awaits further within."

Nier remembered the diary entry where the writer said he'd seen his crewmates eaten right in front of him. The same creature had no doubt consumed both the ferryman and the girl who vanished from home.

Why? he asked himself as his rage began to roil. *Why them?*

"I won't let them get away with this."

He grabbed the ladder beside him and began to climb. He was going to find the thing responsible and end it.

5.

"WE CAN GET in through here!" cried Emil.

Kainé was feeling much better after getting some fresh air and was none too happy about the idea of going *back* inside the ship. Unfortunately, she liked the idea of leaving the search to Nier and Weiss even less, so she steeled herself and stepped into the craft once more.

The moment she did so, she regretted it. The smell was back, and even more powerful than before.

"Whoa, it smells *terrible* in here! The heck is causing that?"

As Emil was about to float down into the bowels of the ship, Kainé grabbed the hem of his robe.

"Better not."

"Why?"

"Because whatever that thing is, it's above us."

Kainé wasn't lying: the smell and the odd aura were coming from entirely different places.

"You hear it, don't ya, Sunshine?"

Yeah, she replied. The noise was a song, one horribly out of tune. The Shade was singing it, stopping every now and then to interrupt itself with snippets of speech.

"Where did he go?" it said. But who was "he"?

"I have to sing and cheer myself up," it said. Sing? Cheer? Could it really be a *Shade* saying this stuff?

"There's something above us?" asked Emil.

"Yeah, and I think it's—"

The rest of Kainé's sentence was broken off by a terrible cracking and crashing from below.

"What was that?!" asked Emil as he and Kainé exchanged glances. "Do you think it's our friends?"

"Stay here. I'll take a look."

She wasn't about to let Emil go down there. But the moment she grabbed the ladder, he reached out to stop her.

"No! It's too dangerous!"

"So what about those other two idiots?"

"Oh. Um . . ."

Emil fell silent, conflicted. It was clear the floor below was dangerous, and there was a decent chance Nier and Weiss were trapped in the space.

As he waffled, Kainé peered down the ladder. It was too dark to see anything. What was going *on* down there?

"So what should we do?" asked Emil as he joined her in peering down the ladder. Suddenly, a familiar tome floated toward them, followed by a mop of silver hair.

"Hey there, you two!" cried a happy Emil.

Kainé noticed Nier looked somewhat pale—and more surprisingly, Grimoire Weiss was silent.

"Hey," responded Nier. "I didn't know you guys came back inside."

"Did we ever! Found a nice hole in the wall to slide through. But *then* we heard a bunch of noise coming from downstairs. You sure had us worried!"

"Yeah, sorry about that," Nier offered before turning to Kainé. "You feeling better?"

"A little, yeah."

"Good. That's . . . good."

Kainé wasn't just imagining that Nier was disturbed. Not only was he pale, but his voice was pitched lower than usual.

"Geez, you seem really down in the dumps. Did something happen?"

If Emil noticed it as well, it had to be true—and Kainé had a pretty good idea what was causing their consternation.

"Tell me, Kainé," said Weiss, further proving his disturbed state by using her actual name rather than some inappropriate term. "That presence you sensed . . ."

"Yeah. It's above us."

"I feared as much. It seems we've little choice but to press onward."

The tome's tone, however, suggested he was reluctant to do so. Even without the ability to sense the presence of Shades, he somehow knew they were up against a foe far beyond the norm.

"The voice pipe led here according to the chart of the ship's layout, right?" asked a glum Nier.

Kainé raised an eyebrow—she hadn't known there was a map of the place.

"Lemme see this chart."

"Don't have it with me; we found it in another room. Why, is there something you want to see?"

"Just curious."

In fact, Kainé was disappointed. She'd been hoping to learn how large the room above them was from the chart.

"Yeah, woulda been nice, right? You coulda figured out just how big this guy is! Coulda tried to get a handle on your fear!"

You wanted it just as much, Kainé replied wordlessly. In an unusual turn of events, Tyrann remained quiet, which meant she'd hit the mark precisely.

Kainé knew the Shade waiting above was powerful—that

much was clear from the potency of its presence. She also knew most Shades grew in size relative to their power, which was the reason she wanted to see the chart. If she knew how big the room was, she might have an idea about the size of their foe.

Still, knowing how large it was at this point wouldn't change much. It clearly wasn't bigger than the ship itself, so perhaps that fact was enough.

Kainé and Nier clambered up the ladder while Weiss and Emil floated behind. Once Emil was far enough away, Kainé turned to Nier and asked in a low voice, "Find anything down there?"

"Some townspeople, actually. They're all . . ."

Nier trailed off, which was answer enough. They'd all been killed—the ferryman, the little girl, the missing boys. All of them.

"Shit."

This fucking sucks, she thought.

"And the stench gets stronger. How you feelin', Sunshine?"

Bad, obviously. But Tyrann, too, was in unusually low spirits. The closer they got to the presence, the further they strayed from their normal selves.

Just then, Kainé heard the strange voice again. It was especially clear now that they were close.

"I want to be able to talk with him. I don't want him to be afraid of me. I don't want him to hate me."

It was talking about a "him" again, and it didn't want "him" to hate it—whoever "he" might be.

"And this is a Shade we're talkin' about here!" piped up Tyrann. *"Really makes you wonder what's going on in its brain, eh?"*

They'd encountered Shades that wanted to protect companions, and Shades that mourned the passing of others. But they'd never encountered a Shade that spoke in so eloquent a fashion. Was that why this situation felt so different? Could it be that . . . ?

No. Kainé quickly dismissed the thought.

"This would be the final room," Grimoire Weiss announced gravely before a door labeled *Captain's Quarters*. "The culprit who murdered the townspeople may be behind this very door. Let us proceed with utmost caution."

Nier wordlessly pushed the door open. Though unlocked, it leaned cockeyed on broken hinges, only opening wide enough to fit one person at a time. He squeezed himself through the narrow gap, and a moment later his companions heard him cry three words:

"It's the girl!"

Grimoire Weiss quickly flew inside. "Hold, lad. This is a lone child sitting inside a hulking ship littered with corpses. Something is clearly amiss."

The Shade was a *girl*?

Kainé could tell there was a Shade in the room—there was no doubt the presence belonged to one, despite how unusual it was. Confused, she rushed in after the others.

"That's it!" she cried. The room was smaller than she'd imagined, and it did indeed contain a small girl. She had pale skin and dirty clothes, and her black hair was tied back with a large ribbon.

"Oh man, this Shade is NUTS! *I think I'm in love!"*

This can't be it, Kainé thought. The sheer potency of the presence couldn't belong to a Shade this small. It *had* to be bigger.

"You can feel her power hangin' in the air, and she ain't even tryin' yet!"

At last Kainé understood why it felt so strange. The Shade before them was mimicking a girl's form, deliberately forcing its enormous body into a human shape. It was expending massive amounts of magical energy in order to preserve the form, which was causing the aura Kainé had never sensed before.

"Yeah, things are finally heatin' up . . . Huh?"

Cold sweat rolled down Kainé's back. The smell of blood hit her nostrils, causing her stomach to turn.

"Could this girl be the presence you were sensing, Kainé?" Nier asked.

Before she could answer, a voice rang out behind them.

"Oh hey, it's you! Been a while."

Not only was the voice far too chipper for the setting, but it belonged to the very person they'd come to Seafront to find.

"You're the postman!" Nier said. "What are you doing here?"

"Oh, I've been coming here a lot lately," replied the postman in a shockingly easy tone. "I think this girl was on the ship when it drifted in. I've been keeping an eye on her until she's well enough to leave."

Taking *care* of her? A human taking care of a *Shade*? Though Kainé heard him say the words, her mind was finding it impossible to comprehend them.

"Hey, so this is kind of awkward," whispered the postman as he drew near to Kainé. "But the girl is . . . you know. Bleeding? I brought a bunch of bandages with me, but, uh . . . how exactly *does* one deal with a woman's 'time of the month'?"

No, Kainé wanted to say, but her voice had abandoned her. The blood was not related to any normal human function. Rather, it was . . .

"S-sorry!" stuttered the postman suddenly. "Sorry. Clearly crossed a line there. Forget I said anything."

In a fluster, he stepped away from Kainé and made his way toward the girl. "Louise!" he called.

"Stay the hell away from her!"

Kainé finally got her voice to work again, causing the postman to whirl around. Behind him, the girl's eyes flashed a devil's crimson.

"She isn't . . ."

Before Kainé could finish her sentence, the Shade wailed. As its body began to swell with darkness, infinite black *somethings* rushed from her. They were tentacles—countless and squirming, each as thick as an adult's torso.

They weren't soft like those of a mollusk, but the fierce appendages of a Shade. As they laid waste to nearby walls and floors, the entire ship began to shudder.

"Aaahhh!"

The postman screamed as he fell through a crack in the floor. A voice shouted, "No, wait!" as the Shade—in the form of a tentacled girl—leaped into the gap after him.

"Kainé! Emil! You okay?!"

Kainé could hear Nier shouting from beyond a cloud of dust. She wanted to move toward him, but the massive hole in the floor made it impossible.

"Yeah!" she shouted back. "We'll figure something out—you just find a way to get the hell outta here!"

As the ship continued to shake, cracks began to spiderweb across the cabin's ceiling.

"You and I must withdraw!" she heard Grimoire Weiss shout.

"Kainé, this way!" came Emil's voice.

"Right behind you," she replied. She began making her way through the cabin by hugging the wall. It had only been moments since Louise's eyes shone red—a dozen seconds at most. Yet the ship was already crumbling to pieces; clearly those tentacles held a fearsome destructive power.

"*Why?*" came a voice from below. The sadness it contained threw Kainé for a loop. The girl's expression as she called after the falling postman seemed pained enough, but this was another level entirely.

No. Now was not the time to concern herself with such things.

She crouched low and held one arm over her head as she pushed forward, trying desperately to get out before she was buried alive.

"Why am I a Shade?"

"Why am I not human?"

She could still hear the voice whether she liked it or not. Neither the sounds of the floorboards ripping apart nor the ceiling crumbling to pieces was enough to drown out Louise's words.

"Goddammit!"

The swirl of dust that had been blocking her view dissipated at last, revealing Emil floating in a patch of painfully bright sunlight.

"Quick, Kainé!" he yelled. "The deck's this way! Can you get up?"

"Yeah. I'm coming."

It was a piece of luck they weren't on any of the lower floors. The deck was fairly close, and it didn't take much effort to clamber up and out of the ship.

Once she was free, Kainé turned her face to the blue sky, basking in the sunlight that poured down around them. Emil clearly felt the same. He was wordlessly tilting his head up toward the sun as well.

"Glad you two made it out in one piece!" said a nearby voice. It was Nier, with Weiss by his side. Kainé was thrilled to see they'd gotten out, but this relief lasted only a moment.

"The poor postman is still trapped inside!" Emil yelled.

"Well, we'd better go help him out," Nier sighed. He turned to head back into the ship, but Weiss stopped him.

"No, lad. We should use this opportunity to ready ourselves."

Regardless of whether they readied themselves now or later, they couldn't reenter the ship. A Shade would have free rein over the darkness inside, and there was no way of defending from unseen tentacles.

"No Shade would dare pursue us into sunlight such as this," continued Weiss. "We'd best—"

Before he could finish his sentence, the ship shuddered violently and a black tentacle burst through the deck. This was followed by another and another and another until the entire sky was filled with flying splinters of wood and metal.

"This cannot be!" cried Weiss.

Kainé watched the surface of the sea swell. What looked like the crest of a wave was, in fact, the body of a Shade. Its round head was reminiscent of a sea creature, while its long arms thrashed in the air like great serpents. She almost wanted to laugh at herself for thinking the Shade couldn't have been larger than the ship; even the small *portion* of what rose from the sea was bigger than the ship. She didn't dare try to imagine how big the entire thing might be.

"Why isn't this Shade being hurt by the sun?" Emil asked. While Shades that covered themselves in armor and straw could survive in the sun for a time, Shades without such protection perished instantly in its rays.

"That is not precisely the case," said Weiss. "It most certainly *is* being burned by the sunlight! However, its regenerative abilities far outpace whatever damage the light is able to inflict!"

Upon closer inspection, Kainé could see black mist roiling from the creature's body—the same dust that usually signified a Shade's death.

The Shade brought its arm down, dust streaming from its skin. Kainé dodged and attempted to counter with her blades, but they barely left a scratch. Nier sliced with his greatsword, and Emil unleashed a barrage of spells, but all their attacks did was kick up more black dust. If they were injuring it, there was no visible sign. Weiss was correct: Its regenerative power really *was* incredible.

The Shade's round head suddenly split in half to reveal a

gaping mouth. But there was something inside it besides teeth: Louise. Though she still retained the form of a girl, her hair and skin were now as dark as any Shade.

"Aw, listen! It's singing! This thing actually thinks it's a person!"

Kainé remembered the girl's voice saying it had to sing and cheer itself up. She wondered if perhaps the postman had taught her about the power of song.

Louise's voice grew until it became a sound wave that gouged a hole in the deck. The ground beneath Kainé's feet rumbled and shook, bringing her to her knees. How were they supposed to even fight such an extraordinary monster?

"I want to maintain a human form!" screamed Louise. *"I want to look at the sun with my own eyes! I want to sing beautiful songs! So if I just eat more people, maybe then I can become human!"*

Become human by eating people? Was that even possible?

"Hold up!" Tyrann's voice crackled in her mind. *"I dunno where the singin' lessons came from, but I do know it's sure as hell tryin' to eat us!"*

"Not happening!" cried Kainé as she leaped into the air and began slicing at the root of the serpentlike arms. If this thing's regenerative power was beyond normality, then her only choice was to attack it with even greater speed.

To her side, Nier and Emil seemed to sense what she was attempting to do. Emil floated in midair brandishing his staff, while Nier unleashed a fearsome strike using magical clones of himself.

"It's working!" cried Kainé.

With the sunlight pouring from the sky aiding their attacks, one arm finally tore free from the body, landing in the water with a tremendous splash.

"Don't stop now!" Kainé called out again. "Focus on the next one!"

So long as they managed to prevent it from attacking with

its arms, their blows would be easier to land. But they knew the Shade wouldn't fall until they attacked the head directly.

"*No!*" screamed Louise. "*Stop! I will become human! We will speak the same language! We will stay together!*"

Tyrann suddenly burst out laughing—exactly the reaction Kainé expected him to have to such a display.

"*Aw, you're doing it for the* postman? *How sad! How precious!*"

As the Shade's other arm fell, the rest of its massive shadowy body slumped to one side—perhaps due to the sudden absence of weight.

"Attack with all that you have!" Grimoire Weiss cried. Nier didn't waste any time; he manifested his magic hand and brought the fist down. The impact split Louise's head from its body, leaving the torso to sink beneath the waves.

"Is that it?!" Nier panted.

No. Not yet. The presence was still there—in fact, it had only grown stronger. An instant later, countless tentacles burst from the wrecked ship. Kainé had only a brief moment to realize the ship would be obliterated before they were all sent flying.

Luckily, they all landed on the beach. Kainé leaped to her feet and readied herself. The ship that once towered over them was gone, and in its place was the largest Shade she'd ever seen—the same one that just reduced an entire ship to splinters.

"To think it could recover from such a grievous wound . . ." Grimoire Weiss muttered in shock.

But the thing had done more than just recover. Arms that had been lopped from its body were back in place—and joined by even more. Kainé could see the girl inside the mouth. Her hair stood on end and her eyes flared with fury as she leered at them.

"*This is for him! So I can stay with him! So we can see the ocean together!*"

The surface of the Shade's body rippled and transformed,

forming thousands of thorns that suddenly shot out. They rained down on the beach—spears from the sky. Kainé was so busy staying out of their way, she didn't have time to counterattack.

"*Hey!*" Tyrann shouted. "*The guy from before collapsed on the beach! That Shade's got some kinda hard-on for him—we should take him hostage!*"

"Shut your yap!" cried Kainé. The idea of using her blades to threaten another living, breathing human made her angry enough that she spoke to her inner Shade aloud.

"*Fine then! I guess we'll all just sit around a campfire and sing songs until we get murdered!*"

The drizzle of spears became a downpour. Somewhere in the distance, she heard Grimoire Weiss cry "My word!" as one of the tentacles sent Nier flying.

"Goddammit, fine!"

Kainé rushed to the postman, who was lying helplessly on the beach. As Louise was preparing to smash Nier into the sand, Kainé pointed one of her blades at the quivering man's throat.

"Hey!" she shouted. "Over here! This guy's important to you, huh?"

Though Kainé considered hostage-taking to be the method of cowards, it caused Louise to immediately freeze in place. Emil, not letting the opportunity escape, let out a volley of the same magic he'd used to destroy The Aerie, though thankfully it was under his full control this time. When it burst to life over the Shade's head, Nier and Kainé leaped into action, attacking the same spot with such force that the head split in two.

But Louise still showed no signs of stopping. The rest of her enormous body remained stubbornly unfazed.

"How can it withstand such an onslaught?!" Grimoire Weiss gaped.

"I'm really scared, guys!" Emil shouted.

Louise's body flailed as she screamed, "*I will . . . become human!*"

Kainé's vision went topsy-turvy as an attack of some kind connected. Her body splayed out on the sand, immobile. She had taken the full brunt of the blast and lost all motor functions—and that was with a Shade inside her. There was no way the others would be able to stand against this for long.

"*What the hell are you doing, Sunshine?!*" shouted a panicked Tyrann. "*Stop that thing already!*"

He should have known that was impossible.

"My body won't . . . Dammit!"

Kainé finally managed to pull herself to a half-seated position. Louise's torso was bent at an angle—she clearly planned to attack again. With no way to defend herself, Kainé took a deep breath, held perfectly still, and prepared for the end.

"Stop!"

The word came from the postman. He was looking up at Louise, a piece of driftwood held in one trembling hand.

"What are you . . . doing?" gasped Nier. "You're gonna . . . get yourself killed!"

But his words had no effect. The postman kept walking, knees knocking as he did. As he approached, Louise leaned over and extended him one massive hand.

"*Do not be scared,*" she said. "*Soon I will be human.*"

But her words never reached him. All the postman could hear was a Shade's unintelligible groaning.

"Don't hurt these people!" he cried as he brought the stick down on Louise's extended hand. Over and over again he swung. No attack like that could ever affect a Shade, for it was neither blade nor arcane.

Louise gazed down at the postman with great sadness. "*But why? Don't you want to look at the sea together?*"

"You've been lying to me this whole time?! You . . . You're a monster!"

She paused. Though humans could not understand Shades, Shades could understand humans.

"I want . . . to be human. I want us . . . to be together."

Kainé knew the pain of being called a monster—and though Louise was a Shade, she must have felt that same pain, if not something greater. She had so wished to be human for the postman's sake after all.

Kainé suddenly remembered a moment. When they were in the ship, she'd picked up a scrap of paper. On it, the words *thank you* had been written over and over in the messy scrawl of a child. Though at first she had no idea who the author was, she now understood. The postman had taught Louise that out-of-tune song. The postman had given her the ribbon that decorated her hair. And the postman had taught her to write as well.

"You *disgust* me!" screamed the postman. The only sounds were his voice and the waves, for Louise had fallen silent. She was frozen in place, staring down at the postman with something like shock.

Suddenly, a magic spear plunged into the Shade's head. Kainé turned to see Nier was back in the fight, as was Weiss.

Louise wailed. Her countless limbs drooped as her massive body tipped to the side. The spear had ripped a great hole in her head, and this time it did not seem to be regenerating. Perhaps she simply felt no need to hold on anymore.

"How could I end up with such a . . . hideous . . . body . . . ?"

As the head tilted back, Kainé watched the figure of the little girl turn to look across the ocean. In the distance, the horizon—the line where the blues of the water and sky met—sat glimmering in the sun.

"And yet . . . this world . . . This world is so full of beauty . . ."

That was all she said in the end.

6.

IT TOOK A week for Nier's wounds to heal.

The postman offered everyone a room while they recuperated. He even allowed Emil and Kainé to have a roof over their heads for once—a gesture of kindness Nier was truly thankful for.

"You really saved our bacon," he told the postman on the morning they were ready to leave.

The postman smiled in turn, though it quickly vanished. "Well, you've all done so much for me. We knew the townspeople were out there being eaten by a Shade, but I never imagined I was taking *care* of it this entire time."

His expression clouded as he finished speaking, and his head drooped. He then went on to explain how he'd heard a child's coughing coming from the ship, which was how he first discovered the Shade.

"I thought she was a human child. I assumed all the adults onboard had died, which was why she was so weak. I thought her lack of speech and fear of the sun were because she'd been trapped in darkness for so long."

The postman's confusion was understandable, for Louise's human form had been convincing indeed. Nier could sympathize; he remembered how befuddled he'd been by the human-like Shades in The Aerie.

"I was going to take her in once she was a little better," the postman continued. "I even asked if she wanted to be my daughter. Can you imagine? A Shade as my daughter? . . . God, I was so stupid."

"The fault lies with that foul creature alone," Grimoire Weiss quickly reassured him. "Not yourself."

The postman gave him a weak smile. "I . . . hope I can believe that someday."

"Well, we'd better get going," Nier said. "There's someone else we need to break this news to."

The prospect of telling the woman with the red bag that her husband was gone had been weighing heavily on his mind. Maybe he shouldn't tell her the truth—maybe he should lie and claim that her husband skipped town for good. She might be happier thinking he was alive somewhere. It wasn't like she was ever going to see him again regardless. Or would the thought of him abandoning her only make her life more difficult in the end?

Nier wasn't sure what to say. Worse yet, he wasn't sure he'd ever find the answer.

REPORT 14

We've sent a number of unfortunate reports lately, and I fear the situation is continuing to deteriorate. I'm also sad to say we lost the trump card we'd prepared to keep the Shadowlord's rampage under control.

A little while ago, we took a Gestalt that drifted ashore at Seafront into our custody. This creature was a powerful experiment with enough magic to sink the greatest ships, and we felt it would prove sufficient to keep the Shadowlord under our control. This was the trump card we were alluding to in our previous report.

However, said Gestalt became obsessed with the idea of becoming human as its intelligence developed, which quickly turned into a serious issue. It eventually came to believe it could maintain a human form so long as it ate people, and began kidnapping and consuming villagers inside its ship. By the time we learned of this, Nier and his party had already destroyed it. The saddest (and most ironic) part is that the Gestalt was an experiment—which means it could *never* be human because it lacked a corresponding body.

Due to this incident, the matter of getting the Shadowlord under control has become even more difficult. We will either have to come up with something that can rival the aforementioned experimental Gestalt in power, or we'll have to push the entire project to the last stage in one fell swoop.

At present, the second option is looking increasingly more likely. However, it will only become available once we can freely enter the Shadowlord's castle, so we will continue our efforts to collect the final fragment, Loyal Cerberus.

End report.

Report written by Popola

The Man 7

1.

I HATE LAB coats, Nier thought. People who wore lab coats were always arrogant in the presence of those who lacked them. He didn't have the slightest idea why that was; he wasn't a doctor after all. Hell, he wasn't even a nurse.

The researchers were always the worst. At least medical professionals saw their patients as human—researchers only viewed them as test subjects. It was always a gamble to trust what they said, and the odds never seemed to be in his favor.

But what choice did he have? He couldn't afford not to take the risk or to throw in the towel if things turned bad. If he didn't do this, Yonah would die. That was all there was to it.

Nier stared at his sister, who slumbered inside a clear, medical-grade capsule. He pressed his forehead against a pane of reinforced glass and stared at the sterilized room beyond. Nier wasn't allowed inside, of course. Cryosleep technology was a well-established technology at this point, and he'd been told the greatest risk wasn't a mechanical or system malfunction but infection.

Don't worry so much, the nurses said with a smile whenever they passed. *The doctors are working as hard as they can. They'll save Yonah.*

Though there was something false in the way they spoke, Nier had no choice but to trust them. If he cooperated with the government's plan, they would save Yonah. If it took months, years, or decades for the new technology to be put in place, he would simply continue on so long as it meant another chance at a life with her.

Hang in there, Yonah, he cheered her on silently. He wished he could give her a word of encouragement as she lay suspended in slumber, connected to countless machines in a sterilized room without the gift of the sun.

"*Will you be going back now?*" said a voice beside him. It was familiar, belonging to the only person he could trust.

Wait. Why isn't it Weiss's voice? His only partner was Grimoire Weiss, and he didn't sound like that at all. Who was speaking to him? This book was—

"Are we sleeping in today, hmm?"

Now, *that* was Weiss's voice. After a moment of darkness, Nier's vision filled with the familiar sight of his bedroom ceiling.

"Oh. I was . . . dreaming."

He sat up, his head heavy. Lately, he'd been having lots of dreams for reasons he couldn't identify—all of which vanished the moment he opened his eyes.

"You seemed to be slumbering quite peacefully from my vantage point, lad."

As usual, Nier remembered nothing of his dream. Not the location, who appeared in it, or what was said.

"Doesn't matter. It was just a dream." If it didn't bother Nier to forget the dream, it couldn't have been anything of value.

"C'mon. We need to get ready."

The trade ship that left the village docks for the desert departed early in the morning, and it was finally time to pay a visit to Facade.

Popola informed Nier that a new ferryman had taken the place of the late man with the red bag, yet he was still surprised to see who was waiting for them.

"Hey there! I'll be taking up the ferryman's mantle from now on."

It was the original ferryman's older brother.

"Oh," said Nier haltingly. "I'm . . . not sure what to say."

"That's okay. My brother was a damn fool, you know? Leaving his whole family in the dust like this?" There was a slight falter in the man's voice, but he quickly composed himself. "Well, what are you waiting for? Hop onboard."

The way he smiled as he spoke was shockingly similar to how his brother used to say those same words.

"Do you think we could stop for a sec once we get outside the village?" Nier asked. "I want to pick up my friends along the way." He worried slightly that the new ferryman might not accept Kainé and Emil. Unlike his brother, who had lived many years in Seafront, he'd been a guard for the village and had a more limited view of the world.

Thankfully, the worry turned out to be needless. The moment the new ferryman saw Kainé and Emil, he said, "The postman told me you were the ones who avenged my brother. You have my thanks."

After a moment's thought, Nier realized letters crossed the world by boat. The ferryman must have had considerable interaction with the postman, so it made sense he had told the other man about what happened at the shipwreck. Perhaps, in fact, Popola had anticipated this and given the new ferryman his job as a result. Once he knew exactly what happened, any prejudices he might have held against Kainé and Emil were likely to fade.

"You're the other man's brother?" Emil piped up. "Oh, I always had so much fun chatting with him. I really looked forward to riding on his boat!"

"What kind of stuff did you two talk about?" asked the brother.

"Oh, you know. Basic stuff. Like how he collected stamps and was always asking the postman to get him ones from all over the world."

"Heh. Yeah, he was into collecting stamps since he was a kid. I'm glad you two talked about it."

The corners of the man's eyes crinkled in nostalgia, and the two continued to chat all the way to the river outside the desert.

"Tell me more about my brother next time," the ferryman said as he waved goodbye. That action, Nier thought, was also performed exactly as his brother would have done.

2.

"THE KING IS getting married! Ah, it does this old book good to see a boy become a man."

Grimoire Weiss spoke these words once they crossed the desert and approached the city gates. It was hard to tell if he was joking or serious.

"Yeah, it's kinda weird how things work out, huh?" replied Nier. He was a poor kid from a destitute village—he never imagined he'd have a friend who was a *king*. But he recalled the first time they'd met at the Barren Temple and how the king later slipped out of the palace to show them around the city. Of course, he recalled Fyra as well.

The more he thought about it, the more it struck him as a strange connection. It was only because Kainé once saved Fyra from wolves that she was allowed in the city—and that was the only reason the rest of them had been able to enter. Though Nier didn't speak the language, Fyra had been willing to help him out, which led to his visiting the temple and saving the prince. If one single piece of that puzzle had been lost, he never would have befriended the king.

How many years had it been since he last saw the king in person? His royal friend was a prolific letter writer, so it never really felt like they were truly apart. However, Nier was certain he'd be shocked to see how much the king had changed once they met in the flesh.

"Oh, you came! It's been so long!"

The moment they entered the palace, the masked king rushed to greet them. Unlike the other residents of Facade, he always wore his mask slightly askew, which allowed the party to see how his face had changed—which, it turned out, wasn't much at all. How he bared his teeth when he grinned, how his eyes constantly roamed every which way—these things were just as they all remembered, as was his devil-may-care attitude. Clearly, being of marrying age had done little to alter his childlike conduct.

"Congratulations," Nier offered. A strange feeling settled in his heart as he spoke; he never thought the day would come where he'd say such a thing.

"Thank you," replied the king. *"And this must be Emil?"*

Nier had mentioned Emil a number of times in his letters, but this was the first time they'd met in person. And though Emil had yet to learn the language of the Masked People, he must have gleaned from the cadence of Nier and the king's conversation that it was his turn to offer his greetings.

"P-pleased to make your acquaintance, Your Royalness. Congratulations on your wedding!"

Grimoire Weiss cleared his throat. "Forgive my prying, but we are all eager to know the identity of your lucky bride."

Even though he liked to tout himself as the pinnacle of human intelligence—and despite how carefully he worded the question—it was clear the tome could barely contain his curiosity.

Nier was glad he asked, however, because he was also desperate to know who the king was marrying. The invitation, sent by The Facade Royal Office of Marriage and Other Legally Binding Contracts and Concerns, had been characteristically formal:

*As per Rule 25,656, please consider this your official no-
tice that the king of Facade has chosen to enter into the
ceremony of matrimony.*

*Please lodge all objections and/or congratulations
through the official channels stated in Rule 38,585.*

*PS: Hey, guys, it's me! The king of Facade! Sorry this is all
formal and stuff. Listen, I'm getting married, and I really
want you to come!*

Even in the added postscript note, a key bit of information—the
bride's name—was missing, and Nier didn't know if the king had
forgotten to mention it, left it out on purpose, or was simply following another strange rule.

"*Oh yes,*" said the king with a smile in his voice that told Nier
he'd left it out on purpose. "*How rude of me.*"

The woman who stepped into the hall behind the king struck
Nier as familiar, but since she wore a mask, he couldn't be certain
who she was. All he felt was a passing sense of familiarity—but
his instincts proved to be correct.

"*It's nice to see you again,*" she signed in a series of gestures.

"Hold on," said a gobsmacked Nier. "Fyra?!"

When she responded with an affirmative gesture, Nier felt himself growing even more surprised. "No way. I hardly recognized you!"

Fyra had been a child when they first met, one barely taller
than Yonah. But now she was all grown up. It made him think
how Yonah must also have grown over that time. Her arms had
likely lost their baby fat, her legs would be longer . . .

No. This was no good. Rather than dwelling on such painful
things, Nier forced himself to speak to Fyra in a bright, cheerful
tone. "Kainé's gonna want to see this!"

"*She's outside, isn't she?*" said the king with a wry expression.
"*What nonsense. She knows she is welcome here.*"

No one discriminated against Kainé in Facade—not for being intersex, nor for being possessed by a Shade. Yet she still didn't want to set foot in the city, much less the royal palace.

"I'll go get her!" cried Emil as he floated out the window. Though they weren't able to follow after him, Nier and the king both moved to the window so they could look down at the city.

"This place hasn't changed a bit, huh?" said Nier. The haze of sand still lay over the city, softening the harsh rays of the sun. Skiffs floated down the rivers of sand, while peddlers wandered the narrow streets. Though the complex maze of weaving passageways bewildered Nier at first, he now found navigating them to be fun.

"The people, the city . . . It's all just like I remember."

"*It isn't though,*" the king murmured, his eyes still resting on the buildings below. His expression was hard, his tone flat. "*The harvest was weak again this year, and my people are beginning to go hungry. Also, our quarrel with the wolves has taken a turn for the worse.*"

The wolves that made their home in the desert had long troubled the people of Facade. Nier himself had been attacked countless times while crossing the desert. Their movements were quick and sharp, and they always roamed in packs, creating a most troublesome foe indeed.

"*The duties of a king are overwhelming. In truth, I feel somewhat guilty about holding a festival to celebrate my wedding.*"

"Everyone needs to blow off steam once in a while," Nier replied. He wanted to ease his friend's worries; the king was younger than he yet bore a burden much greater.

"Indeed," Grimoire Weiss interjected, having sensed the sentiment. "Your people have earned a moment of rest and respite."

It was not the king's fault the villagers' lives were difficult.

Nier knew from traveling the world these past five years that everything was falling to ruin.

"Plus, you want to make Fyra happy, right?" Nier said. "Life is better when you have someone to fight for."

The image of a smiling Yonah flashed in his mind. Her voice calling *Welcome home!* rang in his ears. He did so much for her sake and could withstand anything—no matter how trying or painful—when he pictured her delight. She was truly indispensable.

"*Heh. That's not written in the rules, but perhaps it should be,*" said the king with a smile. "*Someone to fight for . . . Yes, I like the thought of that.*"

For the king, Fyra. For Nier, Yonah. Both of them had someone precious, and they would do anything to make that person happy. *I want her back*, Nier thought. The statement was powerful and unwavering and perhaps a truer thought than any he'd ever had.

3.

AS ALWAYS, KAINÉ was waiting for Nier and the others just inside Facade's city gates.

She had a feeling the place would be filled with festive cheer in the lead-up to the wedding. But while the central areas of the city might have been celebrating, the area around the gates held a leaden, oppressive air. Heavily armed guards were constantly coming and going, and any who ventured beyond the gates spoke with clear tension in their voices.

Kainé wanted to know what was going on but didn't speak their language. Still, something was clearly amiss, so she decided to observe the guards for a while longer. And when a hunting party returned with wolf pelts, Kainé realized the guards had been hunting the creatures on a large scale. It was likely a form of caution to make sure they didn't attack on the grand day of the wedding. Wild animals stayed away from places they thought might pose any danger. And while hunting the animals was a rather dangerous proposition, it just proved how much they delighted in the king's wedding.

As these thoughts ran through her mind, Emil's voice suddenly came out of nowhere, causing her to jump.

"Kainé! You need to come to the palace right now!"

"But I—"

"The bride is somebody you know really well!"

"Huh?"

The only person Kainé knew "really well" in Facade was Fyra. Well, her and the king's advisor who had given her sweets and fruit after she rescued Fyra, but it was unlikely he was slated to be a new bride.

"Is it Fyra?" she asked.

"It sure is! And we need to go celebrate with her, okay?"

"But I can't just go into the ci—"

"Fyra's going to be *so* sad if you're not there! She looked super excited when I said I was coming to get you!"

Despite her reluctance, Kainé thought she should at least give the girl a word of congratulations on her upcoming nuptials.

"C'mon, Kainé!"

"Fine, fine."

With Emil urging her on, Kainé at last stepped into the city.

It had been five years since Kainé saw Fyra, and she'd grown into a fine young woman during that time. Kainé's shock was apparently enough that Nier felt the need to comment on it, a sure sign he'd been equally surprised when first presented with the situation.

"Congrats," Kainé said. But once the obligatory felicitations left her mouth, she found she had nothing else to say. Sure, she was happy to see Fyra for the first time in a long while, but that was where the conversation ended. She had no idea what to say to a person after so much time had elapsed.

But when Kainé awkwardly turned to leave, the king stopped her. Well, to be precise, she was unsure if he was *actually* trying to stop her, but then Nier began translating and removed all doubt.

"He wants us to stay here for the night," he said. "He also wants us to attend the wedding tomorrow."

"Hey, you know I can't—"

"Look, this request comes from the king himself, so I'd probably defer to him. Plus, you know it'll make Fyra happy."

It seemed Emil and Nier both had learned exactly what to say to make Kainé listen.

The royal palace wasn't very comfortable. This wasn't a flaw with the Masked People's hospitality but an issue with Kainé herself. She simply wasn't used to being treated kindly.

Unsure what to do with herself, she roamed this way and that. Though a number of Masked People watched her go, they all seemed to think she was wandering in search of the perfect pillar to lean against. After a number of twists and turns, she was finally relieved to hear the voices of Nier and Weiss nearby.

"To think they even have rules governing the timing and water temperature of a bath!" huffed the book.

"What's it to you?" replied Nier. "You don't even take baths."

Kainé knew Weiss was perfectly fine even in a downpour—perhaps due to some magical protection—so she wasn't shocked to hear discussion on the topic of baths. Still, the Masked People would likely have been shocked to see a tome in a tub.

"Ah, look who it is," said Weiss upon Kainé's arrival. "What is the matter?"

"I don't like this," she replied. "Weddings are festive occasions, you know? Should I even be here?" She hadn't planned on bringing any of this up—it just spilled out when she saw Nier's face.

"We were invited here by the king, remember?" he said.

"Sure, but what about everybody else?"

"This city isn't like our villages. It's all about the rules here. And since there isn't a specific rule about you, I honestly think they won't give a crap."

At that moment, Kainé finally realized why she was so uncomfortable: The Masked People treated her, Nier, and Emil the same, and it was throwing her off. She was a royal guest, and that was all—just as she had once been Fyra's savior. No one regarded her as an unfortunate girl possessed by a Shade.

"Yeah, maybe," she replied half-heartedly. In that case, she'd be happy to attend the wedding. Hell, maybe all these rules weren't so bad after all.

"Will you at least procure a new set of lingerie for the festivities?" quipped Weiss. "Some spring colors, perhaps?"

"Keep talking, book! Let's see how smug you are when I toss you on a campfire."

She could always count on Grimoire Weiss to cross the line.

4.

THE DAY OF the wedding was blessed with good weather. The breeze was calm and cool, and colored scraps of confetti danced in the air. The Masked People's voices echoed across the sandy sky, though whether they were song or commands was impossible to determine.

"Aw, weddings are the best!" said Emil. He was currently floating high in the air—not to get a better vantage point but because his magical power grew as he got more excited. As such, he'd been bobbing up and down before the ceremony had even started.

"By the heavens, boy, calm yourself for a single moment!" snapped Grimoire Weiss.

But Emil would not be deterred. "There's flowers everywhere, everyone's happy . . . It's just great! I'm kinda jealous! Aren't you jealous, Kainé?"

"Meh."

Kainé's utterance was curt, and her head whipped away as she gave it. She did so not because she was upset but because she wasn't sure how to act, and it bothered her. She'd never been to a wedding before and had been worried about the festival since the previous day.

For his part, Nier was disappointed by her level of concern. In Facade, Kainé could celebrate the happiness of a friend without worrying about what others thought of her. It was ironically a reality she could only experience in the world's strangest city. She couldn't do so in Nier's village, nor in The Aerie—or at least not The Aerie that used to exist.

"And thus, in front of these beloved guests—and per Rule 904—I hereby request that you seal your union with a kiss," the masked advisor declared with grave importance. Weddings in Nier's village were officiated by both Devola and Popola, so he found the entire affair to be quite different—though at least the kiss was the same.

With the ceremony concluded, the people gathered in the plaza began to dance. It was a designated dance to celebrate a wedding; the choreography and clothing had been dictated down to the finest detail by the rules, and the wide sleeves on the costumes reminded Nier of large blooming flowers.

Amid the motion walked the masked king and his new queen. Every time they waved, a great cheer went up, and petals and confetti swirled through the air.

Noticing Nier and the others, Fyra gestured to them in thanks. Now that she was an official resident of the city by marriage, she was well within her right to speak. In this case, however, it was simply easier to understand gestures amid the cheers.

But as Nier raised his hand in response, screams rang out from one corner of the plaza, bringing the dancing to a sudden halt. As the people near the plaza entrance parted, a lone figure staggered through. It was one of Facade's soldiers, a man using his spear to drag himself. He was gravely wounded; in the silence of a collectively held breath, the sound of his blood dripping on the earth could clearly be heard.

"Run . . ."

Nier thought he heard the additional word *wolves* before the soldier crumpled to the ground. Nervous murmurs rippled through the crowd, but no one could grasp what had happened or why the soldier was dead.

Then, a black blur raced through the crowd.

"Fyra!" Kainé shouted.

Nier watched as the blur knocked Fyra and the masked king down. Another scream came from a different direction, and this time Nier clearly saw the danger: A pack of wolves had broken into the city.

"It's a Shade!" Kainé yelled again. "That wolf is a Shade!"

She was pointing at a wolf that was abnormally large and covered with writhing patterns on its jet-black body. As she did so, the dark wolf howled. Its voice was mixed with the sound Shades often made, creating a duet that was eerie in the extreme.

The shadowy form leaped high into the air. It gave one last howl when it landed, then dashed away, followed closely by the rest of its brothers and sisters.

"Was that thing commanding the pack?" asked Nier. The wolves seemed to back down as suddenly as they had arrived, and as they were leaving, it looked like the wolf-Shade glanced back at the crowd. There was an intrepidness to the way it carried itself, almost as if it had accomplished what it came to do.

But right now Nier was only worried about the king and Fyra. He quickly scanned the crowd, looking for them. He knew they'd been knocked down by the wolf-Shade, but everything after that was a blur.

He finally spotted the king sitting on the ground. But as he began running toward him, another sight froze him in his tracks.

"Fyra!"

The wrenching grief in the king's voice told Nier all he needed to know.

"Fyra! Say something!"

The masked king cradled the limp body of his new bride. His advisor, who had been examining her wounds, quietly stepped away. Nier could tell by the way his shoulders drooped that the end was inevitable.

"*Enough, my husband,*" whispered Fyra. "*The people . . . are nervous.*"

It was the first time Nier had heard her voice. Though colored by pain, it was still soft and gentle—exactly the sort of voice he imagined she would have.

"*Thank . . . you,*" she said as she extended one bloodied hand to the king. "*Thank you for making someone like me . . . your bride . . .*"

The rules said those who came from the outside were forbidden to speak, which was why Fyra had been forced to hold her tongue. Only now, on the day she had become the king's bride, was she finally permitted speech. The idea her first words would also be her last was almost too cruel to imagine.

"*Fyra, no!*" screamed the king. "*Don't leave! Come back!*"

He shook her lifeless body as if she were a stubborn child refusing to listen. As Nier watched him, he couldn't help but recall the moment they first met, when the king was still a prince. At the same time, he thought of a younger Fyra. When the prince had ventured into the Barren Temple alone, she insisted on going to save him. Her adoration for him was clear, and Nier knew she cared for him more than anyone in the world. The fact he was a prince—and then a king—had been inconsequential.

"*Your life had just begun,*" moaned the king as he clung to her corpse. "*You came from the outside . . . Your existence was hard, but you were finally going to be happy! We were going to travel. To see new things. To be together. We were going to be together forever. We promised each other!*"

Saying this, he threw his head back and let fly a howl of rage and grief before rising to his feet and addressing his people.

"*All men, take arms! The wolves die tonight!*"

"I would rethink this course of action, King," warned Grimoire Weiss. "Ahead lies a battle you cannot win."

It was much the same advice he had given Nier after Yonah had been stolen away and the youth could think of nothing but killing Shades. Alas, sometimes Weiss's advice was heeded, and sometimes it was not—and the king seemed to be falling firmly into the second camp.

"My liege, we mustn't!"

When the advisor stepped forward to admonish his liege, the king still refused to listen. *"Then I go myself!"* he proclaimed.

"You can't, my lord!"

"They must die! Kill the wolves! Kill them all!"

With the king looking ready to dash off at any moment, his advisor suddenly stepped into his path and lashed out, striking him across the cheek with an open hand.

"You can't, my lord," he said quietly. *"The queen would very much frown upon this course of action."*

The king's eyes flew open in realization, perhaps remembering how Fyra had haltingly mentioned the nervousness of the people as she died.

"You are the king and leader of the Masked People," continued the advisor. *"Your duty is to your people and their homes. While the threat of the wolves looms large, we must first solidify Facade's defenses. I beg of you, do not bring shame to the queen's memory. As a ruler—or a husband."*

The advisor's voice faltered, for the king was not the only one grieving Fyra or suppressing the urge to engage the wolves in battle. The king was old enough to understand this, and though he remained silent, he gave a slight nod.

Fyra's body was placed in a casket and a funeral held according to the rules. It was the advisor's job to lead this ceremony just as he had the wedding, and Nier couldn't imagine how difficult the task must have been. His sympathy for the man only strengthened as he watched him speak fluidly and maintain his composure.

"The king's grief is strong," Grimoire Weiss murmured. "I doubt he will stand down at this point."

"Yeah," replied Nier.

Throughout the funeral, the king did nothing but stare hard into space. He didn't even shed a tear.

"I'm guessing he'll run off to take on the wolves anytime now," Nier added.

"Will we let him go by himself?"

"Of course not! Hell, I hate the wolves too."

When they first visited Facade, Fyra had shown them around the city in accordance with the rules. The memory of her jogging ahead was fresh enough in Nier's mind that he could still hear the soft patter of her feet on stone. It was as the king said: Her life had only begun. Her *happiness* had only begun. But the wolves had taken all of that away from her. Of course he hated them.

"Then we must prepare for the fight," Grimoire Weiss stated.

"I know."

Nier's weapon was always at the ready; there was no telling when he would find himself engaged in battle against a Shade. He'd also taken plenty of medicinal herbs for the long journey to Facade, so he was prepared to fight at a moment's notice.

"Let's go see him," said Nier.

"Let us hope we are allowed entry into his palace."

With the funeral just ended, it wouldn't be surprising if there was a rule forbidding visitors in the royal residence. It was also possible the king's advisor would lock the building down to make sure the king didn't run off by himself.

When they arrived at the palace, however, the party was

allowed inside despite the heavy presence of guards. They quickly made their way to the king's room, where they found him standing on the balcony. To no one's surprise, he was dressed for battle.

"There you are," Nier said as they approached him. "You're going to avenge Fyra, aren't you?"

The king shook his head. *"Fyra is not the only victim here. These damnable wolves continue to claim the lives of many people. I will not allow them to suffer anymore. As their king, I must take a stand. And if the rules say I can't, then damn the rules!"* His advisor's eyes would likely have bulged out of his head if he'd been around to hear that.

"Madness!" Grimoire Weiss exclaimed. "The wolves who attacked were only a fraction of the pack. How will you fight them all?"

"I will not be defeated."

"Then count us in," Nier offered.

A look of dismay crossed the king's face, followed by a shake of the head. *"That is too much for me to ask."*

To *ask*? There was no need to ask; their friendship was far beyond such things. After all, Nier had gone to the Barren Temple to save him when he ventured inside five years ago. The idea of doing so again as he flung himself into the wolves' den was simply a given.

However, Nier also didn't feel he needed to say those things aloud. Kainé, though, had a different idea.

"We're not doing it for you, dumbass. It's for Fyra."

"Thank you," replied the king.

"Then let us make haste," said Grimoire Weiss urgently.

Making haste, however, was not in the cards; when they left the palace, they found the king's advisor waiting for them.

"Where are you going, my liege?"

He had seen through it all. There were a number of soldiers

waiting at the ready behind them—it seemed he was going to stop his liege from leaving by force, if necessary.

"*To strike the wolves,*" the king replied. "*The city is yours.*"

"*My liege, that is a violation of multiple rules,*" said the advisor in his typical dry tone, which only caused the king's anger to flare.

"*Did those rules keep Fyra from dying?!*" the king shouted, not bothering to hide his fury.

"*No, my lord.*"

"*What did Fyra ever do? She was so close to knowing happiness, and then she had it snatched away from her.*"

"*Yes, my lord.*"

"*Was it Fyra's fault that she was so frail?*"

"*No, my lord.*"

"*Then get out of my way!*"

"*I cannot, my lord.*"

With a flourish, the king brought his hand to his sword. If his soldiers planned to stop him with force, he would use the same to pass through their ranks. But when Nier followed suit and took on a readied stance, the advisor remained perfectly still.

"*You are behaving like a fool,*" he said. "*Clearly you are still young.*"

"*How dare you!*" hissed the king as the knuckles gripping his weapon turned dead white.

His advisor ignored the outburst and continued to speak. "*Queen Fyra was a kind and gentle woman. All in our city loved her, did they not?*"

His tone was much kinder than a moment ago—clearly he numbered among those who had loved their too-brief queen.

"*Hear me, Men of the Mask!*" the advisor shouted, turning to face the soldiers behind him. "*Who is our leader?!*"

"*The king of Facade!*" replied the soldiers in unison.

"*And who is our king's beloved?!*"

"*Queen Fyra!*"

"*Who stained the court with the blood of our queen?!*"

"*The wolves! The wolves!*"

The king's eyes went wide and settled on his advisor's back as he slowly released the grip on his weapon.

"*Then who are the ones that will vanquish the wolves?!*"

"*The Men of the Mask!*"

The advisor whirled around to face his king again and dipped his head. "*Sire, I request permission to join these men in battle. I apologize; it took time to obtain the blessing of every citizen for the war.*"

"*You visited* all *of them?!*" asked the incredulous king.

"*I did, my liege,*" replied the advisor calmly. "*There are rules about this sort of thing after all.*"

"*Huh,*" the king mused, the corners of his eyes softening in understanding. "*Rules . . .* "

"*Do not exist to bind you,*" the advisor finished. "*They exist so you may know your freedoms.*"

Those were the words of the previous king—the current king's father. But they were also the words the prince taught Fyra when she first came to the city. And she, in turn, had taught them to Nier.

"*My liege, you are a worthy successor to your father,*" said the advisor, his tone that of an old teacher rather than a minister. "*You have my sincerest apologies for the insult against you, but a foolish king attracts a foolish people. Do not forget this.*"

The king's gaze settled on his advisor before scanning the soldiers. Though their faces were hidden by masks, there was no doubt he could see through each and every one of them.

"*You are a foolish people indeed to sacrifice so much for an idiot like myself.*"

The corners of the king's mouth curled lopsided, though whether it was a happy or a strained smile was impossible to determine.

5.

AS THEY NEARED the den, the voice of the wolf-Shade grew clearer by the minute. Kainé remembered the day the creature burst into the plaza, as well as the rage-fueled words it howled:

You razed our forests and poisoned our streams, and now you slaughter our young! You will atone for your sins with blood!

The wedding attack, Kainé learned, was retaliation for the wolf-hunting that had taken place the day before. Though wild animals usually stayed away from places where their kin were killed, it was not the desert wolves' instinctual fear that won out in the end but the animosity born from the deaths of their fellows.

If pressed, Kainé would have said the wolves shared much of the blame, seeing how they attacked humans day in and day out. She had been present when they first attacked Fyra, after all, and she and Nier had to fight off their assaults whenever they crossed the desert.

But really, it wasn't a question of fault, nor of who initially started the conflict. Once lives had been taken, there was no stopping the inevitable result. The murder of someone dear ignites the spark of indelible hatred—as a person who found her life's meaning in revenge, Kainé understood this all too well.

"Death to the invaders!" cried the wolf-Shade as they neared, causing a chorus of howls to rise in response.

As they stood before the den, Kainé saw the king of Facade

apologizing to Nier, likely because he felt guilty for making him come all this way. A moment later, the king turned to Kainé and shocked her by dipping his head apologetically in her direction as well. Rather than respond, a stunned Kainé simply unsheathed her swords and prepared to fight.

"We can ill afford another tragedy!" Grimoire Weiss yelled. When the masked king cried something in turn, his soldiers began to pour into the den.

They were striking with every Man of the Mask available, and the wolves' numbers had dwindled in the hunt before the wedding. Most of the soldiers thought the fight would be over quickly, but it immediately turned into a grueling slog. The wolves were sharp and well organized. They targeted the king and his advisor and knocked back any soldiers who approached. It was a strategy Grimoire Weiss recognized almost at once.

"The wolves appear to be targeting the king!" cried the tome.

"I'm on it!" replied Nier. He placed himself in front of the king and began firing magic at the wolves. Once Kainé saw he had the king's defense in hand, she left his side and began searching her senses for the Shade's presence.

The desert wolves were dangerous because a Shade was leading them. Kainé sensed a degree of intelligence from the creature that set it apart from simple wild animals. It was smart enough to suppress its instincts, the proof of which lay in its choice to retaliate rather than run in the face of its dead comrades. If they could kill the wolf-Shade, the pack's leadership would crumble.

"We can never forgive you, humans! There shall never be peace between us!"

"There he is," Kainé muttered as she dashed off after a dark shadow swaying atop a cliff, a perch from which it was clearly giving orders. As Kainé approached, she sent out a volley of magic. The clifftop was narrow, and no matter how fast her enemy might be, there was no space to dodge. She watched with satisfaction as her attempt struck home. But then . . .

"Oh shit!"

The spell she had fired at the Shade came flying right back at her. Kainé leaped to the side, dodging it with great difficulty.

"The leader seems to have the power to reflect magic," Grimoire Weiss observed, which explained why it was willing to stand exposed on so narrow a perch.

"Kainé, take out the little ones!" shouted Nier. "We'll cull their numbers first!"

"On it!"

If they could eliminate enough wolves, the wolf-Shade would have no choice but to fight. Kainé began cutting down any wolf that approached the king and his advisor. Thankfully, it was obvious who they were targeting, which made their movements easy to read. Also, the other wolves lacked the power to reflect magic, so she cut through them with both steel and spell.

"The humans will pay for what they have done!"

Finally, the wolf-Shade leaped down. It did so with such speed that it looked like a massive boulder plummeting to earth.

"It's here!" cried Kainé. She and Nier turned their attacks to the wolf-Shade. After a number of attempts, Nier's blade finally sank into its shadowy form. Blood sprayed through the air, yet the creature did not slow. Kainé then hit it with her twin blades, but though the attacks were clearly having an effect, the wolf-Shade kept going.

Kainé saw how the surface of its body was changing after absorbing countless blows, which gave her an idea. She launched a bolt of magic at it and was pleased to see the spell strike the wolf-Shade and not be reflected back. Their repeated attacks were slowly wearing it down, and it no longer held the power to reflect magic.

"It's working!" screamed Kainé.

Nier launched his arcane fist, grabbing the wolf-Shade and slamming it into the rocky wall. As it lay on the ground, stunned, the king of Facade leaped at it with spear in hand.

Kainé couldn't understand what the king said, but she heard the wolf-Shade reply, "*Those were my very words, human.*" Clearly the king had said something about avenging his wife.

The king's spear plunged into the wolf-Shade as it attempted to stand. The point pierced its eye socket and slid through the body as the beast lay limp upon the ground.

"*What have we done to deserve . . . such a fate?*"

The wolf-Shade's limbs shuddered, then fell still. Its shadowy body began losing its hard contours, turning to dust. As it disintegrated, Kainé heard it whisper one final word:

"*Grand . . . father . . .*"

Grandfather? What was that supposed to mean?

Though Kainé had no clue who "grandfather" might be, there was no malice in the word—unlike everything else the wolf-Shade had said thus far. In fact, it almost sounded like it was calling out to someone it dearly missed.

The wolf-Shade finally dissolved to dust, causing the king's spear to clatter to the ground. But that wasn't the only thing that struck the ground . . .

"Hey, that's . . ."

A look of surprise crossed Nier's face as he reached down and picked up the object that now lay before him.

"To think that wolf had it all this time," Grimoire Weiss hummed.

It was the last stone fragment: Loyal Cerberus.

Kainé recalled the wolf's last words. If Cerberus referred to the wolf, then perhaps its loyalty was for the one it called "grandfather." Perhaps, once upon a time, the wolf-Shade had even lived with a human.

". . . Nah."

Kainé shook her head to clear the thought, then fell into step behind Nier as they headed back to the city.

REPORT 15

The occurrence of once-rare irregularities has now become commonplace to the point where we no longer consider them irregular. Additionally, we were unable to find anything else that might calm the Shadowlord. In short, the situation continues to decay apace.

More and more subjects are relapsing due to intake of Maso. We surmise this is due to transformations in the Maso itself—likely a result of changes to the Shadowlord's mental state and thought process.

At present, the number of Gestalts falling out of our control due to relapse is increasing. As we believe things will continue to trend in this direction, we must move to the collection stage now or lose the ability to do so entirely.

There are no problems in terms of environmental conditions; the spread of white chlorination syndrome from 178 years ago has come to an end, and Legion has been eradicated. Regardless, the project has hit a sn

The Twins

NO ONE KNOWS where souls come from. We do, however, know where *people* come from. That's the easy part.

Popola stared at the woman on the bed whose rhythmical breathing resonated through the chamber. Despite how slight the sound was, Popola found it unbearably loud in the otherwise deafening silence of the room.

No one visited the library at night. In fact, Popola scarcely heard people talking or the sounds of things being moved around during the day either. It was here, in the deepest chamber of the library, that she now sat: a place the villagers called "the birthing room."

The birthing room was a place villagers were forbidden to enter or even approach without good reason. There were also those who didn't even know the room existed: children, unmarried individuals, and married couples not designated to possess children. Such people had no need to know about birth after all.

But it wasn't just birth—Popola and Devola didn't divulge more information than was necessary on any topic. This was an important factor in safely managing their village charges. Unnecessary information would only cause dangerous variations in their actions, which could then bring about irregularities.

That said, it was often difficult to know how much *was* necessary to divulge. It was rare to have a situation like childbirth, where there was a clear line between information that should and should not be shared. Oftentimes, Popola found herself thinking a piece of information was necessary, only to see in hindsight that it wasn't needed at all. For example . . .

No. Never mind that.

Popola put a pin in her thoughts, turned from the bed, and carried herself to the altar at the far end of the room. All who came to the room believed the altar was used in the rite of childbirth—mostly because Popola explained it that way.

After Popola voiced the authentication code, the altar slid silently aside to reveal a staircase. Once Popola stepped past the threshold, she felt the air around her shift as the altar moved back in place. A moment later, she was shrouded in darkness.

She made her way down, down, down. It was so dark, she couldn't even see the tip of her own nose, but this wasn't a problem; she knew precisely how steep the steps were, as well as their exact number. She could walk up and down them with her eyes closed if she so desired.

Once she reached the bottom of the staircase, she found herself in an underground tunnel built by the people of the old world. Its original purpose was not for walking but for vehicles. The current-day villagers could never imagine a carriage that might carry more people than the entire village's population. Or that it was made entirely out of metal. Or that several such carriages had been linked together to create the whole. At the end of the day, however, they had no need to picture such a thing—or to know about it.

"Why the long face?"

The voice in the darkness belonged to Devola, who had been waiting for her sister to arrive. She'd chosen to do her waiting behind a pillar, which suggested to Popola that she had been hoping to leap out and scare her. She enjoyed playing childish pranks like that.

"My face is perfectly normal, thank you."

Popola reached for a panel on the wall and began flicking buttons and levers to activate an auto-drive mode. She needed a voice-activated authorization code here as well—a safety precaution to ensure none but the twins could enter the area. Even if the code did somehow leak into the populace, the villagers would be unable to recreate the twins' voices.

The moment the code was entered, the tunnel lit up and the lights inside the linked carriages came on. The doors opened, and the two sisters moved inside. As they sat, the doors closed, and the vehicle began to move.

"Something worrying you?" Devola asked loudly. The old-world vehicle was fast and comfortable but made a tremendous amount of noise. For a moment, Popola was going to answer in the negative, but then she reconsidered.

"I honestly don't know what to do with you," replied Popola. "You should be in the middle of performing a birthing rite, but you just up and left without a word."

The ritual lasted a week, and during that time, either Devola or Popola was always on duty in the birthing room. No one else was allowed to enter until the village woman emerged safely with her baby. Such security didn't apply to just the room itself, of course—no one could know of the staircase that led into the earth nor of the metal carriage.

"I mean, it's your turn to be there now, right?"

Popola had library work during the day, which made it hard to step away. As such, Devola took charge during the day, while Popola worked nights.

"Yes. But you know people saw you at the tavern yesterday afternoon."

"Dammit! Shoulda made 'em promise not to say anything . . ."

"And if they wondered why?"

"I, uh . . ."

"See? You can't just ask such people not to blab."

The villagers didn't know Devola was on duty during the day, of course. In fact, aside from the father of the child, they had no idea a birthing rite was going on at all—and the father would have been carefully instructed not to say anything until the rite was over. Such things would have only proved to be unnecessary information for the others.

"Fiiine, you got me. I just wanted to sneak out for a break."

"I understand, but don't take too many, all right? This isn't an event that happens multiple times a year anymore."

Birthing rites had become increasingly rare as more and more people succumbed to the Black Scrawl.

"Still, if it's a break you wanted, why are you taking it at *this* hour?" asked Popola.

"Lemme ask again: Is something worrying you?"

"Devola, it's because you—"

"Aw, you're so cute when you lie. Maybe you can just tell me what *this* is?"

Devola waved a crinkled piece of paper in front of Popola's face: a report she had crumpled up and thrown away barely an hour before.

"I didn't know you enjoyed digging around in garbage."

"So why didn't you finish it?"

There was no smile in Devola's eyes; evading the question wasn't an option.

"I couldn't."

"You're hesitating."

As always, she had seen right through her.

"My miscalculation caused all of this," admitted Popola quietly. "Remember when I gave Yonah unnecessary information?"

"You mean the Lunar Tear thing?"

"Exactly so."

Popola hadn't imagined a child would dare set foot in the Lost Shrine, so when Yonah asked where Lunar Tears might grow, she'd casually given an answer. Things had *always* turned out okay up to that point, after all, so why wouldn't they continue to do so? But that one slip was what led Nier to meet Grimoire Weiss.

"Oh, stop blaming yourself. This all happened when the Shadowlord decided to start acting on his own. It's *his* fault we've got so damn many cases of the Black Scrawl. All we've been doing is trying to stop him so we can fix things."

"You're kind to say so, Devola. But . . ."

Popola had made more than one miscalculation: She'd also attempted to use Nier to stop the Shadowlord's rampage. If Nier could protect Yonah, then the Shadowlord's plans would fall through. Sadly, that caused its own unexpected consequence when the Shadowlord kidnapped Yonah. Indeed, far from being thwarted, his plans had only been pushed into motion. It was a miscalculation that had brought on the worst possible outcome.

"Nier knows too much," said Popola. "He's too close to the core of Project Gestalt."

"Then there's only one thing to do. What's holding you back?"

"Yes, I thought the same. I never expected I'd find myself hesitating now."

Popola had planned to approach all the villagers equally; she never intended to give Nier special treatment.

"Yeah. I'm surprised too. Guess this is what it means to get attached, huh?"

The sickly little girl and her worried older brother—the twins had seen this scenario play out uncountable times before. They should have been able to remain composed even knowing the fate that awaited Nier.

"Look, I agree it would be great for Nier to get Yonah back," continued Devola. "But that can never happen."

"I know. But it can at least wait until the next—"

"Don't you *dare* finish that sentence, Sis. *That* would be a miscalculation."

The stern look on Devola's face told Popola her sister was admonishing herself at the same time—because what Popola was about to say was something she'd once uttered herself.

"Lately I've been thinking a lot about all the time we used to spend with him, you know? I'd like to put it off for a hundred years or so. At least until the next generation—"

"Devola!"

"I know, I know. We can't afford that kind of thing. I get it . . . But I know you feel it too."

"Even if I did, we have no choice."

Having realized Devola's conviction was beginning to waver, Popola had adopted an even more rational air. They both knew exactly what the other felt and thought. If one lost composure, the other had to remain calm. If one hesitated in a decision, the other had to make it. That was how they were meant to be.

"I'm sorry. You're right. You're totally right." Popola knew she was the one who was slipping this time and that her sister's firm language was her attempt to rectify that.

"We're the ones in charge of Project Gestalt after all," said Devola.

Popola knew that—she thought about it every second of every day. It was the reason they observed the villagers and even meddled in their affairs when necessary. They nipped irregularities in the bud and took great pains to ensure generational changeovers were stable.

"So let's do our job. Don't worry. We're not built to run on emotion."

Devola's jesting tone rang comfortably in Popola's ears, causing relief to settle in her chest. So long as she had Devola, all would be well.

I have Devola. She has me. The two of us together will see our mission through.

"We're almost there," Devola murmured abruptly.

Popola didn't respond; she knew exactly what her sister was trying to say. Once they had all the keys, the doors to the Shadowlord's castle would open. It was still hard to believe he'd been hiding right under their noses ever since kidnapping Yonah. They'd used every trick in the book to try and track him down and were dumbfounded when they learned the truth—especially since he'd managed to carefully seal the castle entrance and lock himself inside.

But they'd managed to take down the great Shades guarding the keys thanks to Nier, which meant the castle would soon be open. Then they could stop his rampage in its tracks and push Project Gestalt forward once more.

The vehicle rushed through the dark tunnel for a while longer before slowly gliding to a halt.

"Finally," Devola said as she stretched. "No matter how many times we ride this thing, I always hate it."

"Really? I rather enjoy it. It's much faster than a boat."

"Guess that's true. So we don't have a choice on this either . . ."

Without the vehicle's speed, it would have been impossible for them to get to the facility from the village and back in an hour. The facility was, after all, a place that directly neighbored the Shadowlord's castle beyond the Lost Shrine—a location that took Nier nearly half a day to reach by boat.

The fact the vehicle traveled underground also kept the villagers unaware of their actions. Still, even if the villagers *did* know where they were going, they knew that old-world ruins were strictly off-limits. If they saw Devola or Popola venturing inside, they'd simply tell themselves they were up to important priest business and think no more of it.

The sisters stepped down from the vehicle and walked at a

brisk pace. The area was open and bright, unlike the library base-ment. The staircase was also wide enough for Popola to comfort-ably walk alongside Devola. It had likely been built to accom-modate many people at once. Multitudes had worked here at one time, though it now sat empty.

As always, they voiced the verification code to unlock a thick metal door marked *No Entry* before pushing it open and march-ing inside.

"There won't be any errors at this point, right?" Devola asked.

Popola shook her head, then stopped to input the verification code at a final door.

"The copy was a success," she said when she finished. "So long as we don't find any problems in the genetic data during our final check, everything will be fine."

As the door swung open, a voiceless sigh of air escaped. A wall of air surrounded the room to prevent viruses and bacteria from getting inside. The area contained clear tubes aligned in neat rows, although they were only interested in one. There had been a time when many of the tubes had been filled with cultivating fluid, but that was now a distant memory.

"Tonight marks day seven, huh?" said Devola. She peered into the liquid-filled tube and saw a baby gently bobbing up and down. The previous iteration of the poor thing had fallen into the waterways and died at just ten years old, ruining the promise of long life their genetic makeup had offered. And this time . . .

Well, this time it was likely the child's life would be even more brief.

But perhaps that was for the best. What was there to lose, after all, if disaster struck before the ego took root? In fact, De-vola had long thought Replicants would have been perfectly con-tent without an ego.

People were born in cultivation liquid, lived and grew in the outside world for a brief moment, then returned to cultivation liquid. In this way, their genes were replicated over and over and over again. This was the simple answer to where people came from—and where they went.

"What's the matter?" Devola asked as she readied the transport container.

"It's nothing," said Popola, brushing off the sentimentality brewing in her chest. "Let's hurry."

Devola and Popola planned to awaken this child's "mother" when they returned, which meant they had to be back before daybreak. Then they could place the baby in her arms and recite the line that concluded the birthing rites:

"Congratulations. You've given birth to this baby."

REPORT 15-2

The occurrence of once-rare irregularities has now become commonplace, to the point where we no longer consider them irregular. Additionally, we were unable to find anything else that might calm the Shadowlord. In short, the situation continues to decay apace.

More and more subjects are relapsing despite their intake of Maso. We surmise this is due to transformations in the Maso itself—likely a result of changes to the Shadowlord's mental state and thought process.

At present, the number of Gestalts falling out of our control due to relapse is increasing. As we believe things will continue to trend in this direction, we must move to the collection stage now or lose the ability to do so entirely.

There are no problems in terms of environmental conditions; the spread of white chlorination syndrome from 178 years ago has come to an end, and Legion has been eradicated. Regardless, the project has hit a snag: We are unable to execute our contract with the Shadowlord.

Humanity was unable to develop technology that could stop relapses and return things to the way they once were. If they had, it would have solved 99 percent of the problems we currently face. But they didn't, and now the Shadowlord is trying to annul the contract of his own accord. He's grown impatient, if you will, and it's hard to blame him—a thousand years is a long time to wait.

Ironically, it was his defection that allowed everything to fall into place. Our only question is how much of Grimoire Weiss's dysfunction we'll be able to fix, but I suppose we'll just have to trust in this thousand-year-old human technology.

Once we send the Shadowlord's Replicant into his castle, we can initiate the merging program. And with his route to the castle secure, we hope this happens in short order.

We are now initiating the final stages of Project Gestalt. End report.

Report written by Popola

NieR Replicant
ver.1.22474487139...

The Man 8

1.

ONCE THE FINAL fragment was in his hands, Nier ventured to Seafront for materials, then he brought them to the Junk Heap to improve his weapons. He remembered how powerful Grimoire Noir was, and there was no doubt the Shadowlord was stronger still. He needed his weapons to be as capable as they possibly could be.

As Kainé and Emil prepared camp, Nier hurried to the village. He wanted to leave as early as possible the following day. But—

"What's the matter, lad?"

At some point, he'd apparently come to a halt. Grimoire Weiss, who had been floating alongside as they approached the northern gate, came back to collect him.

"Oh. It's nothing."

"Does something trouble you?"

"Guess I'm just amazed I'll finally be able to save Yonah."

"Aye, lad. That you will."

It had been five long years since Yonah had been stolen away. Since then, Nier had kept his attention forward and forged ever ahead. Now that the end of his journey was in sight, he found himself looking back on the path he had tread.

"And?" continued Weiss. "What is it, lad? You've quite the pensive look on your face."

In hindsight, his path had been both long and cruel. *That* was what gave him doubts.

"Listen, I need your advice. It's about Kainé and Emil."

"Out with it then."

"The Shadowlord is strong, and our fight with him is going to be harsher than anything we've faced so far. And even though I'm doing this for Yonah, that doesn't make it okay for me to put Kainé and Emil in harm's way."

His friends had proven to be powerful allies. He would doubtless have died at The Aerie or the Seafront shipwreck had they not been at his side. Still, did that make it right to bring them all the way to the Shadowlord's castle?

"*Now* you question the integrity of your actions?" Grimoire Weiss asked with an exasperated sigh.

"I know it's pretty late in the day, but—"

Before Nier could finish, the ground at his feet burst into an explosion. He grunted and leaped back, but his leg took the brunt of the blast wave, leaving it stinging.

"What the hell?!" he cried.

"I'm sorry! I'm so sorry!"

Nier whirled around to see Emil floating up, his staff gripped in his bony hands.

"Emil!" Grimoire Weiss exclaimed. "This was you? How terrifically violent!"

"K-Kainé told me to do it . . ."

"I needed to get the attention of a certain coward who was spewing a bunch of hot garbage," explained Kainé as she marched up to Nier. Clearly she'd overheard his conversation with Weiss.

"Kainé, Emil, look. I just—"

"Wanted to leave us behind? Why, so we'd be *safe*? Fuck that."

"Kainé's right!" chimed in Emil. "You accepted me. You told me we'd be together no matter what happens. Now it's time for us to return the favor!"

"Don't make me start talking about loyalty and debts and all that—you know I hate mushy shit."

But . . . Nier thought. *But that's why* . . . He opened his mouth to finally say something, but Emil gleefully cut him off.

"If it makes you feel better, we're not doing it for free! After we rescue Yonah, we're totally gonna call in a favor of our own!"

"Wait. You two need help from . . . me?"

"Yep!" Emil nodded vigorously. "We're going on a journey to cure Kainé's possession and restore my body. It's gonna be tons of fun! Just think of all the delicious local foods we can try along the way!"

"I'm gonna eat way more than my fair share," said Kainé. "So you better get ready to pony up."

Though there was no proof the group would come back alive, Kainé and Emil were already planning the after-party. The strength of that belief was a weighty gift filled with warmth, and there was only one way for Nier to reply.

"Thanks, you two. We're gonna rescue Yonah. I swear it."

2.

"YOU'RE REALLY GONNA do it?" Devola asked.

Nier nodded, noting how odd it was to see both sisters in the library. His original plan had been to say goodbye to Popola in the library, then meet up with Devola at the tavern. Clearly Devola had caught wind of the plan and made her way to her sister's side.

"The whole village is buzzing, you know? They say you're going to rescue Yonah."

Nier could tell Popola was consciously brightening her tone out of concern for him.

"I'll bring her back. I promise."

"I guess it's really happening, huh?" said Popola as she dropped her gaze. She opened her mouth to speak again but seemingly changed her mind at the last second.

"Nothing. Never mind."

"Popola just loves to worry," Devola piped up.

Nier knew Popola was about to warn him that it would be dangerous. This was no surprise, seeing as she'd worried about Nier during this entire journey. But no matter how many times she told him what he was doing was dangerous, he never stopped hunting Shades. That's why Popola had fallen silent. If she couldn't keep him from killing Shades, how could she possibly hold him back from the Shadowlord?

"Anyway, you be careful," Devola added.

"Thanks, you two." Nier whirled on his heels and opened the door, but Popola's voice stopped him.

"Yes. Do be careful."

Nier peered over his shoulder and saw she was smiling. Closing the door behind him, he started down the narrow stairwell.

"I marvel at how relatively simple a task this retrieval process proved to be," Grimoire Weiss muttered dubiously. "It is almost as if someone deliberately set us on this path."

"You're overthinking again, Weiss."

"But—"

Nier knew he was about to suggest it was a trap, but if they started listing things that didn't add up, they'd be standing there forever. Besides, the presence of a trap meant someone had set it up, and the fastest way to find out who was behind such a thing was to leap in headfirst.

"I don't care if it's a trap. Yonah's waiting for me, and I'm going."

"I see" was all Grimoire Weiss said before falling silent.

Countless villagers spoke to Nier on his way to the docks, starting with an old man who clapped him on the shoulder as he reached the bottom of the library's hill.

"You're up against the king of Shades, boy. Take care out there."

"Can we play with Yonah once she comes back?" asked the children by the fountain.

"Sure thing," replied Nier. "So long as you all get along."

As he reached the stairs leading to the docks, someone mentioned how much brighter the village would be once Yonah was back in it. It reminded Nier of how Popola said the village was buzzing. These kind people had been a support system for him and Yonah as they desperately fought to survive as children, and he wanted to bring the Shadowlord down for them as much as for himself. *Everything* would be better without that demon around.

The ferryman was waiting for him at the docks and asked where he was going with his usual chipper air. Considering how word of Nier's activities was drifting through town, the ferryman likely already knew the answer. But Nier saw a kind light in the man's eyes and realized he thought repeating the phrase like everything was normal would help ease Nier's nerves.

"The Lost Shrine," Nier answered. The ferryman simply smiled wider and set off.

3.

THE JOURNEY WAS the same all the way to the docks behind the Lost Shrine. But once they cut through the short cavern beyond it, everything changed.

"Shades?! What are they doing here?!"

Nier had never encountered Shades outside the shrine, but now the wooden bridge and ladders were swarming with them. And not the small, weak creatures they had come across inside the last time—these Shades were clad in armor and wielding swords.

"It seems the Shadowlord has prepared a welcoming party," said Grimoire Weiss, sighing. "How very kind of him."

Weiss was correct. After the loss of the guardians of the key fragments, the Shadowlord must have realized they were coming and strengthened his defenses.

When they made their way inside the shrine, they found the Shades there were armored as well. Though there weren't as many as before, they proved much stronger opponents, and it took the group a considerable amount of time to reach the roof.

"And now the path is open," said Weiss when they finally opened the doors to the altar room. His tone suggested how moved he was by the prospect, and Nier felt the same. Looking back, it seemed like all the time it had taken to collect the fragments, complete the key, and get to this point was worth it.

Nier approached the altar with slow, reverent steps. No Shades burst through the ceiling to attack, and no tiny Shades welled up from the ground.

"Such an ominous sight," the tome continued. "And yet I find it strangely nostalgic."

"Yeah," Nier nodded. "This is where Weiss and I first met—and first fought together."

"Wow!" Emil marveled. "This is where you used to live, Weiss?"

"Well . . . Yes, I suppose. In a technical sense."

He'd actually been sealed here rather than actively choosing it as a home, but he must have considered that too much of a hassle to explain. He was happy to settle things with "in a technical sense."

"Pretty nice digs for a floating magazine."

Kainé wasn't holding back, as usual, and Weiss chose to respond in kind.

"At least it was free from annoying hussies like yourself!"

Despite how the walls were crumbling and the floor was pockmarked—clearly as a result of their fight against Kainé—the barrier over the altar remained as stout as ever, likely because it was an extension of the Shadowlord's power. As Nier considered this, he fit the five stone fragments snugly in place over the engraved pattern.

The Stone Guardian.
The Memory Tree.
The Law of Robotics.
Sacrifice.
Loyal Cerberus.

Once the pentagon was complete, the door beyond the altar shuddered. The patterns that suggested the presence of a barrier vanished, and the door heaved open with a metallic scrape.

"Is this an elevator?" asked Nier as he stared into the opening.

"It appears so," replied Weiss.

It wasn't as rusted as the elevators in the Junk Heap, nor did it reek of oil, but the way it opened and the tiny gap between door and floor were exactly the same.

What made Nier wonder if it was an elevator was the fact there were no buttons to tell them where they were going; the sides were completely smooth. He ran his hand along the wall thinking perhaps it would trigger a mechanism, but nothing happened.

"Maybe they're hiding somewhere," said Emil as he floated toward the ceiling.

"Oh, I got this one. Fuck you, door!"

As Kainé lifted her leg to kick the door, it rolled shut. While the elevator was quieter than those at the Junk Heap, the sound and vibration when it started moving were similar. Apparently this version simply started working on its own a certain period of time after someone entered it.

When the faint shuddering came to a stop, the doors slowly opened to reveal a corridor with a high ceiling. The floor sloped gently upward, leading to a set of doors at the opposite end.

When the sound of scraping metal rang out behind them, Nier turned to see the elevator door close. But unlike in the Junk Heap, there was no button to summon it back.

"It seems intruders are trapped in this place," Grimoire Weiss mused.

"We just have to defeat the Shadowlord," said Nier confidently. "Once we do, his influence over this place will vanish."

It wasn't as if he had any intention of leaving before the Shadowlord was dead.

"Let's keep going," he said. The corridor wasn't all that long, and once they reached the end, Nier pushed the doors open, causing brilliant light to pour from the space between them.

"I never knew a place could be so beautiful!" Emil exclaimed.

The next room was a gorgeous garden built of stone and greenery. Bright sunlight showered trees, flowers, and shrubs in their orderly rows. After a short staircase, a flagstone path appeared and extended into the distance. The path was flanked by statues of women, each of exquisite make. They were so tall, Nier had to crane his neck to see their faces, and he noted that one of them was damaged.

The center of the garden was enclosed by a circular metallic fence and pillars. There was no roof over the spot to keep out the elements, which meant the pillars were purely for decoration.

"The meticulous maintenance here boggles the mind," said Weiss. While beautiful, it was difficult to discern any practical use for the place. A considerable amount of water and fertilizer would be needed to grow the varying flowers—water and fertilizer that could easily grow enough wheat to support an entire village.

What a waste of resources, Nier thought. Eventually, he spied a shallow basin with slender legs sitting atop the fence. Two small white birds were perched on the edge—enjoying a bath, most likely. Nier quietly approached so as not to spook them.

"That must be the exit," said Emil, pointing some distance away from the birds. He was right—a brief glance around the area showed nothing else that looked like a way out. The only other door was the one they'd come through, which now lay far behind them.

"Let's check it out," Nier offered.

"This is clearly a trap," Grimoire Weiss muttered.

"I don't care."

Let it be a trap. Even if a sudden horde of Shades leaped upon them or they were plunged into the jaws of a vicious mechanism, Nier would kill them all, break everything, and keep going.

But despite how he'd steeled himself, what awaited on the other side of the door was just another beautiful garden.

"This looks like the place where we just were," Emil pointed out.

It didn't just *look* like it; one of the statues was even damaged. There had to be a magical explanation.

"We just have to keep going," Nier insisted.

But when they reached the end and pushed through the door on the other side, they found themselves in yet another identical garden.

"Okay, hold on," Emil piped up. "Is it just me, or are we looping around the same path over and over?"

"We should head back," Nier said. He turned to grab the door they'd just passed through, but it wouldn't open. No matter how hard he pushed or pulled, it refused to budge.

"Move," said Kainé, who then shoved Nier aside without waiting for him to do it himself. She kicked the door with a solid thump, but all it did was mar its flawless surface with a footprint.

"Could we be . . . ?"

"Weiss? What is it?"

Grimoire Weiss did not answer Nier's question. He only pressed farther in, forcing Nier to follow with quick steps.

"The door," the tome commanded.

Nier did as he was told and pushed it open, only to see the same garden extending before them. The door closed behind them as they entered and wouldn't budge no matter how they pushed or pulled.

"Now look there," said Weiss. The group stared and saw a faint footprint, which raised the question of how Kainé's print could be visible on a door they'd just passed through. There was only one possible explanation: They were not walking through similar gardens, but the *same* one.

"He means we're stuck," Kainé muttered with a click of the tongue.

"Not necessarily. There may be another exit that is not this door."

Nier scanned the area. What sort of exit would there be if not the door? If he were to create a puzzle that would lead them out, where would he put it?

While he began investigating every railing and pillar, Emil floated around treetops and peered down at roots—but neither of them could find anything. Frustrated, Nier sliced the fencing with his blade, but nothing happened. In a fit of even greater rage, he knocked over a stack of crates beside him with a clatter.

At that point, he noticed something odd: The birds sitting on the bath hadn't moved at all. He'd caused an unholy ruckus, yet they showed no sign of flying away. He strode forward and reached out to touch them, but they didn't even spread their wings. All the birds he'd ever seen flew away at the sight of a human, especially one who invaded their space.

"*To whom does the true voice speak?*" came a low voice.

Nier blinked a couple of times, wondering if he was now imagining things.

"*To whom does the true form show itself?*"

Nope. Not imagining things.

"*You must answer.*"

"Whoa!" Emil yelped. "It can talk!"

This was clearly their puzzle; no normal bird could speak the human tongue.

"*I ask: Why did humans disappear from the world?*"

"The hell?" said a bewildered Nier. "What's it talking about?"

"Hold, lad," Grimoire Weiss said sharply. "I believe this is some manner of password."

"A password?"

"One that will allow us escape from this place. A magic word that will let us proceed into the castle. I feel confident I have heard this somewhere before . . ."

Grimoire Weiss fell silent, leaving the question of where he'd heard it a mystery.

"*I ask: Why did humans disappear from the world?*"

The birds repeated the same question, seemingly content to do so until they received the password, just as Weiss suspected. Unfortunately, Nier didn't know the answer. Popola probably did, but it wasn't like they could turn back and ask.

"I answer: because of a black disease."

"Uh, Weiss?"

"Silence! I remember now."

Nier could tell Weiss's answer was correct because the birds moved on to the next question.

"*I ask: How can humans extend their lives?*"

"I answer: by separating body from soul."

"*I ask: What is the destination of souls?*"

"I answer: They are placed in their corresponding shells."

There came silence. After a lengthy pause, the voice finally returned.

"*Very well. You are acknowledged as master. You may enter.*"

The birds flew off, and the sound of a door opening filled the room. As they made their way to the correct exit at last, a question came to Nier:

"How did you know the password, Weiss?"

"As much as I wish to reprimand you for doubting my myriad talents, the true answer is that I do not know."

"You don't?"

"Perhaps I heard it once long ago. But where that happened— or who told it to me—has been lost to time."

"Of course the dusty old magazine can't remember," muttered Kainé.

"Speak up, hussy!" Grimoire Weiss spat as they moved toward the door. But as they reached the threshold, he came to a sudden stop and remained floating in the doorway. Nier came up beside him and began to ask what was wrong, then froze in astonishment. Before them was a vast open courtyard—one that contained people who could not *possibly* be there.

"Popola? Devola? What are you doing here?"

Nier rushed toward them, but his feet froze in place halfway. All of his instincts were telling him to be careful; there was something cold and distant about the way they were looking at him.

"Hey," said Devola. "Any chance you'll just . . . go back to the village?"

"This is a very dangerous place," added Popola. Though the two seemed to be speaking in their usual candid way, the tone of it was *cold*.

"Even if you can find Yonah here, you probably can't—"

"How did you get here?" Grimoire Weiss interrupted.

"Shhh," replied Popola, keeping her eyes fixed squarely on Nier. "*We're* asking the questions now."

"Well? Are you going back or not?"

Retreat wasn't an option; no matter what either of them said, Nier had made up his mind long ago.

"Of course we're not going back."

"No dice, huh?" said Devola. "I guess we don't have a choice then."

The twins slowly lifted their staves into the air—the same ones they carried when performing weddings or funerals in the village. But this time, they were pointing them directly at Nier.

"We didn't want to fight you," Devola said.

Nier couldn't believe his ears. *Fight?* Why would they *fight?*

"We really, really didn't want to," Popola added.

"What's happening?" asked Nier.

Devola swiped her staff through the air, her way of saying she wouldn't be answering. "Sorry, but this fate was predetermined."

"Still, we spoke the truth," Popola continued. "We really wanted to avoid this if possible." Despite her words, there was no hesitation in the way she brandished her staff.

"We were hoping to put it off for a hundred years or so. Until the next generation came along."

"What are you *talking* about?!" cried a bewildered Nier as he dodged their staves.

"Are they Shades?" Grimoire Weiss asked.

"I don't think so," replied Kainé. But her answer did little to ease the situation as the twins continued to press their attack.

"It's a lie!" Nier shouted. "I don't believe it!"

He dodged Devola's attack, then blocked Popola's with his sword. That was enough to tell him that they were fighting in earnest.

"This is madness!" Grimoire Weiss cried. "Why do you block our path?"

"*You!*" Popola said sharply, her tone causing a shiver to jolt down Nier's spine. "You have no cause to speak so with us, Grimoire Weiss. You are a traitor!"

Without warning, Devola and Popola began casting a spell, pointing their staves not at Nier but Weiss. As their hands began to glow, the same light enveloped him, causing him to groan.

"Weiss!" cried Nier as the light faded. "Are you okay?!"

"They . . . copied my powers . . ."

Before Weiss could finish speaking, a barrage of bullets flew from Popola's hand—a magic Nier had seen countless times before.

"Oh, shit on a shingle," muttered Kainé. "They can use the Sealed Verses."

"Of course we can!" replied Devola as she deployed the magical hand. "The power came from us in the first place!"

"You were simply loaned a small portion of it," Popola added.

The massive fist flew down at them from above.

"Why are you siding with the Shades?!" Nier yelled.

Devola smiled. "The answer to every riddle lies within the heart of the Shadowlord."

The Shadowlord? His heart? The way she spoke almost made it sound like . . .

"You've been on his side this whole time?!" Nier demanded.

"You must search for that answer yourself," said Popola.

"You've gotta face your own truth now," said Devola.

The magic stopped. A red light enveloped Popola's and Devola's bodies—the same light flying Shades used when they cast magic.

"Please, enter the Shadowlord's castle," said Popola.

The light obscured them completely. As the two shot away into the air, Nier could only watch with his mouth hanging open.

4.

BEYOND THE COURTYARD was another corridor. Kainé glanced over her shoulder to see Nier plodding behind her with his head low. He'd trusted Devola and Popola his entire life, yet now they'd attacked without provocation or reason. It was only natural he'd be confused. Perhaps things would have been better if he'd always viewed them as unlikable women—like Kainé did.

Either way, the twins were a serious problem. Not only had they thrown Nier for a loop, but they'd knocked Grimoire Weiss completely haywire. The tome had been acting loopy ever since they copied the Sealed Verses with their weird magic. In fact, he could barely articulate himself or string a sentence together. Even Kainé couldn't find humor in watching a talking book struggle to speak.

When they reached the halfway point of the dim corridor, a peculiar noise reached Kainé's ears.

"Is that music?" Emil asked, tilting his head. "It sounds like a waltz."

No wonder Kainé hadn't been able to identify the noise; she had no interest in music and couldn't tell a waltz from a rumba. But Emil, who had serious musical chops, had been able to identify it right away.

The closer they got to the door, the more Kainé understood the sound as music. And once they pushed it wide, she found herself dazed by the grandiose sound. Put concisely, it was *way* too loud.

"It certainly is a grand affair!"

Kainé ignored Weiss's unbidden opinion, because who gave a crap about any of that when silhouettes of men and women were gliding gracefully across a floor?

"Buncha dancin' bastards," she muttered. She could feel her left half squirming, and while Tyrann didn't say anything, she knew he found the whole thing just *delightful.*

A moment later, she heard the music warp. A pair of white-silhouette dancers vanished, only to be replaced by . . .

"They're all Shades!"

Nier yelled as the Shades screeched and lifted massive clubs in the air.

"Defilers! This is a holy sanctuary for humans! Leave at once, beasts!"

One silhouette after another began transforming into Shades.

"None of you are human!"

Words Kainé never wanted to hear struck home as more and more Shades began to appear. The idea that perhaps they should retreat for a while popped up in some small corner of her mind.

"I think we're locked in!" Emil shouted from the door. Clearly he'd beaten her "let's run" idea to the punch.

"I wasn't planning to leave," Nier snapped.

"Yeah, it's a bit late for that," agreed Kainé. Even if they *did* manage to get out of this ballroom and back into the corridor, the door leading to the courtyard would likely be locked. If there was one thing she knew about the Shadowlord's castle, it was that there was no turning back.

"This sanctuary must remain under our protection. It is our final bastion. For the sake of those we love, we will not allow it to be destroyed."

The Shades continued to spout irritating nonsense, and Kainé was getting mighty sick of it.

"Dammit!" cried Nier. "They won't stop coming!"

His voice was filled with both panic and irritation as more Shades popped into existence. And more. And more. And *more*. Once all of the white silhouettes had become Shades, more started appearing out of thin air. In addition to wielding clubs, some could even fly.

"I'll open the next door!" Kainé called. "Cover me!"

If they couldn't turn back, they'd just have to push forward. The other door in the room was their only chance. Kainé stomped a path through the swarming shades, kicking her way to the far end of the ballroom.

"No! You cannot go that way! You can't enter! You mustn't!"

The Shade's voice came from behind her, but she ignored it and grabbed the handle, only to find it locked. Frustrated, she reared back and kicked it.

"No, you idiot!" Grimoire Weiss shouted. "What are you doing?!"

"Doesn't wanna open? Fine! I'll just break it down!"

"Stop, you impatient fool!"

Kainé had no interest in Grimoire Weiss's warnings. Swearing loudly, she rose up and booted the door with all her strength. Something snapped, hinges groaned, and the door swung wide.

"Got it!"

She whirled around to look at the nagging tome, perhaps to remind him there were, in fact, some things only brute force could accomplish. But then . . .

"Kainé! Look out!"

The book was shouting again, but why should she care? Pleased with herself, she turned back to the door, only to be greeted with an unexpected sight.

". . . Muh?" she said eloquently.

The space beyond the door was shrouded in darkness. But this was no mere absence of light—it was a mass of writhing spherical Shades. They spilled out of the open door and quickly overwhelmed her, sending her crashing to the ground. Her head smacked the floor with a sickening thud, stunning her.

Through stars, she saw Nier cutting down the Shades that roiled around him. She kept telling herself to get up and help, but her traitorous body refused to cooperate.

"*Stop! Please, stop! They're just babies! They don't know any better!*"

Babies? The black spheres were *babies*? The moment the thought entered her head, Kainé realized she could hear them laughing and crying. Mild amusement overcame her; who knew Shades could have *babies*?!

"*Spare the lives of the children! We waited for so long, and now we finally can recreate them! Please! I beg you!*"

Apparently the Shade that had been caterwauling this entire time was the babies' mother.

"*Get up, Sunshine! It's slaughter time!*"
Cram the reminder, asshole. I'm on it.

Strength finally flowed back to Kainé's limbs. Though she was still light-headed, her swords served as a form of balance that let her pull herself to her feet.

"You okay, Kainé?" Nier called.

"Yeah. But I think we got even bigger problems now."

Kainé could hear the mother Shade calling the babies over to her and realized they were forming into something much, much bigger.

"Uh-oh. This is bad, guys!" Emil understood perfectly, for he had learned his own painful lesson in how powerful combined Shades could be in The Aerie.

As the mother and child Shades came together, they began absorbing all their companion creatures in the ballroom. As their outlines began to blur, they briefly took on the form of a large undefined mass. A moment later, the mass resolved itself into the shape of a boar that looked exactly like the beast that roamed the northern plains.

"*There is no justice in the slaughter of innocents!*" roared the Shade-boar. "*How many have you killed? How many? Your actions can never be forgiven!*"

To the boar, Nier had committed a crime by killing baby Shades. But to Kainé, it was the *Shades* that couldn't be forgiven, for they were the ones that slaughtered her helpless grandmother.

Yeah, and how many have you *killed?* she wordlessly asked.

The same was true for the king of Facade, where a Shade-wolf had murdered his beloved and countless of his people. Yet for that creature, the humans were butchers who had cut down most of its pack. Neither could forgive the other; those being killed could never accept those who were doing the killing. It did not matter what reasons they had—that was simply how things were.

Hearing Shades speak always filled Kainé with guilt. She found it difficult to kill anything with intelligence and a sense of self. But she could only marvel at her egoism, for despite that guilt, she chose to kill anyway.

"*We will never forgive you! Never!*"

Of course you won't, Kainé thought.

It was a thought of such urgency, she suddenly turned to the Shade-boar and screamed.

"We don't need forgiveness, asshole!"

She would never ask for absolution while she continued to murder Shades. The days of pretending not to see her own blood-soaked hands were over.

"*Wait a second. Waaaaait a second!*" Tyrann crowed. "*Your heart is . . . different. What's going on here, Sunshine?*"

"How should I know?" Kainé spat. Frankly, the garbage musings of Tyrann were the last thing she was interested in right now.

"Kainé! Are you all right?!"

A worried Emil began to float toward her. Neither he nor Nier could hear the Shades, so she must have appeared to be saying strange things to herself.

"I'm fine. Let's just kill some shit and move on, all right?"

The massive boar bellowed and charged. Kainé dodged at the last second and fired off a volley of magic in return.

"*Iiinteresting,*" crooned Tyrann. "*Oh, how very interesting!*"

Shut your trap. Don't talk to me. I'm killing this thing right now.

"Dammit!" she yelled. "How can something so big be so fast?!"

The beast was incredibly quick. Kainé could barely target the thing while it was charging. And even if she did manage to land a hit, it was covered head to hoof in a thick, tough hide that acted like armor. But it had another similarity to a wild boar: Small precise movements were a problem. Whenever its momentum carried it into the wall, it would lie there for a second, stunned.

"Hit the thing while it's down!" she called.

She stood at the edge of the room, waiting for it to charge, then dodged at the last moment. After it smacked into the wall, she attacked for a few seconds, then retreated to a different part of the room and began the process all over again. As she kept it up, the Shade-boar finally vanished in a puff of signature black dust.

Kainé's breath came in harsh, ragged gasps. Her legs wobbled. But they could move on.

"Oh dear," said Weiss. Kainé whirled at his voice and noted

with horror that another massive Shade-boar had entered the room.

"What the hell?!"

And unlike the previous enemy, this one was clad in *literal* armor.

"Don't fall victim to such distractions!" Grimoire Weiss reminded them.

"Come on!" Emil added. "We have to keep going!"

Kainé agreed. The door she had kicked earlier was still open, so they exchanged nods and rushed to the exit. As they hurried up a spiral staircase on the other side, a deep, earthy rumble from behind revealed the giant Shade was giving chase.

"How can we deal with this th-th-thing?!"

Grimoire Weiss's articulation was still faulty, and it worried Kainé that she could occasionally hear static in his voice. But frankly, she had bigger concerns at the moment.

"Oh, you pissed her off now!" Tyrann cackled in regard to the Shade-boar. *"Look at her! So full of scorn and hate! She's just like you, Sunshine!"*

Like you're any different, Kainé thought as she ran.

"Eh?"

Hate is just another crutch for you. You're in pain. You're lonely. No one likes you. So you try to hide it under violence and hate.

"I'm not like that at all!"

It's okay.

". . . It is?"

Look, I'm the same way.

Tyrann fell silent. Because he *knew*.

Kainé had realized something as she listened to the Shades scream at them. She realized she wanted forgiveness for her selfish actions. She realized she chose to keep killing despite fearing the weight of her guilt. And she realized that despite it all, she continued trying to hide everything under a wave of violent tendencies. Because all these disparate parts of her were simply too much to handle.

But would such realizations change anything?

It's too late for us now. We're too far gone, you and me.

No. That wasn't right. Nier had accepted her for who she was—accepted her cursed, wrong self without question. *He* had given her forgiveness.

And maybe that was enough.

They rushed up the seemingly endless staircase with the Shade-boar hot on their heels. Suddenly, Emil's voice called out from somewhere above:

"There's a door up here! Hurry!"

The rest of the group slipped through the door, but their pursuer couldn't manage the nimble turn in time and ended up rumbling right past them.

5.

RELIEF LASTED BUT a moment; when they ran to the door at the far side of the new room, they found it locked. Though Nier wasn't explicitly trying to imitate Kainé, he kicked it anyway. Sadly, this one wouldn't budge.

"Oh no!"

Emil's cry prompted Nier to turn around and see the massive Shade he thought they'd escaped standing in the center of the room. He wondered briefly how it had gotten there, then cast curiosity aside and took his blade in hand. If escape wasn't an option, they'd just have to kill the thing.

The group repeated the strategy of attacking the beast while it was stunned, but their blows barely did anything—likely due to the armor covering this one's body.

"Our attacks are not w-w-working!" Grimoire Weiss exclaimed.

"My magic isn't either!" Emil agreed.

Nier leaped and plunged his sword into the back of the Shade's head—a spot fatal for the boars of the northern plains—but this creature would not be so easily defeated. A shudder rippled through its body, causing the sword to ring with a terrible sound.

The vibration knocked Nier to the ground. He immediately took up a defensive position, but a terrible pain shot through his back, causing his breath to catch in his throat. Sensing an opening, the Shade bared its fangs and opened its mouth, emitting a foul-smelling, acrid smoke.

"That mist is poison!" Emil cried. Nier clapped his hand over his nose and mouth, but it was too late. The noxious smell burned the back of his nose as his vision began to waver.

"Stay focused, Kainé!"

Grimoire Weiss's voice caused Nier to turn his head, where he saw Kainé struggling to stand. Sadly, he couldn't help because he was in the very same position—and the massive Shade was closing in on them both.

I guess this is it, he thought.

But then, with no warning or fanfare, the great Shade fell onto its side. Sticking out from its back were a number of spears; behind it were soldiers armed with the same.

"I'm surprised this one gave you so much trouble."

That voice belonged to the king of Facade. As he spoke, fresh air blew in from the now-open door behind him, dispelling the mist.

"Unseal the exit! Let our friends through!"

Nier knew that voice: It was the king's advisor.

"The People of the Mask owe you a great debt," cried the soldiers. *"And now is the time to repay it!"*

"They could stand to loosen up a bit, huh?" laughed the king, his voice bright and cheerful.

"What are you doing here?!" asked a bewildered Nier.

"My citizens were speaking of your latest adventure."

Nier remembered how the citizens of his village all seemed to know he was heading out to get Yonah. Clearly the rumor had made its way to Facade, likely by way of the ferry.

"This is the castle of the Shadowlord, is it not?"

"You are correct," Grimoire Weiss replied.

"Then we have a common enemy. I swore upon Fyra's grave to

become a good and just ruler. A king who would protect others from the Shades."

"But—"

Nier began to object, but the king's advisor cut him off.

"We shall hold this one off. Please keep moving!"

The king turned to the soldiers and brandished his spear high above his head.

"We are the People of the Mask! We will stand our ground until our last breath!"

Soldiers suddenly appeared on either side of Nier and grabbed his arms before doing the same to Kainé and Emil.

"Hey!" he yelled. "Stop! Let me go!"

He'd guessed what the soldiers were trying to do—what the king had *ordered* them to do—and desperately tried to pry himself from their grasp. But they were surprisingly strong, and they lifted him up and off the floor like a feather. He tried to fight back, to thrash himself into some kind of desperate escape, but the soldiers only continued to drag him along in silence.

"Now go!" the king shouted. *"Rescue the one you hold most dear!"*

As Nier and his companions were tossed unceremoniously through the open side of the door, he managed to scream a single desperate word:

"KING!"

"We'll meet again, you and I, once all of this is over." The king smiled, flashing his teeth—the same smile he'd displayed when he and Nier first met. *"Until then."*

As the door swung shut, Nier scrambled to his feet and began pounding on it.

"No! Open the door! You can't fight that thing on your own!"

"It's all right!" came the king's voice. *"You have to keep going! Get your sister back! You must once again know the joy of having one you love by your side!"*

"King! Open the damn door! Please!"

He pounded again. Again. Again. Suddenly, Kaîné appeared from behind him, whipped him around by the collar of his shirt, and smacked him across the face, causing fireworks to explode across his vision.

"Knock it off already!" she shouted. Hearing her voice was like being doused with freezing water, and it suddenly brought Nier to his senses.

"He's fighting for you," she continued, her voice unusually quiet. "And for Fyra. Don't let him die for nothing."

The words pierced his heart more painfully than any blow. Having delivered them, Kaîné whirled around and started off down the hall, seemingly unconcerned if he followed or not.

When Nier first saved the king of Facade, he thought their relationship was something akin to fate. But he was wrong—it wasn't fate at all. Their friendship was something far beyond the power of a single word to describe.

Please survive this, King. Just hold on until I've killed the Shadowlord.

With that silent wish echoing through his mind, Nier balled his hands into fists and set off after Kaîné.

6.

THEY PASSED THROUGH many corridors, climbed several staircases, and killed countless Shades.

As Nier pushed open yet another door, he thought, *This must be the end.* The door was so grand and stately, he figured the Shadowlord had to be waiting behind it—or at the very least a Shade larger and more wretched than any they'd yet faced. But all he found was an open room smaller than the ballroom. One wall was filled with large glass windows, while a bridge led across the room and even farther into the castle. There was no gigantic Shade nor a Shadowlord. Instead, there was only a pair of familiar faces Nier had fervently hoped to not see again in this place.

"Oh, look," said Devola. "You made it."

"We've been waiting for so long," said Popola.

"Why?" Nier whispered in a voice that sounded weak even to him. "Why are you doing this?" He recalled Popola telling him to search for his own answers, but now he was facing them again with all his questions still a mystery.

Grimoire Weiss, however, had always regarded the twins with suspicion. The tome mentioned how their search for the Sealed Verses and then the key fragments all felt too convenient—as if someone had set the whole thing up. Nier had dismissed such concerns, so the tome had dropped the topic but had never forgotten it. Still, while Weiss was cautious, he never doubted something without good reason, and Nier found himself ruing the fact he hadn't given more weight to those suspicions.

"It began thirteen hundred years ago," Devola said ominously.

"Humanity," Popola continued, "finding itself on the brink of extinction, undertook a last-ditch rescue plan called Project Gestalt."

"Ges . . . talt . . . ?"

There was something strange about the way Grimoire Weiss spoke; it had been happening ever since Devola and Popola copied his powers.

"Do you still not remember, Grimoire Weiss?" asked Popola in a chilly tone.

"Then let's give you a refresher!" Devola's mouth curled into a smile Nier had never seen her wear before—one where her lips almost seemed to tremble. This was followed by a grating sound like a blade dragging across metal, which caused Weiss to groan loudly.

"Weiss! You okay?!"

Nier received no answer. The tome merely hung in midair.

"My . . . mind . . . Gaggghhh!"

Weiss had frozen in a similar way back when Grimoire Noir attacked them. And Nier wasn't the only one to remember this: Kainé and Emil clearly recalled it as well.

"Get a grip, book!" screamed Kainé.

"Weiss!" begged Emil simultaneously.

Five years ago, it had taken Kainé's insults and rage to pull Weiss back to reality. But this time, it seemed that would not be necessary.

"I . . . I remember . . ." began Weiss as the sound from Devola and Popola abruptly went silent.

"You okay?" Nier asked.

"Worry not for me," he replied before turning to the twins. "Devola . . . Popola . . . You are not human."

While this fact would have knocked Nier to the floor a few hours earlier, knowing they'd been on the Shadowlord's side this entire time allowed him to take it with a kind of eerie acceptance.

"In fact," continued Weiss. "Oh no . . ."

Devola chuckled. "Yeah, sometimes the truth can be a real bitch. You wanna finish that thought for him, sister?"

Popola turned her attention to Nier, the expression in her eyes as soft as when she'd bid him farewell back in the village.

"All of us, every person standing in this room, are mere shells created by the true humans."

"What are you saying?!" cried Nier.

"You still don't get it?" griped Devola. "*You aren't human!*"

Nier had no words. He couldn't even begin to comprehend what she was trying to say.

"So then humans—I mean, the true humans—are extinct?" Emil asked in a quivering voice.

It was Weiss who answered. "No. They still live on. You know them as Shades. Each Shade is a twisted remnant of what was once a human being."

Wait. The Shades Nier despised and loathed from the core of his very being were *human*? And he and his friends *weren't*? It was madness. Absurd. Far from being shocked, he found himself having to suppress a bark of laughter. Sure, killing a Shade had felt like killing a human the first time he brought one down, but when he noted how it bled, he'd been told it was the same as goats and sheep. That was how he'd continued to think of them to this day: as goats and sheep.

"Your bodies each have a rightful owner," said Popola. "A human in the form of a Gestalt—a being composed of soul only. Replicants are kept alive so that one day the Gestalts may be revived."

"Replicants?"

"Yes. That's you. Humanity—*true* humanity—now exists only in the form of souls separated from their corporal vessels. This was done in order to survive white chlorination syndrome. *This* . . . is Project Gestalt."

The words of the small white birds suddenly came back to Nier.

Why did humans disappear from the world?

How can humans extend their lives?

What is the destination of souls?

And Grimoire Weiss had replied to each of the questions with answers of his own:

Because of a black disease.

By separating body from soul.

They are placed in their corresponding shells.

The exchange clearly signified Project Gestalt, in which souls were separated from their bodies so they could be replaced and revived at a later hour.

"You are tools for Project Gestalt," said Devola in a voice tinged with sadness. "Nothing more than empty containers for a soul. But Popola and I are tools as well. Our endless existences have a single purpose: to control the lives of others in accordance with the will of the true humans."

The villagers had trusted and looked up to Popola and Devola. They coordinated all the rites, and they were always there to provide a helpful word or a shoulder to cry on. They were a constant source of advice, kindness, and warmth, yet it turned out that had merely been a method of control.

As Nier tried to take everything in, all signs of emotion vanished from Devola's face. "Right then! Let's skip the part where you stand there with your mouths agape and just get down to business. We're gonna be needing that shell of yours, because the rightful owner has been waiting a veeery long time."

Somewhere deep down, things were starting to make sense to Nier. The twins had told him where the Shadowlord's castle was, then sent him on a quest to collect the keys. All for a human who supposedly owned him unilaterally.

"Please don't be angry with us," Popola added. "We are only doing our duty."

"I *still* don't understand what your duty's supposed to be!"

Popola was done giving answers; she ignored the question and held her staff at the ready.

"You have your own motives," she stated. "Your own desires."

"And we have ours," added Devola, raising her own staff high. "I fear it really is just that simple."

"Don't speak such foolish-n-n-ness!" cried an irritated Weiss. Though his faltering speech made him sound like a child trying too hard, Devola lowered her head and whispered a single word of apology:

"Sorry."

A moment later, the twins sent a magic spear flying, the same one Weiss once conjured from the Sealed Verses.

"Please don't do this!" Nier screamed. Once his mother passed away, the twins had been his lifeline. Popola read books to Yonah. Devola cheered him when he was down. The two of them had practically *raised* the siblings.

"I don't want to do this! I don't want to fight you!"

"Those two have watched the world wither for time imme-morial," Grimoire Weiss remarked. "The cruelness of such a fate is difficult to imagine."

"But . . . but still . . ."

Thousands of spikes burst out from the ground around Nier's feet—another instance of magic Weiss has used countless times against the Shades. Nier quickly raised a magical barrier to block it, but in the next moment, the magic hand crashed down upon him.

"You cannot win this with defense alone!" Grimoire Weiss shouted to him. Devola and Popola were taking the fight seriously and were out for blood. Though it had taken Nier a long time, acceptance and realization of this fact finally came to him in that moment.

"I know!" he replied as he let fly a spear and magic bullets. Neither of the twins' expressions changed in the slightest; they sang as they cast spells and danced as they fired off magic. It was almost as if they weren't fighting people but merely dispatching animals—or Shades.

Nier recalled how Devola had called him a tool, then named herself the same. "No!" he cried suddenly. "I'm nothing like you!" He wasn't a *tool*. He wasn't a *vessel*. He loved his family, worried for his friends, and had hopes for the future. He was alive. He was *human*.

"Stop bitching and start fighting!" cried Kainé. "It's the only way!"

She laid her twin blades into their foe as Emil launched magic of his own. As his companions attacked, Nier raised his own blade high.

I have my friends—we belong to us. *I'm not giving that up or letting anyone steal it away!*

He fired off magic with the help of Weiss—whom he thought of as a partner and not a tool.

And then . . . a scream.

It was Popola. A volley of magic had pierced Devola and slammed her to the ground.

"Devola?!" Popola howled as she fell to her knees beside her sister. "*DEVOLA!*"

Popola lifted Devola's limp body in her arms and desperately began to shake her. Worry filled Nier's heart, along with pain and sadness. At the same time, he'd been attacked, so he had fought back. He'd thought they were going to kill him, so he had responded in kind. He'd matched their earnestness, and the result was fatal.

"Devola!"

"Are you crying?" Devola finally replied, her voice terribly weak.

"No . . ." Popola whimpered. "Don't die . . ."

Popola's tears spilled onto Devola's face, rolling down her cheeks and to the floor. The effect made it seem as if the injured sister was the one who was crying.

"You know, Popola, I understand now why we're twins . . . It's because . . . because we were born without souls . . ."

"Devola, I can't stop the bleeding. Oh god, I can't stop it!"

"This world is too . . . *lonely* for one without a soul. There's too much . . . emptiness."

Devola reached up and wiped away the cascade of tears on her sister's face with a trembling finger. "Our souls are missing, yet somehow our tears still work . . . It's kinda weird . . ."

"Devola? Devola! Don't you go!"

"Sorry, Sis. I . . . love you . . ."

"No!" cried Popola as she shook her sister's still form. "No, don't go! I can't be alone!"

Despite her sister's pleas, Devola's hand fell limp on her chest. Her eyes slowly slipped shut. She took a breath, then another, and then there was nothing at all.

"DEVOLAAAAAAA!"

Popola had always been so calm and composed—Nier had never seen her unleash her emotions like this. It was a horrifying sight he wished he'd never had to witness.

"Popola, let's stop this now," he offered as he lowered his sword. If they kept fighting, one of them would surely die. He didn't want to die, much less watch it happen to someone else. He was done.

Popola's head snapped up.

"Stop? *Stop?* Now you want to *stop?*"

Despite being a mess of tears, Popola had a sharp and dangerous glint in her eyes.

"You think you have the luxury to *stop?* You cut down my sister like a goddamn animal and now you want to *STOP?!*"

Her eyes began to glimmer with madness. There came a sound, then—a peculiar noise from deep within her throat that could have been a sob or laughter.

"No one *stops!* It's way too late to *stop!*"

A whorl of magic enveloped Popola as her powers reached a frenzy.

"Popola, wait!" Emil called out. He could tell she wouldn't be able to maintain this at this rate. "It doesn't have to—"

"NO ONE STOOOOOOPS!"

Nier begged her again not to fight, but her maddened laughter drowned out his plea. Rampaging magic swelled, shaking the entire room. Cracks split the floor at his feet as the glass in every window shattered.

"Blast!" Grimoire Weiss exclaimed as the bridge leading up and out began to give way, showering them with debris. "We're t-t-trapped!"

"I've got an idea!" Emil exclaimed. He lifted his staff, causing a ball of magic to envelop the four of them. The spell quickly took the form of a transparent cocoon that slowly lifted them into the air and safely through Popola's storm of arcane energy.

"*No stopping EVER!*" Popola screamed.

Nier sensed fierce power and vindictiveness emanating from

her; the magic she'd cast earlier was child's play in comparison. As she spread her arms wide, a dark power in the form of tendrils lashed out and grasped the cocoon, arresting its progress.

"I fear we're done for!" Grimoire Weiss yelled.

"It'll be all right," Emil responded calmly. He turned to look at Kainé, then Nier, before speaking again.

"You know, when I was young, I hated my eyes. And now that I'm older, I hate what my body has become. But there's something else there now. Something like . . . pride. You know? I mean, without all this, I couldn't have become your friend."

He paused, looking at the rest of them in turn.

"Goodbye, my friends. Thank you for everything."

"Emil?" said Nier hesitantly.

"For so long, all I could do was destroy. But now I have a chance to save something."

Nier suddenly realized what Emil was trying to do. He knew he had to stop him, but Kainé reached out first.

"No!" she cried as her hands grasped futilely at empty air.

"Now, get going, okay?"

The magic cocoon shuddered and pitched in midair. As Emil slipped free of its grasp, dark tendrils began to envelop him from all angles.

"Emil, you jackass!" cried Kainé.

"Don't worry about me. I'm gonna be fine!"

He brandished his staff, pushing the cocoon farther away as the tentacles dragged him back toward the earth.

Grimoire Weiss shouted his name in the loudest voice he could manage, Kainé kicked wildly at the inside of the cocoon, and Nier slammed his fist against it over and over. But there was nothing he could do—there was nothing *any* of them could do. Kicking and screaming meant nothing against the magic of the world's most powerful weapon, and the cocoon simply floated gently away. Eventually it reached the upper floor of a neighboring building, where Nier continued to scream until his throat was raw.

Through the noise and turmoil, he thought he heard Popola roar with laughter. At the same time, he saw an impossibly dark magic swell in the distance—one Popola was using all of her remaining power to create. It enveloped the entirety of the building for a moment, then suddenly winked out as if it had never been there at all.

There was no more Popola. No Devola. No Emil. All that remained was a dark and empty void where all of them used to be.

7.

"IN THE YEAR 2003, a red dragon appeared over the skies of Tokyo as a white giant materialized in Shinjuku. This was the beginning of everything."

The corridor was long. Every time there was a break in the waves of enemies, Grimoire Weiss would recount the details of Project Gestalt. For Nier's part, he simply listened quietly. The pain of losing Emil was hard to bear, and he couldn't find the energy to speak. Kainé was the same, and the two of them plodded forward in complete silence.

"The red dragon killed the white giant before being shot down by something called the Self-Defense Force. As the dragon fell, it was impaled on a red radio tower; I hear it took a considerable amount of resources to remove the remains."

A red tower. A scene flashed in the back of Nier's mind of a strange, swordlike tower. He felt like he'd seen it somewhere before. Was it in a dream? Or something else?

"Is anything the matter, lad?"

"Nothing. Keep going."

He was imagining things. Or perhaps it was an illusion shown to him by a Shade in the Forest of Myth.

"Upon dying, the red dragon spewed out a previously unknown substance called Maso, which introduced two things to our world: magic and a disease known as white chlorination syndrome."

Nier remembered what Popola had said: *This was done in order to survive white chlorination syndrome.*

"As the name suggests, white chlorination syndrome was a disease that turned humans into salt. There was no cure nor a way to prevent it from running unchecked. One by one, the people of the world began transforming into salt."

Another sight arose unbidden in Nier's mind: a thick layer of salt strewn across the ground. Perhaps these were memories of the one to whom his body originally belonged. Although, who could say if it was possible to inherit memories from a time before he was even born?

"A few rare individuals survived the illness without turning into salt. These poor souls would soon lose their sense of self and turn into monsters that attacked indiscriminately. Such creatures quickly became known as Legion."

Sounds a lot like Shades, Nier mused. That meant the people of the time must have agonized over how to deal with the newfound foes, much like he and his friends worried about the damage caused by Shades.

"And so, various research institutes were established to find a way to rid humanity of both white chlorination syndrome and Legion. There were a small number of proponents for Project Gestalt, but they lacked both voice and influence in the beginning. Furthermore, the project's research had run into something of a snag."

Weiss went on to explain that while separating a soul from the physical body was technically possible, such separated souls quickly lost all sense of self. It was a problem for which researchers had no solution. Gestalts who lost their sense of self were considered to have relapsed, and there was no meaning in returning them to their physical body once that happened.

The researchers, however, continued to experiment on live

human subjects in secret, and at last found a case where the separated soul did not relapse.

"That was the only successful case, however," intoned Weiss. "Though the experiments continued, all subsequent subjects relapsed. Progression for a blood relative of the successful subject is rather slow going, so that case did not reach total relapse. Both subjects, however, are outliers, and it is likely there is a genetic component to their unusual qualities."

"Hold on," Nier interjected. "You said the progression *is* slow going? Not *was?*"

"Indeed. She is essentially being kept in a state of mid-relapse."

"She?"

"Yes. The successful subject's little sister is currently preserved in cryosleep. The older brother—the only successful case in the project thus far—wanted so desperately to save his kin that he made a deal with the research institute."

The successful test subject possessed a unique type of Maso, and the researchers soon realized they could prevent others from relapse by having them absorb it. Knowing this, the research facility approached the subject with terms: If he allowed them to extract his Maso, they would devote all of their resources to finding a way to restore relapsing Gestalts. Though it would not happen for hundreds or even thousands of years, once the world was free of white chlorination syndrome and Legion, humanity would be revived, and the boy and his sister could be together once more.

"Thus was Project Gestalt put into motion. Gestalts survived thanks to the boy's Maso, and they soon came to worship him."

And why not, seeing as he held the fate of all Gestalts in the palm of his hand? Maso was connected to the donor's mental state even after being harvested, so even if it was taken when the subject was doing well, it didn't mean things would remain that way. If the donor's psychological state ever grew unstable, any Gestalts that absorbed the Maso would likewise grow volatile. And if the original donor happened to lose his mind, any Gestalt in possession of his Maso would lose their sense of self and relapse.

"The one thing they wanted to avoid at all costs was relapse."

"Why?"

"Because relapsed Gestalts cannot return to their human form. Do you remember The Aerie?"

Nier nodded. How could he ever forget seeing all those villagers possessed by Shades? Watching regular villagers having regular conversations suddenly morph into Shades had been a nauseating sight.

"That is what happens when the body rejects a relapsed soul. One may try to force the two together, but they immediately separate."

Which was why the research institute not only requested that the test subject provide Maso but that he remain mentally stable as he continued to live far into the future. The reason Gestalts began to worship him was to ensure he remained sane—which was the only way they themselves could continue to live.

"But things do not always go as planned. A thousand years is a long time—too long, in this humble tome's opinion—to be separated from one's beloved sister. Who could blame him if such solitude began to eat away at him? No matter what he does, he cannot stave off the loneliness that comes from the absence of his kin."

"Even if he was worshiped as a king?"

"Even so." Grimoire Weiss nodded.

It was all clear now: The king of the Gestalts was the king of the Shades, as well as the single successful test subject. And that man . . . was the Shadowlord.

"It seems the Shadowlord's psychological state has rapidly declined these past few years. The proof lies in how the Gestalts that absorbed his Maso have now begun to relapse."

Ever since that fateful day five years ago, there had been a marked increase in Shades—and an increase in their ferocity. Once that thought crossed Nier's mind, he felt his heart practically leap out of his chest.

"The Shadowlord had a little sister . . ."

"I believe you may have pieced it together already, but they say her name is Yonah."

Now everything truly fell into place. The Shadowlord stole Yonah away because that was his sister's body. And the reason Devola and Popola had called Nier a shell was because he was the Shadowlord's . . .

"Is the Shadowlord trying to return to a human form along with his sister?"

"Very likely."

"I bet Devola and Popola knew everything, huh? They must have really been laughing at me when I was searching so desperately for Yonah. I bet they've been laughing for the past five years."

All Nier could find within himself after learning why Yonah had been taken—where she was and what she was doing—was a painful silence. It was as if he'd been shattered into a thousand pieces.

"Not necessarily so, lad," said Weiss. "It's likely what happened five years ago was the Shadowlord acting out erratically of his own accord—the twins could well have had nothing to do with it. In fact, if they did, they'd likely have brought us here sooner. All the conditions for humanity's revival have been met after all."

"And what are those?"

"White chlorination syndrome is a dead disease, and Legion has been stamped out. These two things ensure humanity's survival. Once all was in order, it was the duty of myself and Grimoire Noir to activate the program that would return the humans—who are presently Gestalts—back to their physical bodies."

Was that even possible? No, that was a silly question—Project Gestalt had taken off because humans from a millennium ago had decided in the affirmative. They'd not even considered that the Shadowlord might lose his sanity, resulting in their fellow humans losing their senses of self.

"Hold on!" Nier exclaimed. Grimoire Weiss had just told him that relapsed Gestalts could not return to their human state. Which meant . . .

"So if Gestalts relapse, they can't go back to their bodies, right? That means we, um . . ."

He carefully considered his word choice; he didn't want to call himself and his friends Replicants and the Gestalts their owners.

"I know what you are considering, but unfortunately, no. Once a Gestalt relapses, the Replicant dies of the Black Scrawl."

"What?!"

"Gestalt and Replicant were originally a single entity. When a Gestalt relapses, the corresponding Replicant develops the Black Scrawl. There has been a significant increase in hostile Shades of late, no? The rise in Black Scrawl cases began at around the same time. The causal relationship between the two should be quite clear to all."

Now that Weiss mentioned it, Nier realized the Black Scrawl *was* considered an unusual disease back when Yonah caught it. While their mother, the lighthouse lady, and the previous king of Facade had succumbed to it, it remained a rather uncommon occurrence.

But lately, every village and town had a patient or two. Though it remained a terrible—and terminal—illness, it was now a depressingly common one.

"Due to my memory loss," continued Weiss, "I'd not realized the true significance in the rise of Black Scrawl cases."

"Yeah. And the Shadowlord's little sister was relapsing, even though that had been stopped in its tracks."

Which was why Yonah developed the Black Scrawl.

"But wait," Nier said. "Does that mean she'll never be cured?"

If they couldn't prevent the Shadowlord's sister from relapsing, Yonah would have to live with the Black Scrawl forever.

"That can't be," he said to himself. "There *must* be a way. I just have to think. I'll figure something out."

Grimoire Weiss did not reply. Instead, it was Kainé who spoke.

"Yeah, yeah, blah, blah, enough with the chitchat. I sense a Shade nearby. It's incredibly large, incredibly powerful, and it's right fucking *there*."

She pointed to a door, then turned back to stare at them. Nothing else needed to be said: What lay behind it was clearly the Shadowlord.

"All right," Nier replied. "Then let's go kill him already."

He could think about everything else once he finally had Yonah back.

8.

THE ROOM WAS large, open, and somewhat odd.

I'm sick of big rooms, Kainé thought.

And yet there was something about the place that set it apart from all the others they'd come across so far. Long curtains covered the wall from floor to ceiling. Every so often, a ripple would run through them, revealing not walls but windows; a breeze from outside was causing the fabric to flutter. Though they moved, they were thick enough to block all incoming light.

And there was one more thing: At the far end of the room, in the very, very back, was a small bed with a figure lying atop it.

"Yonah!"

Nier dashed forward. He seemed barely able to believe he'd finally found his sister. But Kainé held back and scanned the room, searching for the Shade whose presence she felt everywhere.

A dark shape suddenly fell across the floor, as though telling Nier he was not allowed any closer. As it began to swirl, Nier stopped in his tracks and drew his sword, while Kainé braced herself. The moment she knew *something* was coming, the Shadowlord and Grimoire Noir appeared from within the writhing swirls.

"How could a mere tool hope to stand against our Shadowlord?!" boomed the unforgettable voice of Grimoire Noir.

"Fool!" snapped Grimoire Weiss. "Don't speak in such a

manner! I am nothing like you!" He then turned to Nier and commanded, "Strike hard! Hold nothing back!"

Nier nodded firmly. "This ends here!"

Nier rushed at the Shadowlord, but Grimoire Noir blocked his path. Magic poured from his open pages, thousands of blades flying straight at Nier. He knocked back and dodged as many as he could, but many found their way through. Before they could cut him to ribbons, Kainé leaped into the fray and used her own blades to knock away the incoming missiles.

"Careful!" she shouted.

"I know!"

It was times like these that Emil would come to the rescue. If Kainé or Nier recklessly ran into a fight, he would protect them. If they got hurt, he would hurry to heal them. It had been such a given—such a *habit*—that Nier and Kainé had adopted a reckless fighting style in response. But perhaps they would not have survived for as long as they did if they hadn't.

As Kainé turned her blades against the magic barrier surrounding Grimoire Noir, Nier and Weiss fired off bolts of magic. While the book roared in anger, Nier brought his blade down on him again and again and again. As his sword rose and fell, Kainé continued to support him with magic. But this only made it more obvious that Emil was gone.

"*Hey, Sunshine?*" came Tyrann's voice. "*I ain't certain about this, but I think your heart is . . . evolving.*"

Meh. Who cares?

Tyrann's words washed over her as she continued to fight.

"*The hate is gone. The sadness is gone. It's just a buncha white light now. What the hell's goin' on here?!*"

You can't tell, Tyrann?

She could feel the corner of her own mouth curling into a smile.

You're not the only voice in my life anymore. I've experienced fear, hate . . . and now sympathy.

The barrier around Grimoire Noir shattered.

I'm a curse. A freak. I know that.

The blades protecting him vanished.

But guess what. He still accepts me. He still forgives *me.*

"You're doin' this for him?"

Kaihé nodded as she brought her full might down on the black book.

I'm tired of this world and everybody in it. But I'll become his sword one last time!

Kaihé watched Grimoire Noir sink to the floor as Nier followed up with magic to obliterate him for good. The tome howled like an animal as his pages fluttered through the air before vanishing on the wind.

Only one enemy remained.

9.

NIER LOOKED UP to see wings the color of darkness and flame undulating above him.

"Shadowlord . . ."

The writhing outlines, typical of a Shade, looked like a silhouette on a wall. He could feel the Shadowlord's eyes, and even though he couldn't see the features of his face, he knew the king of the Shades was glowering at him.

They both fired off magic at the same time. Spell clashed with spell, creating shock waves in the air.

Nier dashed in with his blade, but the Shadowlord blocked it with a sword that suddenly appeared in his hands. As they sparred, Nier noticed the Shadowlord attacked with movements similar to his own and also used a familiar defensive stance. It was a terribly uncomfortable experience; as much as Nier hated to admit it, it felt like fighting himself.

Kainé fired magic at the Shadowlord as he glided through the air. The moment his altitude dipped, Nier leaped at him, bringing his sword down on the enemy while dodging magic bullets.

The difference in strength between them had been overwhelming five years ago, but now Nier scarcely noticed it. It had been an insurmountable hurdle then, but now it was nothing—and Nier knew the Shadowlord had not weakened in that time. As Grimoire Weiss was wont to say, *You've grown strong, lad.*

He thought back on how he had gained this strength and

realized it was the years he'd been ripped apart from Yonah that had allowed him to grow strong. When he considered this devil's bargain, the rage and hatred inside him swelled anew.

He was going to kill the Shadowlord—for Yonah's sake. He didn't care what he had to give up in exchange or what might happen to the people who used to be human. He didn't care what might become of the world. Such things weren't his problem.

This was all for Yonah.

He narrowly dodged another shower of bullets as he made his way toward his goal. His blade sliced at the red-and-black wings before plunging into the body covered in writhing black patterns.

The Shadowlord staggered. Nier cut him again. Even if his foe tried to block or dodge or even run, he would never relent.

At last, the Shadowlord fell to his knees. Just one more. One more hit, and the Shadowlord's life would be forfeit. Nier tightened his grip on the handle of his blade and . . .

"Wait!"

It was a familiar voice, and Nier froze despite himself. When he whirled around, he saw Yonah sitting up in bed. She dropped her feet to the floor and slowly made her way toward them on unsteady legs.

"H-hey."

Her voice was a reminder of simpler days. How many times had he heard it in his dreams?

"Yonah . . ."

She's all grown up, Nier thought. Her hair was longer, and her cherubic, childlike face had matured into that of a young lady.

Nier reached for her as she walked toward him. When was the last time he'd caught her in an embrace as she leaped into his arms, shouting how much she had missed him?

But then, a most unexpected thing happened: She did not leap for him. Nier's eyes went wide. His gaze dropped first to his own empty hand, then back to Yonah as she walked right past him.

"Brother . . ."

She was speaking to the *Shadowlord*.

"Just stop. Please. I . . . I don't want this anymore."

She gazed down at him, watching as his wounds left him crawling miserably on the ground.

"I don't need someone else's body. I don't want it."

In that moment, Nier finally understood: It wasn't Yonah who was speaking but the Shadowlord's sister.

"There's another girl inside this body. I can hear her. She won't stop crying. She says she wants to see her brother."

It was *Yonah* who was crying. His precious, only little sister— the one for whom he'd been searching so tirelessly.

"This girl loves her brother as much as I do. It's not right that she can't see him."

At last, the Shadowlord's sister turned to look at Nier.

"It's you. Isn't it?"

Nier sheathed his sword; he didn't want to frighten the other Yonah, even if she was the Shadowlord's sister. As he did, the Shadowlord howled something he couldn't understand.

"Yes," Nier replied. "It's me. Let's go home."

He gently extended his hand to her, and the other Yonah nodded. The expression on her face told him she knew exactly what that meant. She then began to walk toward the window. The curtains fluttered as the small, delicate hand grasped the fabric.

The Shadowlord howled again. He seemed to be desperately reaching for her, but he couldn't move—and yet he clearly wanted to stop her. Even though Nier couldn't understand his words, he could tell that much.

The other Yonah turned to look at them.

"I'm sorry. I'm just so very sorry."

The curtains flew open. Light flooded the room as black mist began to seep from her small frame.

"Just know that . . . I love you."

For a brief second, the black mist took the form of a person. Then it dissolved into nothingness and drifted away on the breeze.

"Hurry!" Kainé shouted. "The Shade that possessed her is gone!"

The other Yonah—the Shadowlord's sister—had walked into the sunlight and chosen death. The Yonah who remained staggered and fell to the floor, but Nier reached out and caught her on the way down. He was shocked to realize how thin and light she was.

The Shadowlord wailed. He gripped the floor and squeezed out all the air inside him, unleashing the entirety of his self in a blizzard of noise and rage. Magic whirled around him, much as it had Popola in the moments before her own death. And if that was the case, they were in danger; without Emil, they had no way to combat such an attack.

"Watch over Yonah for me, Kainé!"

Nier had to put a stop to this before the magic went out of control. He drew his sword, intending to end the Shadowlord for good this time.

"You want me to understand your pain?" he growled. "You think I'm going to sympathize with you?"

The Shadowlord screamed. He sobbed. Even though they didn't share the same pain, Nier could still guess what he was about to do.

With unsteady movements, the Shadowlord got to his feet. Despite scarcely being able to act moments before, he managed to take a series of staggering steps. At first, Nier thought his bright crimson eyes were looking directly at him, but then he realized they were boring into Yonah.

Nier and Weiss unleashed a barrage of magic that sent the Shadowlord flying, yet he still clambered to his feet and attempted to walk. Nier had no idea what the king of Shades was trying to say, but he *did* know he was after Yonah. His little sister had been taken away, and now he was trying to get her back.

"I swore to protect my sister and my friends!" cried Nier as he conjured a magic hand to slam down on his opponent.

The Shadowlord stood again. It was a miracle he remained on his feet, yet he kept going. His body was oddly angled in one direction, but still he walked.

"If someone puts them in danger, they must stand aside or be cut down!"

But no matter how much magic Nier shot at him, the Shadowlord would not relent.

Suddenly, the air around the king of the Shades changed color and formed into a barrier of red and black. His wings, which should have been broken, unfurled with a horrifying noise. The twisted, crooked wings flapped, carrying the Shadowlord into the air, almost as though telling Nier he would remain forever out of reach. As Nier pondered this new development, a strained burst of static rang out beside him.

"Weiss!" Nier shouted. "What's wrong?!"

It was no ordinary noise—Weiss was groaning in pain.

"F-f-fine! All is weeeeell . . . W-w-wellllll . . ."

"You're freaking me out here, Weiss!"

Nier provided cover for the tome while dodging a deluge of magic bullets from the Shadowlord.

"Wh-wh-what are you doing?! To come so f-f-far . . . D-d-do it! Strike the k-k-killing blow!"

Nier could tell that the tome was mustering everything he

had to scold him, but he was so concentrated on fighting off his opponent's magic, he couldn't possibly move to the offensive.

This is bad. At this rate . . .

Before Nier could finish the thought, a light bloomed from Grimoire Weiss, and he dropped to the floor.

"It seems some headstrong idiot has decided to push me beyond my limits. I should have taken that job as a cookbook when I had the chance."

Nier knew he'd pushed Grimoire Weiss beyond his limits by how strange he'd been acting this entire time.

"Weiss, I'm sorry. I just—"

"Only joking. I hate cookbooks."

The tome slowly took to the air again.

"Let's go, out of the way! I have one final task to fulfill."

"Where are you . . . ?"

Weiss didn't answer. Instead, he moved between Nier and the Shadowlord, filling the space with that strange, brilliant light.

"Where am I going? Why, to stop him, of course."

As the light grew brighter, Nier belatedly noticed it was swallowing up a great number of magic bullets.

"But the rest is up to you. Only you can see this battle to its conclusion. I wish you luck . . . my friend."

Nier felt like crying. He had lost an irreplaceable companion, as well as two women he looked up to like sisters. He *couldn't* lose Grimoire Weiss now, the partner who had been by his side from the very beginning.

"You can't! I swore to fight by—"

"Bah! You are an exceedingly stubborn lad. You know that, yes?"

When next he spoke, Weiss's tone was almost blithe. "Perhaps that's why I've so enjoyed our time together."

Me too, Nier thought. Though theirs had been a life of

constant danger, Weiss had been a reliable ally in that regard since Nier was a young boy. And once Yonah was taken and he was spurred on a journey of anger and hate, only the presence of Weiss had allowed him to maintain some semblance of human emotion.

"But I fear this is where our journey ends."

"Weiss!"

"Oh, and remember what I told you about using my full name?"

The light around the tome grew brighter; Nier could barely make out his friend beyond the brilliant glowing veil.

"Well, forget it. I've grown rather fond of Weiss."

"I knew you'd come around," said Nier as he forced the corners of his mouth upward into a smile. He didn't know if it looked good or not, but he was going to try. If he couldn't stop his friend, he could at least do that much.

"Don't let it go to your head, now."

Grimoire Weiss's tone was the same as it had been whether they were chatting leisurely aboard the ferry or strolling around town. Nier couldn't believe it was all about to come to an end.

But end it did. There was a blinding flash of light as Grimoire Weiss scattered, and his separated pages become a torrent that rushed the Shadowlord. As the enemy collapsed with a scream, Nier thought he heard Weiss yell one final word:

"NOW!"

Nier didn't hesitate. He leaped forward, sword in hand.

"I have something to defend! I have a reason to live!"

He wasn't a tool. His body was more than just a vessel for a soul. And he was going to keep *living*.

The tip of Nier's blade caught on the abyssal form of the Shadowlord. The force against his hand was no different from the other countless Shades he'd killed; once he'd cut through, a dreadful shock wave erupted in response. Black wings crumbled to the ground. The barrier around his foe vanished without a trace. All that remained was a young man on his knees with slumped shoulders.

The Shadowlord.

The other Nier.

Nier plunged his blade straight down. Blood rushed out, and then the body became dust and was no more.

10.

AFTER CALLING AND calling and calling for Yonah, she finally woke up.

"Is that . . . you?"

This was Yonah. She sat up in Kainé's arms as Nier helped her to her feet. *She's grown*, he thought once more.

"Is this . . . my body?"

Bewildered by the change in her vantage point, she lifted her hands, picked up her feet, and tilted her head.

"Yes. It's yours—and yours alone."

It wasn't a vessel for a Gestalt. *Yonah* owned that body.

She looked up at Nier quizzically. "You look bigger than before. Like you've grown up."

"Well, yeah, I guess you haven't seen me for a while."

Five years had passed since she'd been taken away, and he was so happy he could now call that time period "a while."

"Have I been asleep?"

"Something like that."

"Wow. It's almost like I'm a princess from some fairy tale."

While Yonah beamed and Nier pulled her into a hug, reality welled up inside him: He'd *finally* gotten her back. It was a moment he'd so often seen in his dreams, and he held on to it with everything he had.

Then the sound of quiet footsteps reached his ears. Nier lifted his head to see Kainé walking away. She stopped when he called her name but didn't turn around.

"You and your sister . . . You have a good life, okay?"

"Where are you gonna go? You could stay with—"

Us was what he'd been going to say, but Kainé's forceful tone cut him off.

"Thanks, but I'll pass. You know how it is. I got my own shit to take care of."

"What do you mean?"

"Personal shit, all right? Anyway, take it easy, yeah?"

She briefly glanced over her shoulder before setting off again. Was she worried about her possession? Did she really think she needed to care about something so trivial anymore? It wasn't like Devola and Popola were around to keep her out of the village.

As Nier opened his mouth to call for her again, Yonah tugged sharply on his arm and pointed out the window.

"Hey, look! It's beautiful!"

The skies were clear. There wasn't a single cloud, and the sun's rays shone brightly overhead. Nier had come to dislike blue skies while searching for Yonah, because cloudy days made for better Shade hunting. Sunny days were inefficient, which annoyed him—especially since the Shadowlord had flown off in just such weather. But as he looked up to the brilliant azure sky now, he genuinely thought it was beautiful. It was a hard-earned sentiment indeed.

For a brief moment, Nier forgot about Kainé; he was enraptured by the sight beyond the window as he stood beside Yonah. Had there been no unusual sounds behind him, he might never have remembered her. What a cruel thought.

But there *did* come sounds: a groan, followed by a hard thud. When Nier whirled around, he saw Kainé crumpled on the floor, the left half of her body shuddering. She seemed to be attempting to stand, but her hands simply scrabbled across the slick floor in a search for purchase.

"What is it?!" cried Nier. He rushed over and lifted her up. Her breathing was ragged.

"The Shade inside of me is growing . . . and I can't stop it. Soon—*real* soon—I'm gonna go berserk."

Black patterns spread across her body, moving from her limbs up to her face. It was the same as when she turned into a Shade and lost control back at the Lost Shrine.

"Kainé, you have to fight! You have to—"

"Just shut up and listen to me! Emil is gone, which means there's no way anyone can stop me. So before it comes to that, I want you to kill me."

"*No!*"

He'd killed the Shadowlord. He'd gotten Yonah back. Things were just getting started. Life was coming back. This *couldn't* happen now.

Nier grasped her blackened hand. He had to stop this precisely *because* Emil wasn't around anymore. Without Grimoire Weiss, Kainé was his only friend left.

"I am who I am today because of *you*!" he cried. "I'm not going to give up on you!"

As black patterns encroached over her entire body, he held her tighter and screamed, "I'm going to save you. I swear it!"

But then came a voice.

"There might be one way to save her."

"Who said that?!"

"Just shut up and listen."

The voice was compelling. It almost felt like it was coming from inside his own head while simultaneously emerging from the patterns on Kainé's skin.

"Wait, are you—"

"*I said* listen!*"

This was the Shade possessing Kainé. Nier was sure of it.

"*There's a way to save Kainé's life, all right? But you're gonna have to make a difficult decision.*"

"I'll do whatever it takes!"

"*One way is to plunge your sword into her chest. That's what she wants after all. Freedom from burdens. Freedom from life.*"

"What's the other way?"

"*The other way is to make her a normal human being again. But to make that happen, you gotta trade your own existence for hers.*"

"Is that even possible?!"

Could they really make Kainé a normal human again? Grimoire Weiss had told him relapsed Gestalts couldn't go back, just as there was no cure for the Black Scrawl.

"*Sure it is! Oh, uh, but you'll disappear from the world. Your sister? Your wittle fwiends? Everybody in your life will forget you. You—and any sign you ever existed—will be erased.*"

That's it? Nier thought. *What's wrong with that?*

He'd been prepared to give his life for this fight since day one; he could not have carried on without that conviction. And yet, after losing Emil and Weiss, he knew the pain of being left behind. If all proof of his existence were to vanish—if everyone he'd ever met forgot about him—he was okay with that. In fact, it might even be *better* if Yonah and Kainé never had to live with the pain of losing him.

"Make Kainé human again."

"*Well, THAT was easy! Kyaaaa ha ha ha!*"

"You're the Shade inside Kainé, right? Why are you trying to help her?"

"*You mean 'cause no Shade would ever try to help a real person? Good question, kid. See, I spent yeeeears inside Kainé's body.*"

Tormenting her from within. But now . . . Well, I guess I'm helpin' her for the same reason you are."

The Shade's tone became dubious.

"So, uh, ya sure you wanna trust me on this? No questions or doubts or nothin'?"

"Yeah. I trust you."

"But why?"

The Shade said it had spent years tormenting Kainé, but that wasn't all it did. Had it brought pain and nothing else, she wouldn't have wrapped the left side of her body in bandages to keep it out of the sun. There was no way she lived with the Shade for years *solely* to take advantage of its power. There had been some kind of connection that couldn't be explained by common cause alone. And if Kainé had been able to trust it that far, Nier figured he could do the same.

"Of course I trust you," Nier said again. "For the same reason you trust me."

Emancipation

THERE WAS LIGHT. Even with her eyes closed, she could tell it was bright. When she eventually lifted her lids, it stung with surprising ferocity.

As Kainé slowly pushed herself into a seated position, she realized it wasn't as bright as she had first thought. It only felt that way because she'd opened her eyes so suddenly.

But where *was* she?

She felt as if she'd been through something similar before. Once, she'd awoken in a building with no roof—a library. It had been a lot like this, in fact, but . . .

Nope. No good. Her mind wasn't working like she wanted it to. Had she been hit on the head?

A moment later, she heard the soft tapping of bare feet on tile. Before she could turn to see who it was, a voice spoke:

"Are you all right?"

It was a girl, a familiar one who was peering at Kainé with worry. What was her name again? Kainé desperately forced the molasses in her brain to move around and eventually found the answer.

". . . Yonah?"

That was the girl's name, all right, but Kainé had no idea how she knew that.

"Are you the one who helped me?" the girl asked.

Helped her? Helped *Yonah*? Why? With what?

But Kainé *had* helped the girl: She saved her from the clutches of the Shadowlord after he stole her away.

That's right. She was in the Shadowlord's castle, and she had defeated him . . . Probably.

Kainé's eyes roamed her surroundings. She didn't sense any Shades, which meant the Shadowlord was definitely gone. But somehow it just didn't feel *real*.

She must have hit her head; that was the only way to explain why everything was so fuzzy. All she could remember was a barrage of magic bullets, the Shadowlord with his wings spread in the air, and . . .

"You hurt?" Kainé asked.

Yonah shook her head in a precious way that emphasized her still-childlike nature.

"Thank you so much!" she cried suddenly, the worry on her face replaced by a smile like a blooming flower. Seeing it, Kainé suddenly understood why someone would go to the ends of the earth to make her happy.

"I'm glad you're all right," replied Kainé.

I get it. This is how he *felt.*

The moment that thought crossed her mind, Kainé felt like she'd been thrown into a deep, thick fog. Whose memory was she trying to dredge up? Maybe it wasn't even a "who" but a "what." The harder she tried to remember, the more it seemed to slip through her fingers.

"What's wrong?" asked Yonah as she stared at Kainé with concern.

Huh. She reminds me of someone.

"I mean," Yonah continued, "you defeated the Shadowlord and everything, but you don't look . . . happy."

"I don't?" Kainé replied. "Huh. I guess saving people is a little out of character for me."

She was shocked when a jeering voice didn't interject after she spoke, and a moment later a flash of realization struck. She didn't even need to look at her left side to know that Tyrann was gone—the dark, writhing sensation she'd kept under wraps for so long had vanished without a trace.

Perhaps she hadn't noticed right away because the lack of Tyrann wasn't unpleasant. Indeed, the uncomfortable sensation and dull pain that had bothered her for ages—even in her sleep—was completely gone. If it had brought her discomfort instead, she would have noticed the moment she'd woken up.

Why did Tyrann leave? The room was bright, so to leave her body would mean his death. But Tyrann wasn't the kind of Shade to take his own life, nor the type to be easily forced out. Besides, Tyrann couldn't depart even if he wanted to; he'd resided in her body for so long, he'd become unable to leave it.

Whatever happened, it was something beyond Kainé's imagining. Tyrann was gone—that much was certain—yet she couldn't remember *why*. And it wasn't just her memories surrounding the fight with the Shadowlord that were affected—there were holes all across her recollection of the journey to this place. Hell, even memories from months or *years* ago were like moth-eaten sweaters hanging—

"This is a Lunar Tear! How pretty!"

Yonah's voice drew her back to reality. The girl had plucked the flower from the ground with a cry of joy.

The myth of the Lunar Tear claimed it could make a wish come true. Long ago, Kainé's grandmother had found one blooming on the outskirts of their village, plucked it, dried it, and made it into a hairpin for her granddaughter. The one Kainé wore now wasn't the same—it was a little crooked, a bit lopsided. But she knew someone had worked hard to make it for her all the same . . .

The petals of the white flower suddenly blurred in her vision as clear drops fell onto the blossom.

"Are you crying?" Yonah asked.

"Uh, yeah," Kainé replied. "I guess I am."

Though she couldn't remember, her tears didn't stop. All her memories surrounding the hairpin had vanished, but it seemed whatever mechanism controlled her tears knew exactly what it meant.

"It's like I just found something special. Something . . . very special."

She couldn't help the overwhelming loneliness inside her. Though she felt that she'd found something special, she also felt she'd lost something equally so. She was free of her Shade-wrought body, but at the price of something else being bound to her.

Kainé stood. Though her balance was unsteady, she was otherwise unharmed.

"What's wrong?"

She turned to see Yonah looking up at her with unease. Was the girl experiencing the same feelings of strangeness as she was? Kainé was about to ask what was wrong, but she stopped. She didn't want to make her unease worse if she didn't have to. Kainé couldn't abide the idea of causing this girl concern.

Kainé grasped Yonah's hand. "C'mon. Let's go home."

She would bring Yonah home. That was her first task—the first mission she had been entrusted with. And once that was done, she would venture out on a search, even though she had no idea where to go or even *what* she was searching for.

But she had to go, and quickly. Before it was too late.

Thus decided, Kainé tightened her hand around the smaller one within it, and she began to walk.

REPORT XX1

Due to android recklessness in Precinct XXXX, both the Original Gestalt "Nier" and the ignitions system for the merger program, Grimoires Weiss and Noir, have been lost. As a result, we are no longer able to proceed with Project Gestalt.

What caused the Devola and Popola model androids from the above precinct to lose control of themselves remains unknown. It may have been a fault with their programming or perhaps the result of some initial defect. Regardless, the possibility of the same phenomena occurring in other androids of the same model is now a very real concern. From this point forward, all Devola and Popola model androids will be suspended and placed under observation in consideration of future disposal.

Additionally, disposal of Replicant residents in the above precinct is currently on hold. Any intervention is to be minimal while observation of the increasing number of relapses in other precincts is being carried out. The reestablishment of Project Gestalt will be detailed in a different publication. End report.

Report written by Devola

Rebirth

1.

——'S VOICE POURED in with the light.

"Don't give up, Kainé! You're stronger than that!"

Give up? Give up on what?

"Don't you dare give up now!"

The voice tugged at her memory for reasons she couldn't understand.

Warmth was approaching. It was a comfortable warmth—one she desperately wanted to touch—and she found herself reaching for it.

"This woman is more trouble than she's worth" came another voice.

A talking book, she thought.

Then it was gone.

That dream again.

Her awakening came abruptly, as it always did after the dream. She placed a hand to her cheek and found it damp. She'd been crying. Why? She didn't know. No, she *did* know—because the dream was sad. But she couldn't remember what kind of dream it was or why it had *been* so sad. All she knew was that it was a dream of overwhelming pain and grief.

She sat up and looked around. Her home was the same as it had always been: One sword sat nearby while the other lay abandoned. They were her twin blades—ones she'd used so often in the past. The blade of the second was snapped in half, broken during the heroic battle she'd waged against the Shadowlord.

. . . Or so she thought. But that memory was also strangely misty.

And then there was a staff—a memento she'd found on the ground on her way home from the battle with the Shadowlord.

"Emil . . ."

A precious friend who gave his life to . . .

Ah, but these memories were hazy too. Emil had protected her, and she had survived. This was fact, so why was her recollection so vague?

On the day she'd saved the girl called Yonah, Kainé had suddenly found herself crying. Tears had poured down her cheeks for reasons she didn't understand.

Why? Why am I crying?

For three long years, she had searched for the answer to that question.

"Guess it's time to kill some Shades," Kainé murmured to herself as she took up her sword. She stepped out from her abode and looked to the brilliant blue sky. Stony cliffs surrounded her home, giving her only a small glimpse of the blue, but the breeze was dry, which meant it would be perfect weather for hunting Shades. Luckily, the only Shades that found their way into sunlight were the strong ones clad in armor, not the weak ones.

Kainé always killed Shades when she had that dream, and only Shades so strong that she could fully devote herself to her swordwork. Sitting around moping at home would only make her depressed, and she'd doubtless find herself wondering if she'd forgotten something important when that was the last thing she wanted to be thinking about.

Was that "something important" the reason why the Shade, Tyrann, who had occupied the left side of her body ever since her grandmother died, had gone? Tyrann had definitely existed—she remembered the discomfort, unease, and dull pain that accompanied him. And yet she couldn't recall some things he had said. She had a feeling they'd engaged in a deep, serious conversation right before he vanished, yet all she could recall was his cackling laughter.

Kainé also had a feeling she'd kicked and grabbed at someone in the Shadowlord's castle but was never certain if that had actually happened or was simply a dream from the road.

And there was more. When Kainé took Yonah out of the Shadowlord's castle, she came across the bodies of masked soldiers. She'd sped past them, not wanting to frighten Yonah, but the sight of one body in particular had made her heart clench. Perhaps it was simply because that particular person had their mask askew, unlike the rest of the bodies. But was that truly enough to make her feel so uncomfortable? She didn't know the answer to that question.

These mysteries had remained unknown for three whole years. Life would have been easier if she could have simply forgotten them, but that would never happen. The haze in her mind and the repeated dreams remained as intense as the day they began. But weren't memories supposed to fade with time?

Kainé had memories she desperately wanted to remember and other memories she desperately wanted to *forget*. Each of these feelings constricted around her and refused to let her go.

When Kainé entered the northern plains, there were almost no Shades to be found. The smaller ones being absent was no surprise, but there were no armored ones either. Such days happened, she supposed. Not even Shades had the duty or obligation to appear regularly.

"Guess I'll go beat up some robots."

Robots roamed the halls of the Junk Heap regardless of the weather. As a bonus, Kainé could collect materials to sell to the weapon shop while she was there.

But Kainé had lost her superhuman recovery and healing power when Tyrann vanished and also couldn't use magic anymore. This meant being caught in an explosion had gone from a minor annoyance to a death sentence—and without the ability to attack from range, the Junk Heap was a very dangerous place. Still, the materials she harvested from the machines sold for good money, so she'd adopted a strategy of hitting them in their weak spots and leaping away as fast as she could.

Why do I know how to do this? Who taught me?

Fog clouded her mind again, causing the answer to slip through her fingers and vanish into the mist.

"Goddammit!"

She lent all her strength into destroying a nearby crate. At some point, she'd come to the metal bridge in front of the Junk Heap. Traversing the northern plains really was a quick and painless process without any Shades around.

She clambered up a ladder, leaped over crates, and climbed more ladders. It was a bothersome route, but she had no other way to reach the Junk Heap. Once she crossed the bridge, the familiar fence and gate came into view—but today, things were slightly different.

"Is that a sign?"

The scrawled writing on the sign read:

REGARDING THE CLOSURE OF THE JUNK HEAP

We've discovered that the number of robots being produced in the Junk Heap has been increasing with each passing year. For safety purposes, passage beyond this point is now forbidden.

—Two Brothers Weaponry

"Goddammit," muttered Kainé as she rattled the locked gate on its hinges. "Came all this way for nothing."

The guy who ran the shop had probably packed up and moved, which was perhaps for the best. The look in his eyes had been a little more crazed each time she'd visited. Last time, he'd even *squealed* when she'd brought out the materials she had for sale.

Sadly, the Junk Heap's closure was only the first thing to go wrong. When Kainé arrived at the dock on the northern plains, the ferryman told her it was out of service.

"Shades damaged the canal." He frowned as he scrubbed the boat moored at the dock.

"There are Shades in the canals now?" asked Kainé.

"Yeah, and no one's got the time to fix it. I know it ain't great, but you'll have to get around on foot for a while."

Shades weren't supposed to appear in the water—that was the reason people could sit back and get to their destination in the blink of an eye on a boat. He used to laugh about it, saying it was the best transportation ever . . .

Wait. *He?* Who was *he?*

"Uh, you okay?" asked the worried ferryman.

"Yeah," replied Kainé as the question snapped her back to reality. "Thanks." She then spun on a heel and left without another word.

But there was some good news in the day as well: Once Kainé returned to the northern plains, she realized Shades were out and about again. Perhaps they'd just been hiding earlier.

As on any sunny day, she only came across the powerful Shades. She'd close the distance in a single bound, stab her foe, then swipe its feet out from under it. Once the Shade was on the ground, she'd hack it to pieces—and if it didn't cooperate and fall down nicely, she'd put distance between them and start the process all over again.

Thankfully, Tyrann's absence hadn't hampered Kainé's Shade-hunting skills at all. Though she could no longer use magic, her swordsmanship was as skilled as ever. Her physical prowess was also above that of an average person, likely because she'd honed her body through constant battle.

She killed every Shade she encountered; they gave off strange noises as they melted into black dust and disappeared. For some reason, that made her think about how she'd killed a countless number of Shades while rescuing Yonah. But now she had a strange feeling they weren't all bad.

So weird. Why did she know that?

A robot and a little Shade. Stone statues. A wolf. These images flashed through her mind for no reason before departing just as suddenly. She swung her sword, mowing down Shades, desperate to shake the discomfort that clung to her.

The next thing she knew, Kainé was at Yonah's village. It faced the northern plains, which made it vulnerable to Shade attacks—an especially grave prospect considering how the creatures' numbers had been steadily increasing in recent years.

It was all because she'd killed the Shadowlord—*that*, at least, was a piece of her spotty memory she could recall. She remembered that Project Gestalt had collapsed after the Shadowlord was killed and that Shades began to lose their sense of self once they lost their king. This, in turn, led them to start indiscriminately attacking Replicants—people. Kainé had paid a grave price indeed in order to rescue a single girl. To save Yonah.

Of course, Kainé was worried about the girl she'd sacrificed so much to save—although it was almost like she *had* to worry. She couldn't remember the reason why, other than she may have been tasked with doing so.

Kainé cut across the northern plains while mowing down Shades and peered into the village from just beyond the gate.

Things seem fine here, she thought. She heard no screams, saw no smoke from fires. She could even hear children laughing and playing.

But Yonah was not among them; the Black Scrawl had made her too weak to run about. Thankfully, the kind villagers took turns looking after her, busily bringing her food and flowers throughout the day. Though they claimed they did so to repay a debt, it was more likely they felt guilty about leaving an ill, dying child to perish alone. The desire to avoid a guilty conscience was the real motivator.

Convinced she had nothing to worry about, Kainé turned around and left rather than venturing inside. Her clothes reeked of Shade blood, after all, and there was no reason to frighten Yonah by reminding her of the Shadowlord.

As Kainé left the village, she came across a guard being attacked by Shades. The man likely worked in Yonah's village, and knowing it would be less safe if he were to perish, Kainé immediately leaped to his defense.

"Hey, get back!" cried the guard. "It's dangerous here!"

"I think that's my line, buddy," Kainé quipped. The guard was surrounded by a number of Shades wearing hats. Though small, they were constantly in motion, which was annoying. There were also four or five adult-size Shades wearing armor and armed with clubs, which were likely the ones the guard had been referring to when he warned Kainé to stay away.

On sunny days like this, the first order of business was to remove the Shades' hats and armor. No matter how agile or how powerful, all Shades grew weak in the light of the sun without anything to block it. With that mindset, it didn't take long for the pair to square the threat away.

"Thanks for the save," said the relieved guard.

Kainé could see he was young and likely inexperienced. "Shades have been on the rise around here lately. So go home."

He may have been a guard, but he was barely an amateur when it came to combat. So many soldiers had lost their lives in Shade attacks that they were running out of replacements—and the local Shade population was a weighty burden for any new soldier to bear.

"Believe me, I want to," said the guard. "Thing is, I've got a job to take care of."

"Oh yeah? What's that?"

"See, we haven't been able to get in touch with anyone in the Forest of Myth for almost a month now. Somebody's gotta go over there and make sure they're all right."

The Forest of Myth was far away, and the road there thick with Shades. To top it off, the guard was injured: There was a massive rip in his sleeve, with blood staining the fabric. An injury to his dominant arm would be fatal if he was attacked.

"Not looking like that," growled Kainé. "You won't make it ten feet before some Shade mauls your ass. I'll go."

"What, really? Thanks a million!" The relief that swept over the guard's face proved he knew he'd never make it back alive. "Oh wait. You should take these."

He handed her a small hide bag containing medicinal herbs. Kainé nodded and took it. You could never have too much medicine after all.

"I'll wait for you around here. Thanks again."

"No problem," Kainé replied as she dashed away.

2.

KAINÉ HAD HEARD that the residents of the Forest of Myth were talkative and good-natured.

Probably the exact opposite of me.

Though she couldn't say that reputation was the reason, she'd still never set foot in the place. Her knowledge of it ended at the stone gate at the entrance; everything beyond was always shrouded in mist.

As she stood before the gates, she was overcome by an intense sense of déjà vu. She *knew* this place. Once, she'd leaned against the gate for a long time waiting for someone. There were also colorful berries involved, ones so good, she'd asked for more, earning someone's annoyance in the process.

Who was it? Who was she waiting for? Who gave her the berries?

"Dammit. Not this again."

She couldn't remember, and the absence of recall made her sick.

With a click of the tongue, she started off again. No one to blame but herself if she started dragging ass now; better to get the job done and get back.

She found the mailbox just inside the entrance. Not long ago, people heard from the Forest of Myth more than once a month because the postman would come to collect letters and parcels.

But with Shades growing more violent, the postman rarely ventured out of Seafront anymore.

"It's too quiet here," muttered Kainé. The stillness was so heavy that she felt compelled to speak her thought aloud. As usual, a thin mist hung over the village, making it impossible to see what was happening.

"Anyone in here?"

She strained to listen, expecting to hear the chatter of talkative residents at any moment. But all she could hear were her own footsteps and . . .

Wait. No. There was something else.

"Machinery?"

It sounded a lot like the robots that roamed around the Junk Heap. As she approached the source of the noise, it took only a few steps for her to learn why the village was so quiet.

The villagers were dead. And not just one or two—dozens of bodies lay strewn across the road, all of them facing the gate. They had died trying to escape.

As Kainé moved farther in, she found bodies facing different directions. That meant they didn't even have a chance to run before they died.

Suddenly, she tensed and readied her sword; a number of robots were shambling toward her. They were mobile types, shaped like boxes with metallic arms strapped to the side—the same as those she'd encountered in the Junk Heap.

"The hell are machines doing here?"

There was a not insignificant distance between the Forest of Myth and the Junk Heap, a distance filled with both mountains and rivers. So how on earth had these robots managed to get *here*?

Kainé had no time to ponder the problem before the machines began their assault. The way they moved and their general strength was also like the robots from the Junk Heap—the same ones Kainé had her heart set on smashing so recently.

"Looks like things are finally going my way!"

She thrust her blade into the gap between a robot's plating, causing it to tilt askew. Then she leaped backward and out of the way of the ensuing explosion before approaching a different unit. This time, she waited for its compatriots to approach before thrusting her blade between the plates. It was more efficient to catch them in a single explosion, plus, it kept her blade from getting coated in oil. But just when she thought she'd taken out all the robots, a new batch appeared.

"Oh come on. *More?!*"

She repeated her strategy of catching this new group in a single explosion. Luckily, the footing was sound—making it an easier battleground for her than the Junk Heap. The footing also dulled the movements of the machines, which clearly hadn't been designed for places where the ground was broken up by tree roots.

Once all the robots were rendered into husks, quiet returned to the forest. Kainé strained her ears but didn't hear any more machinery.

This was the point where she should have pulled back. The robots were clearly done for, and it was unlikely there were any village survivors. Yet she continued onward all the same. Even though the chances of her having missed a machine were low, if they weren't zero, she felt a need to make sure.

She slowly moved forward, keeping her steps as quiet as possible. The earlier robots had appeared after she'd made a loud noise, so she wanted to ensure they wouldn't attack if they sensed her presence.

Finally, a mighty, ancient tree rose up in her path. Its thick trunk was oddly twisted and almost ugly in a strange way. The tree was so tall, she couldn't see where it ended even if she strained her neck.

This seemed to mark the edge of the village, beyond which she could no longer proceed. With a shrug, she turned around and made to head back—but then something caught her eye.

A villager was lying on the ground, twitching slightly. She'd assumed all the bodies were corpses, but seeing an actual survivor gave her a rush, so she hurried over and helped him sit up.

"Hey, wake up," she murmured. Her words caused the villager's eyes to open slightly. After a moment, his lips began to move.

"Machines . . . came from . . . the Divine Tree . . ."

"The Divine Tree? What the hell is that?"

Kainé received no answer. The villager was dead. She laid the body down and got to her feet, thinking. The villager had clearly been trying to help, and the only "Divine Tree" she could think of was the massive one in the middle of the path.

When she returned, she examined a large hollow in the trunk. She knew hollows and cavities were a given with old trees like this, so she hadn't paid it much mind at first. But if the robots had come *out* of there, that changed everything.

And indeed, the hollow was large enough for the box-shaped robots to pass through. As she looked inside, the faint scent of machine oil tickled her nostrils. The hollow seemed deeper than she'd anticipated, and upon sticking her head inside, she realized it was actually *enormous*. Stepping fully inside, she found a path that sloped gently down.

Why is this in a tree? Does it lead to the Junk Heap?

It was silent. No machine noises, no anything. Kainé ventured deeper and found the path to be both wide and covered in tree roots. It was hard to think a person could have made it, but it clearly wasn't a natural phenomenon either.

The scent on the air was a strange mix of foliage, earth,

machine oil, and rubber, as well as other scents she'd never before encountered. Metallic fragments and machine parts were
scattered across the path, scraps of something Kainé couldn't
make out. As she stared at them, she realized the path was bright
enough for her to view the metallic fragments on the ground.

Suddenly, Kainé came to a stop and strained her ears to pick
up a new, distant sound.

Robots.

She flattened herself against the wall and waited as the noise
grew louder. Soon, two dots of light that were clearly part of the
box-shaped robots came into view. She lured them as close as
possible before taking them out with a single blow, then ran as
fast as she could as they exploded behind her.

She'd been lucky to take them both out in one strike; had
she been attacked by multiple machines on such a narrow path,
she'd undoubtedly have been caught in the blast. Kainé knew she
should retreat before she ran into a pack of robots she couldn't
handle. And yet she was *so* curious to see where the path led.

But then . . .

"Welcome to the sea of humanity."

It was a boy's voice. Kainé's head whipped around, but she
didn't see anyone, even though it seemed to come from nearby.

"Welcome to the cemetery of sin and punishment."

A girl's voice that time—and again, there was no one.

"You are a Replicant."

"A manufactured existence."

Kainé raised her sword and squinted into the dim. The voices
sounded as if they were coming from nearby yet also from farther
down the path.

"Who are you?" she shouted. "Show yourselves!"

Her voice echoed down the tunnel, something the children's
voices didn't do. So where had they been coming from?

"Individual name: Kainé."

"Individual name: Kainé."

Kainé's eyes widened. How did they know her name?

"Remain calm."

"Do not be hasty."

Suddenly overcome with a feeling that the speakers were somewhere deeper inside the tunnel, Kainé set off at a run.

"Soon we shall meet."

"Soon we shall meet."

Creepy little freaks, she thought as she ran. Suddenly, the sound of her footsteps changed; it felt like she'd stepped on something hard. Where the tunnel floor had previously been covered in vines, there were now long lengths of . . . something. They looked to Kainé like the cables she collected in the Junk Heap, but those were small, while these appeared to be quite long.

As Kainé tried to determine if this was another machine part, the boy and girl spoke again. She hoped they might answer her original question, but that wasn't about to happen.

"This is an integrated information-management database designed to resemble a perennial plant."

"It transmits phenomena recorded in its memory unit."

I don't understand a godddamn thing you're saying, Kainé thought. *Total bullshit.*

"Observations of you have been recorded as well."

"You brought an end to Project Gestalt."

"You killed the Original Gestalt. Now the remaining Gestalts run wild because they have nowhere left to go."

"Your actions have caused the deaths of countless Replicants."

The way they said that grated on her nerves. It felt like she was being scolded like a child who didn't know any better, which *royally* pissed her off.

"Show your damn faces already!" she yelled.

The sound beneath her feet changed again as she ran across piles of metallic scrap.

"Do not be hasty. Soon we shall meet."

"Soon we shall meet."

She kicked aside the debris and ran on, ignoring the shrill noise that grated on her ears. The metal soon changed to black tendrils again—but this time they were not roots but a tangled mess made from black vines of various sizes.

Suddenly, her vision opened up. The round room reminded her of the Junk Heap, save that tendrils of all kinds—black, green, metal, thick, and thin—were tangled across the floor, the walls, and the ceiling. It was an eerie place.

The tendrils on the floor suddenly writhed and shot into the air. They squirmed as they reached up, splitting into two bunches that quickly took the shape of a boy and girl.

"Ahh. How nice of you to join us," said the boy.

"Yes. How nice of you to join us," echoed the girl.

So these are the freaks who talked to me, Kainé thought. Their upper halves looked like human children, but their lower halves were bunches of green and black tendrils. Whatever this was, they clearly weren't living creatures.

"We are—"

Kainé didn't let them finish before she swiped at them with her blade. Had they been real humans, their heads would have gone flying. But as they weren't, their upper halves exploded and scattered, filling the room with the smell of metal and oil.

"How full of life you are."

"We won't get anywhere like this."

Kainé whirled around at the voices and saw the children, even though she'd run her blade through them moments before. Well, she didn't care if they could speak to her or not, because she had no intention of carrying on a conversation. She was going to kill them. That was all.

"Now then. Let us fight."

"Now then. Let us fight."

The boy and girl returned to their original state of black and green tendrils. They began coalescing again—this time pulling in thicker tendrils and metallic poles that weren't part of either child. Before Kainé could even blink, she found herself face-to-face with a massive robot—a horrifying patchwork thing made of metal pieces.

The robot stomped its ugly, warped legs, causing the ground to shake so violently that Kainé could barely keep upright. The vibrations became shock waves that raced toward her. She leaped out of the way, barely rolling aside when she struck land and the robot's arm crashed down.

"My name is——."

"My name is——."

Though the boy and girl gave their names, Kainé couldn't make out what they said. Honestly, she didn't really care—plus, she was busy slashing at the robot as she dodged the shock wave.

Suddenly, she heard Emil's voice play in her head: *Aim for the legs! Knock it down!*

That's right: They'd fought an enormous robot at the Junk Heap. She remembered plunging her sword into the leg joint to keep the robot from moving, and she let her memory dictate her actions in this moment. The creature's movements dulled slightly when her blow struck, but that was all. Though the enemy before her *looked* like a robot, its makeup and weaknesses were entirely different.

"We are the administrators."

"The administrators of this forest."

Though Kainé ignored them, the children kept talking at her. Oh, how she *hated* that.

"We have long been watching."

"We have long been listening."

"The stories of recycled vessels."

"The voice of a recycled world."

The false robot moved fast. She couldn't simply aim for the legs, so instead she started hacking at whatever opportunity presented itself.

"What will you show us?"

"Will you show us your potential?"

What the hell are you talking about? Shut up! You're pissing me off!

She wished she could yell but held herself back. She felt like she'd end up biting her tongue if she opened her mouth.

"Entertain us."

"Entertain us."

She *also* hated that these two idiots were intent on turning her into some kind of toy for their amusement.

"Enough, you fucking brats!"

She let anger guide her blade and brought it down on the false robot, leaping into the air to split its head in two.

Except it didn't work.

Kainé brought her blade down again. And again. And *again*. Clumps of metal poles bent. Sparks flew into the air. Finally, the false robot's movements began to grow choppy and unstable. She dodged the arm as it came down in an unnatural manner, responding with her own blade. As the false robot teetered, the acrid smell of smoke filled the air.

"Eat shit!" cried Kainé.

She put her whole body into the thrust. The false robot shuddered erratically, then finally exploded. If only she could have blasted those damned brats to smithereens along with it—then she wouldn't have to put up with their inane demands to entertain them.

Once the false robot was debris, the black and green tendrils began to writhe before taking the shape of the boy and girl again.

"How truly fascinating you are."

"You are just as we expected."

They sounded so *arrogant* for a couple of kids. She hated it. But before Kainé could swing her sword at them, they vanished.

"Come this way."

"Come this way."

The wall behind them crumbled, revealing a path that led further into the tunnel.

Perfect. Sure, I'll invite myself in—then I'll find you shits and smash you to pieces!

When Kainé stepped inside the new area, she was greeted by a smell that reminded her of the Junk Heap. She hated it. Also, she now knew how cats felt when all their hair stood on end. As that thought crossed her mind, she realized she'd had the same thought at the Junk Heap, even though the memories surrounding the thought were missing.

Flowers bloomed in places along the corridor, the petals and stems both unnaturally white. Not once did Kainé think them beautiful.

As she came to another open space, the boy and girl were waiting. The gray tendrils strewn across the floor began to squirm, and Kainé braced herself for whatever was coming. The tendrils began to split into groups, meaning there were going to be multiple enemies.

Yawn. Boring. She was tired of this.

"You are strong. We have taken the liberty of sampling that strength."

The gathered gray tendrils took the form of women.

"We have reproduced you at the point in your journey in which you were strongest."

The women all had blades in each hand.

"Son of a . . . Are those things *me*?!"

They look nothing like me is what Kainé wanted to yell—and yet she could see the resemblance in certain respects. How very irritating.

"They are copies of you, shaped by machinery."

"A collection of microscopic, plant-based propulsion units bound together with Maso particles."

All the "copies" rushed Kainé at once and were much, much faster than the false robot from earlier. Kainé knew she couldn't let herself get surrounded, so she took off running to put some distance between them. One at a time she could handle, maybe two, but that was all.

"The same as this very forest."

"A massive forest of memories coalesced by the triumphs of quantum mechanics and Maso research. A forest that records anything and everything about the world."

"If you wanted me to follow any of this, you're gonna be real fuckin' disappointed!" screamed Kainé. Not only were the voices annoying, but her copies were angering her in a very specific way. She never could see how she looked while fighting, but this setup gave her an idea—and that pissed her off even more.

"Your comprehension is unnecessary."

"After all, all you care for is killing. Is this not so?"

Kainé swiped her blade to the side, sending the torso of a copy flying.

"These other mes are brittle as hell. I oughta be insulted!"

She smashed another one of their heads in but was shocked when the corpse vanished and a new one appeared in its place.

"It matters not how many copies you destroy."

"They will simply disperse and immediately reconstruct themselves."

Shut up! Just stop talking!

"There is still much fun to be had."

"We have finally come to an end."

Kainé hated how the copies' breathing remained calm and measured no matter how much they ran or jumped.

"God DAMN, you're annoying! I'm gonna tear these freaks apart, eat the pieces, and shit 'em into a trash can!"

Her voice cracked and broke as she yelled. She hated that she was losing control of her breathing.

"Have we reached the end?"

"Have you reached your limit?"

She took the full brunt of a kick and landed hard. Though she managed to sit up, she couldn't get to her feet. Another kick came, and she could only roll out of the way.

"How unfortunate."

"How unfortunate."

She was surrounded. There was nowhere to run.

"God . . . *dammit* . . ."

This is it, she thought as she gritted her teeth and closed her eyes. But then . . .

"Hraaah!"

Kainé's eyes snapped open. She could hardly believe the voice she'd just heard.

"Kainé! Are you okay?"

A bright white magical barrier stretched around her. How long had it been since she last saw that spell?

"Emil . . . ?"

"You betcha!"

The response wasn't from a ghost. It wasn't from a recreation. It was from *Emil*.

"First things first. I'll do something about this! Hiyah!"

The voice. It really *was* Emil. As Kainé struggled to accept this new information, the copies on the other side of the barrier were sent flying.

"It's good to see you safe!" said Emil as he extended a hand to Kainé. For some reason, he had *four* of them now. Kainé wasn't sure which one to take, so she grabbed one at random and pulled herself to her feet. Even with the additional limbs, his hand still felt like him.

He'd somehow been alive this whole time. Kainé wanted to ask where he'd been for the past three years—and where he found the extra hands—but there wasn't time. New copies were approaching quickly.

"I sense tremendous power over there," Emil said, pointing to the magical barrier on the far wall. "I think it's acting as an energy source. If we can destroy it, all the other Kainés should disappear!"

"Got it!"

"I'll take care of the barrier—you focus on kicking some Kainé butt! Er, I mean the *other* Kainés' butts. Not *your* Kainé butt. *You*, the real Kainé, should—"

"I get it, Emil! Just focus!"

A warm laugh bubbled up from her throat despite how tired she was—and despite how relentlessly the copies threw themselves at her. She had Emil now, and that alone was enough to give strength to her exhausted limbs. She ran again. Ran and sliced, sliced and ran. Suddenly, her body felt lighter; Emil had cast a restorative spell.

"Number 7: a magical weapon forged by humans."

"A being who absorbed the power of Number 6 and transcended humanity."

The children's voices echoed around them. Emil, who had used all of his magical strength on the barrier, turned to Kainé with a confused expression.

"Um, who's that? Who are those voices?"

"Just a coupla little fucks." There was probably a different expletive that would more accurately describe exactly how pathetic Kainé thought they were, but she wasn't sure what it was.

"Gosh, it feels like it's been forever since we fought together!" Emil exclaimed loudly. Just as Kainé was about to respond, she experienced a familiar, almost-dizzying feeling. Memories of battle came flooding back: Emil used to support her as she rushed at the enemy, but there was also someone else. She was always fighting with *someone else*. So there was another person, and . . . ?

"Unusual phenomena-fluctuation observed."

"Singularity signature detected in Replicant Kainé."

"Fascinating."

"Terribly fascinating."

Good fucking god, just shut UP and get out of my way! My memories . . . I need to . . .

"Are you all right, Kainé?!"

She had apparently come to a stop. "Yeah," she replied as she focused her concentration on destroying the copies in front of her. Without warning, they all suddenly vanished.

"Kainé! I did it!"

Emil had successfully destroyed the barrier. When Kainé turned to look, she saw a hole where it used to be—another passage. As they ventured inside, she saw it was different from the others. It wasn't covered in tendrils or sticks but instead a haphazard mess of boxes of varying sizes and shapes.

"Is that a doorway?" asked Emil. At the end of the corridor was what appeared like a stack of blocks. It was a bit of a strange look for a door, but at least it wasn't a wall. As Kainé pondered it, the boy and girl appeared before them again.

"Beyond here lies that which was lost."

"The final hope—for you to reclaim."

After those suspicious parting words, they disappeared again.

"Kainé . . ."

Kainé nodded. "There's no going back now. Let's end this— *all* of it."

And with that, she threw open the door.

3.

EVERYTHING BEYOND THE door was white. The sky, the constructs—everything.

"Whoa. What *is* this place?" Emil gaped.

"Don't ask me," replied Kainé as she scanned the area, trying and failing to make any sense of it.

"Well, at least there don't seem to be any bad guys around."

A bridge of pure white stretched before them, long enough that they couldn't see the other end. But it was clear their destination lay on the other side.

"Look, Emil," began Kainé as they started crossing the bridge, "I didn't get a chance to ask with all the fighting and shit, but what happened to you back then? And where have you been? And why the hell do you have *four arms?*"

"Kainé, it's gonna take way too long to get into all that now."

Kainé nodded. She figured it had been too much to ask but still had to try.

"I was worried, you know?" she continued—and it was true. When she saw his staff on the ground, she'd assumed he was dead. After all, how could anyone have survived an explosion of such magnitude?

"But look at us now," said a chipper Emil. "Team Kamil, back together again!"

"Yeah, I guess so."

She was glad they were together again—happy, even. And with every step, those feelings grew stronger. Emil was floating by her side, and the notion it was *really happening* made her want to cry tears of relief.

"Kainé, I . . ." began Emil before grinding to a halt. Sensing he had something on his mind, Kainé gently encouraged him.

"What's up, Emil?"

"I feel like I've forgotten something really important."

"Yeah, tell me about it," she deadpanned.

"You too?" said Emil, his voice rising in shock.

Relief and shock spread through Kainé's chest at the realization she hadn't been imagining such things. "Yeah. I can't really describe it, but it's like my mind is filled with this weird fog."

"Me too! But . . ."

"But?"

"I think . . . I made a promise to somebody? Like, that we would go eat something delicious?"

Laughter spilled from Kainé's lips. That was *such* an Emil promise to make.

"Well then, we'll just have to get those memories back."

"Yeah!"

Kainé and Emil continued across the long bridge. Before she knew it, the bridge had ended. *Did we really walk all the way across?* was what she was going to ask, but when she opened her mouth to speak, something entirely different came out.

"The Shadowlord's castle."

She and Emil were looking at the garden inside the Lost Shrine, but one devoid of all color. The flagstone paths, the trees, the flowers— all these things were pure white. Only the birds that asked for the password were gone.

. . . The password? What the hell is that?

"Uh, what's going on?" asked a befuddled Emil.

"Hell if I know."

The door that should have stood at the far end of the garden was simply a continuation of the corridor—and at the end of that was another familiar door.

"I feel an enormous magical power ahead," whispered Emil.

If Kainé recalled correctly, there were traitor priestesses at the end of the corridor that led from the garden at the Shadowlord's castle.

"Just don't do anything rash. Got it?"

"Got it," Emil nodded. "Same goes for you, Kainé. I don't want to be alone anymore."

Kainé nodded firmly and pushed the door open. If this was really the Shadowlord's castle, the garden should have been on the other side. Instead, she found herself in the room where they fought the Shadowlord.

"This is a very special place."

"To you—and to the world."

Those voices again. What did she need to kill this time—and what could she stick her sword into to make them shut up?

"The magical energy over there is incredible!" breathed Emil as he pointed to a large box. It was perfectly square, as though each side and angle had been measured and cut precisely. It also floated in midair, giving off a dim glow as it shuddered faintly. Though Kainé didn't sense any magic, she knew right away that something wasn't right about it.

"That has to be the source . . . Let's smash it!"

Emil didn't have to tell her twice. Kainé rushed forward, delighted that her instincts to destroy it had been validated.

"That is the core frame of this forest, within which a great variety of information is stored."

"Inside it exists all that this world is, including the memories you have lost."

"Though rather than memories, it might be best to say the 'world' you have lost."

"In any case, it is surely the answer you ought to seek."

"Would you two shit sacks *please* shut up?!" Kainé yelled as she brought her blade down on the square. All she had to worry about was hitting this thing until it broke—but the moment that thought crossed her mind, she was flung backward.

"You don't get to decide who lives and who dies!"

Another voice, different from the children's. One Kainé knew.

"That's the voice from my dreams," she murmured.

"I've heard that voice before," agreed Emil. Kainé readjusted her grip on her sword and turned her attention to the box. In a surprising development, it fired magic at her—the same magic the Shadowlord used.

"These are your memories."

"Memories you repeatedly clung to."

"Memories you repeatedly rewrote."

Kainé ran, ignoring the children's words. She dodged the magic and leaped at the cube, but when she thrust her blade into it, she was knocked back again.

"We made it this far because you were with us, Kainé! I'm who I am today because of you!"

That was a different voice from the one in her dreams—an older one—but she still knew it. She knew the voice belonged to the same person she kept hearing in her dreams.

"Do you suffer?"

"Are you pained?"

The boy and girl were really pissing Kainé off now, and she had a keen desire for a sword that could smash noises to bits. Lacking one, she just got back to her feet and ran at the box again. She didn't care what it was saying about the world—she was going to destroy it. If the world broke when she did so, then too damn bad.

She ran straight at the box. It fired a magical blast that hit her directly, but she kept going.

"You pathetic fucking shit purse, just *die already!*"

She put everything she had into the attack. The moment blade and box connected, a numbing sensation ran up her arm and a crack formed along the box's surface. Light poured out of it, causing her vision to go white.

A moment later, she could see again.

"Where . . . am I?"

What lay before her wasn't the Shadowlord's castle. The space wasn't white but light gray and was formed entirely of straight lines, including some that formed the path that extended before her.

Emil, however, was gone. Did that mean she'd been the only one transported to this place?

"These are your memories."

"These are your records."

"This is your world."

"This is your world."

The damn voices, however, had gleefully followed her. *Wish you would get lost*, she thought, but she kept her mouth shut and began swinging her sword at the multitude of Shades that were now attacking from all directions.

"Shades: human souls that have gone Gestalt."

"These Shades are but data reproduced via your records."

"They are the true humans you slaughtered on your journey."

"They are the true humans you slaughtered on your journey."

She knew that, but it didn't matter if they were real or fake—she killed them because she decided she was going to. That was all.

Once Kainé felled all the Shades in front of her, another box appeared. It was black this time but otherwise exactly the same as the previous one. She brought her blade down on it without hesitation.

"Beepy, wait! That's enough!"

"I can't live without you!"

"I don't wanna be alone again!"

She knew these voices as well. When she looked up, she saw a large robot on the ground with a little Shade beside it.

"Goddammit, enough with this bullshit already!" roared Kainé. The little Shade rushed toward her, and she cut it down before doing the same to the robot.

"You have heard many voices."

"Fear. Hate. Rage. Suffering."

Every time the children spewed their nonsense, a Shade and another box appeared. And every time Kainé killed a Shade and destroyed a box, she heard a voice she knew and saw another foe she recognized.

"Each of them has meaning."

"Each of them has meaning."

They *all* had familiar voices—voices she never wanted to hear again. It didn't matter if they meant anything.

"Stop it, stop it, *stop it*!"

Kainé brought her blade down so hard on her foe that her sword hand went numb. "I kill Shades! That's all there is to it!"

She killed until all the Shades were gone. Strangely enough, she didn't feel tired at all. She felt pain if she got hit, sure, but she didn't get tired from running around. What a strange place this was.

"You are a foreign entity in this world."

"An error created by a discrepancy between memory and record."

Kainé whipped around to face the nauseating voices. "I have not understood a *single fucking thing* you shitty little ass-grabbers have said since we *started* this goddamn adventure!"

When she lifted her head, she saw the boy and girl floating in midair, along with the black box. She hated the feeling of being looked down on like this.

"This is the deepest place in your memories."

"Memories you had sealed away."

Bullshit.

"And this one . . . is your worst memory."

"And this one . . . is your worst memory."

When she heard that, she braced herself. As the boy and girl touched the black box, it shattered to pieces, bringing forth both mist and an enormous Shade.

"Motherfucker . . ."

Standing there was the Shade that killed her grandmother—a Shade she already killed ages ago.

"I'll kill you as many times as it takes, you goddamn shit-fucking despicable piece of garbage!"

She brought her blade down on it, etching cuts across every inch.

"We upgraded the data that was recreated from your memories."

"Can you defeat this nightmare?"

She ignored the kids and concentrated on the sword. She would kill this thing as many times as she had to. Only . . .

That's right—someone else had been here. She was *sure* someone else was with her when she knocked this Shade down. Someone who dealt the killing blow.

"*Fuuuck!* Why can't I *remember*?!"

She was hit and went flying. Her head spun. When she opened her eyes again, she was greeted not by the sight of the Shade but by people from The Aerie.

"*Get out, half-breed!*"

"*You brought these Shades here!*"

"*We don't want you!*"

The villagers rushed to attack her. Even though Kainé knew their only talent was bad-mouthing and gossip, they were still trying to bring the fight.

"You pieces of shit! You could never—"

—*take me on* was how she wanted to finish, but the villagers vanished as a Shade swept its taloned tail into her. She couldn't dodge. Exhaustion had finally overcome her, and it took all her strength just to stand. And once she did manage to get to her feet, she couldn't run. She could scarcely even walk a straight line.

Another attack came her way, and she didn't dodge it so much as awkwardly roll out of the way. Her arms and legs were hardly doing what she asked of them anymore.

"Don't you dare call yourself human!"

"Get out!"

"Get out of our village!"

The villagers began throwing stones at her, and these were just as painful as the abuse. As far as Kainé was concerned, words, sticks, and stones were all in the same ballpark; each hit caused her to groan in pain.

"Shut up, shut up, shut up, *shut up*! I don't want to hear your—"

Sticky mud covered her eyes. Darkness came to her then, along with burning pain.

KAINÉ opens her eyes. It's bright. She leaps to her feet and looks around.

KAINÉ

The hell? What happened? Wasn't I just fighting Shades?

Her right hand searches for her sword. The place that greets her is entirely different from the one she was just in. Rope

bridges. Tank houses. A weather vane. And
villagers, all of whom are looking at her
with confusion as she mutters to herself.
She is in The Aerie. She is home.

GRANDMA
Is something the matter, girl?

KAINÉ spins around and sees a woman
ravaged by time. A shawl, thin from years
of use, hangs over her shoulders.

KAINÉ
. . . Grandma? Is that really you?

GRANDMA
What's wrong, you fool girl? Is your head
lost in dreams?

KAINÉ wonders if this is a dream.
GRANDMA's worried face and the way her
shawl flutters in the wind make it feel
very real. And yet she knows GRANDMA was
killed by a Shade a long time ago. Could
this be . . . ?

KAINÉ
That must be it. I'm dead. I'm dead and
this is he—

GRANDMA
Oh, stop with that nonsense already!

KAINÉ flinches as GRANDMA raises a hand
in the air, expecting pain to come as
correction for her foolishness. But

instead, GRANDMA places a hand on her
cheek. The warmth of her wrinkled hand
spreads from KAINÉ's cheek and fills her
entire body.

KAINÉ

Sorry, Grandma. Not sure where my head was
at there.

GRANDMA

Well, just make sure you keep it attached.

KAINÉ decides she doesn't care if this
is a dream or the afterlife, so long
as she's with GRANDMA. Doing so makes a
weight lift from her heart.

GRANDMA

Let's go home. Hold this.

GRANDMA holds out a sack filled with fruit
and vegetables.

GRANDMA

(laughing)
It's important to treat yourself every now
and again.

KAINÉ understands that she has been
shopping. The villagers treat them
horribly, but they still sell them
things—business is business after all.

GRANDMA

Well, what do you know? I forgot to buy my
medicine.

KAINÉ

You go home and rest. I'll get the medicine.

GRANDMA

You sure?

GRANDMA looks at KAINÉ with worry, her odd behavior from earlier still fresh on her mind.

KAINÉ

Really. It's fine. Go home. I've got this.

KAINÉ wrenches the wallet in GRANDMA's hand free and takes it. She doesn't want her to worry.

KAINÉ

Besides, you know how stubborn I am. Once my mind is set, there's no changing it.

GRANDMA

Hmph! I wonder where you get that from!

GRANDMA laughs in defeat as she exits. KAINÉ watches her leave before turning and heading for the apothecary.

APOTHECARY

Ho there! Here for Kali's medicine, are you?

GRANDMA and the APOTHECARY are old friends, which is why he is so kind to KAINÉ.

KAINÉ

Uh, yeah. If it's not a bother.

*The APOTHECARY immediately begins his
work, deftly pulling bottles and herbs
from the shelves and mixing them with a
practiced hand. A peculiar smell fills the
store, one that immediately reminds KAINÉ
of her childhood.*

*Not long after, the APOTHECARY holds out
a bag of medicine.*

APOTHECARY

*Oh, say. That was a fine portrait you drew
of your grandmother. Looks just like her,
it does! I've never seen Kali so over the
moon about anything. She brags about it
every time she stops by!*

*The picture was one KAINÉ had only drawn
on a whim. It wasn't meant to be shown to
others.*

APOTHECARY

*It's been a long time since I've seen
something so wonderful.*

*KAINÉ hesitates. She doesn't know if he's
just being nice to her. The APOTHECARY
senses this and keeps talking.*

APOTHECARY

*I could really tell you put your heart into it.
It was simply wonderful.*

*KAINÉ doesn't know how to take
the compliment and just wants the*

*conversation to be over. She grips the
bag of medicine tightly and turns to
leave, making a mental note to tell
GRANDMA to cease her little traveling
art show. But when she reaches the door,
she hears a loud thud from somewhere
back in the shop. KAINÉ turns to see the
APOTHECARY crouching on the floor.*

KAINÉ

Uh, hey there. You okay?

APOTHECARY

*MY LEG, MY LEG, MY LEG, MY LEG, OH GOD,
WHERE IS MY LEG?!*

*KAINÉ rushes over. The APOTHECARY's leg
is gone.*

APOTHECARY

HELP ME! HELP ME!

*KAINÉ grabs the APOTHECARY's hand, but
his fingers begin to shimmer and vanish.*

APOTHECARY

Heeel . . . Iii caaannn . . .

*The APOTHECARY's face warbles out of
existence, causing a stray eyeball to roll
out of its socket and onto the floor. A
moment later, what remains of the pitiful
shopkeeper collapses into a heap of ash,
releasing a small puff into the silent air.*

*KAINÉ stumbles backward. She hears
screams coming from outside. She bursts*

*from the store and finds herself in a
nightmare. Homes sluff off the side of
cliffs. Villagers run in mad circles
before exploding into dust, their
clothing drifting this way and that
through the air.*

KAINÉ

Grandma!

*KAINÉ runs. She needs to get home as soon
as possible. Flecks of ash blow into her
face, her mouth, her eyes. Ash, ash, ash.
Buildings and people reduced to cinders
in the wind.*

KAINÉ

Grandma!

*Her home is gone. Her oasis in this
maddening world is now nothing more than
a pile of ash.*

GRANDMA

Kai . . . né . . .

*GRANDMA is alive! KAINÉ begins digging
through the ash and unearths her
blackened form.*

KAINÉ

Come on, Grandma. We're getting out of
here.

*KAINÉ gathers GRANDMA in her arms and
breaks into a run, hoping to escape the*

chaos. But the wave of ash has become a
tsunami—her leg gives out, and she falls.
Her right leg has vanished at a point
just below the knee.

KAINÉ

It'll take more than that to stop me.

KAINÉ cradles GRANDMA in her arms and
tries to run with just her left leg.

KAINÉ

We're going to make it. We're going to
live.

The weight in her arms suddenly vanishes.
Ash slips through the gaps in her arms.

KAINÉ

This can't be happening . . . Grandma!

KAINÉ tries to pull the ashes back to
her, but she can no longer tell which
particles used to be her grandmother.

KAINÉ

I was supposed to belong here!

As she continues her frantic digging,
her hand suddenly closes around a
piece of soft, ragged fabric: GRANDMA's
shawl.

KAINÉ

Come the fuck on!

Kainé knows this place is a lie yet still can't do anything. She can't save anyone. She can't even escape. She feels peace and so desperately wants to accept it. But that's why everything vanished: her reason to live, as well as her goals. And that is why . . .

???

. . . say . . .

KAINÉ hears a new voice.

???

I say, can you hear me?

The voice calls out again. It is louder. Clearer. Familiar.

???

Now then! You wish to get him back, mmm?

KAINÉ

Him? Who are you talking about?

???

Oh, for the love of all the heavens.

I always did know you were a handful.

The voice immediately begins to grate on KAINÉ's nerves, but there is also a sort of warm familiarity about it.

???

Are you truly so daft that you have already forgotten one of your beloved traveling companions and friends?

*Something deep in KAINÉ's memories surges
forth.*

KAINÉ

That's right. I had friends.

And I was fighting to get one of them back.

*Light fills the ashen world. KAINÉ turns
to the light and reaches for it.*

???

Do hurry back now . . . hussy.

Before her stood the damn enormous Shade. As its tail came
rushing down toward her, it suddenly froze in midair. It was then
she saw a black spear neatly piercing the tail—a magic spear.
Magic she knew.

The enormous Shade, its tail skewered, bent backward and
howled. It writhed.

The one who cast the spell was . . .

Kainé whirled around and was greeted with the sight of
a floating book with a face on its cover bouncing lightly in
the air.

"What is the matter?" asked the book. "Do you still not
remember?"

As she unconsciously reached for the book, the thrashing
Shade got to its feet and slammed its tail down on her again.

"You've not time to become lost in your thoughts," the book
reminded her.

"Right. Okay. Let's get him back!"

Strength had returned to Kainé's numbed limbs.

"Use my magic to topple the beast!" instructed the book. "I
presume you know how to use magic, yes?"

Kainé nodded. Using magic was like breathing until Tyrann disappeared, even though she was crap at it.

"Then give us a show, hussy!"

Don't need to tell me twice, she thought.

Because she knew. She knew that Grimoire Weiss's magic was ostentatiously grandiose, annoyingly loud, and unbelievably powerful. She'd seen it in action thousands of times thus far—so she knew.

"Hey, Weiss?"

Without the tome, she would have been trapped in a facsimile of her hometown, drowning in her memories, reduced to nothing.

". . . Thanks."

"Have you been in your cups again?"

The book hadn't changed a bit. He had awful manners, did nothing but lecture, and was irritatingly overbearing—so Kainé replied as she always would.

"Fuck your face."

"Ah! That's more like it!"

She let fly magical bullets. She fired out magical spears. She absorbed a barrage of the Shade's own bullets, then launched them back at her foe. All spells she knew well.

Her defense, however, faltered, likely because she had been so eager to use the magic. One of the Shade's bullets hit her, sending her flying. When she scrambled to her feet, she found herself standing before The Aerie's villagers.

"Let not your resolution waver before mere illusions again, hussy!" cried Weiss.

"Don't worry!" she called. "I'll do what needs to be done."

She rushed at them and swiped her blade through the air. One, two, three people fell to the ground. They weren't human but merely illusions the enormous Shade was subjecting her to. The technique of casting illusions to confound its enemies was its specialty, but though Kainé had fallen victim to it once, that wasn't going to happen again.

The villagers vanished. As the Shade began to weaken, Kainé shot out a magical spear.

"Are you sound of mind, hussy?" Weiss asked suddenly, as though the thought had just come to him. "What you are attempting is extremely—"

I know, Kainé thought. She'd pretended not to realize it out of frustration from being told nonsense about memories and the world, but she knew. This was a world of memory—memories *of* the world. All the enemies she faced here were under some degree of the children's control, but they were still enemies from her own memory.

She understood now: She would be violating the order of *something* if she took back the memories she had lost. And that would come with great danger. She knew. And that's why she shouted:

"Cram it, book! I'm *doing* this!"

"I see," Grimoire Weiss murmured.

She sent a bundle of spears flying at the massive Shade, causing it to thrash its tail about.

"It's working!" she yelled.

"Do not relent in your assault!"

"Time to close this out!"

A magic fist hurtled toward the massive Shade—the same attack she had seen that day in The Aerie. The hand grabbed the Shade, plucked it from the ground, and sent it flying. She shot out another volley of magic, causing the boy and girl to melt into the light she and Grimoire Weiss emitted.

"So this is a Replicant's potential!"

"Possible futures are blending with the time we currently inhabit!"

"The light . . ."

"I hear a song . . ."

Peaceful looks, as though thinking back to a simpler time, graced the children's faces as they vanished. They had been enigmas to the very end. Kainé watched as the massive Shade crumpled to the floor before her eyes.

"Let us finish this!" yelled Grimoire Weiss—and as he did, she heard another voice:

"*. . . iné . . . Don't . . .*"

It was a boy's voice, the same as in her dreams. She remembered now. She remembered *everything*.

They'd met at The Aerie. He mistook her for a Shade. They exchanged blows. He helped her gain revenge. They became friends. They traveled together to save his sister. His village was attacked. She became stone. They reunited when her petrification was removed. They traveled together again.

She remembered it. All the pain, the hardship, the joy. They were friends, and there was a happiness in simply traveling together.

"*. . . go back . . . Don't . . .*"

Don't? Don't *what*? What was that supposed to mean?

Cut the crap already!

"I already made up my mind!" she shouted. "Nobody tells me what to do! I swore I would be a sword! I swore that I would be *your* sword! Do you hear me?! So I am going to get you back, and I don't care what it takes! Who the *fuck* do you think you are to just up and disappear like that, huh? *I'm* the one who gets to decide what my life means to me! It's *my* life, and I'll do whatever I want with it!"

It all spilled out at once, and when the words were finished, she unleashed all the magic she had. She didn't even know what sort of spells she was using anymore—all she knew was that she was subduing the Shade and ending its life.

"So get your ass back here *right* now and quit wasting time like a—"

A loud, deep rumble drowned out the rest of what she said. But she could feel her hands grabbing hold of *it*—a piece of the memory of this world. The piece she had been looking for. A person most precious that had finally come back.

"I leave the rest to you . . . hussy."

Kainé nodded to Weiss as he faded.

Then she called a name.

4.

WHEN POWERFUL MAGIC erupted from the box, Emil figured that was the cause of everything. The Kainé copies, the barriers blocking the path—all of it seemed to be using the box's magic, which was why he suggested they destroy it.

I think I made a mistake, Emil thought as he tried to hold back tears.

As Kainé bashed her sword against the white box, cracks ran through it, and the Shadowlord's castle began to crumble. And though the "coupla fucks" were gone, they weren't the only ones to disappear. As he looked on, Kainé also vanished. Emil had been planning to escape the crumbling castle with her, but now he had no idea where she'd gone.

He dodged walls and ceilings as they fell, flying as fast as he could as he frantically called her name. Neither of them wanted to be alone anymore. They'd *promised.* But he had been alone since that day three years ago when he'd been caught in the magical blast and sent to the farthest corners of the world.

In his hopelessness, his sister's name unwittingly slipped from his lips. The tearful waver in his word caught him by surprise, and he stopped for a moment to shake his head.

"I'm okay," he said to himself. "No more crying. I promised."

He recalled Halua saying she wanted him to be happy, right after she had protected him that day when he had been on the verge of being consumed by that brutal magic.

Emil, wake up. Please, wake up.

His body had already begun to fall apart back then. His consciousness had begun to dim. Without Halua's voice, he would have readily given himself over to oblivion.

I'm just here to keep my promise.

Her voice and face were just as kind and comfortable as they'd been when they merged in the underground facility.

I told you I'd always be watching over you, didn't I?

But both voice and face were fading.

Sorry, Emil. Looks like I'm out of magic. But I'll always watch over you—and we'll always be together.

After they merged, Emil always felt like Halua was inside him. Even though they couldn't have actual conversations, he felt like she was watching over him. That was how he knew she'd used all of her magic and was about to disappear.

Don't cry, Emil. I want you to be happy.

He didn't want that—he didn't want to say goodbye. But all he could do was throw a fit and sob.

Promise me that you'll live for both of us.

As Halua's voice drifted away on the wind, Emil was ejected from the Shadowlord's castle. His body was gone. His head flew far, and the next thing he knew, he was in a desert.

But he survived. And he journeyed. He created a replacement body and set off to reunite with his friends. He would not cry anymore. He would live in happiness, fulfilling his promise to his sister. He would do so because he wanted to see the others.

For three years, he traveled alone. He was successful in creating a replacement body—so successful, in fact, that he ended up creating an extra set of arms. Once this was done, he set off for the village where those he held most dear lived, looking forward to the day they could travel together again.

But on the way, he'd felt an odd magic coming from the Forest of Myth—and when he came to investigate, he found Kainé. At last they had been reunited, and the two of them swore to find whoever it was they had so unfortunately forgotten.

"Kainé?! Where are you?!"

Emil had no idea where he had flown, but the next thing he knew, he was outside beneath a clear blue sky.

"Is the air shaking?" he asked himself. A moment later, a deep rumble came from the earth, and Emil shot up in the air. He knew what was going to happen, and he raced straight toward the event.

The forest trembled. The trees shuddered. All the birds resting among their boughs flew into the sky as one.

"What's going on in the Forest of Myth?"

The great, ancient tree toppled as the ground shook ever more violently. With splintering cracks, the other trees did the same. Then a white tower slowly rose from the earth. It grew and grew and soon stood at a height far above the mountains of the northern plains.

"What's that supposed to be?"

Emil approached the tower, hoping to get a better look. It continued to grow as he got nearer, and it stretched to a height above the clouds. He soared to the top and found it to be strangely shaped, with a pointed tip. In fact, it looked just like . . .

A flower bud.

Suddenly, it split down the sides.

"It *is* a flower!" cried Emil. "And it's blooming!"

White petals unfurled. The bud above the clouds bloomed into a flower as large as the entire northern plains.

"That's . . ."

There were people inside. Emil knew one was Kainé right away, just as he knew she'd reclaimed their treasured memories. Their precious person. Though he was some distance away, Emil could never mistake the other person for anyone else. The boy looked just as he had the day they first met—and though it was the first time Emil been able to see him with his own eyes, he knew it was *him* in an instant.

Memories flooded back to him. He recalled the name he had forgotten and absently wondered if this was not allowed. A sensation came to him, as though they were going against the very fabric of . . . *something*. And yet . . .

He didn't care if it wasn't allowed. Or if it was a mistake. Those he held most dear were now right before his eyes, and that was all he needed.

Even if it meant facing a day in the future where they would come to regret this choice.

JUN EISHIMA was born in 1964 in Fukuoka Prefecture. Her extensive backlist includes stories set in the *Final Fantasy*, *NieR*, and *Drakengard* universes. Under the name Emi Nagashima, she has also authored *The Cat Thief Hinako's Case Files*, among other works. In 2016, she received the 69th Mystery Writers of Japan Award (Short Story division) for the title "Old Maid."

YOKO TARO is the game director for the *NieR* and *Drakengard* series.

TOSHIYUKI ITAHANA is an artwork and character designer at Square Enix. Major works include *Final Fantasy IX*, *Chocobo's Mystery Dungeon*, and *Final Fantasy Crystal Chronicles*.

    Cover Illustration: Kazuma Koda

    Frontispiece Illustration: Akihiko Yoshida

    Interior Illustrations: Toshiyuki Itahana

    Japanese Edition Design: Sachie Ijiri

JASMINE BERNHARDT is a translator of Japanese popular media, including such works as *NieR Re[in]carnation*, *Spice & Wolf*, and *My Happy Marriage*. She lives in Wales with her husband.

ALAN AVERILL has worked on dozens of video games, including *NieR:Automata* and *Hotel Dusk: Room 215*. He is also the author of *The Beautiful Land*, a novel about love and time machines.

8-4, Ltd.

    Translator: Jasmine Bernhardt

    Editors: Alan Averill, D. Scott Miller

    Coordinator: Tina Carter

    Special Thanks: Graeme Howard

English Edition Cover Design: Ti Collier
English Edition Text Design: Jen Valero